WHAT'S MINE IS YOURS

C.L. JENNISON

To Mum and Dad, for always encouraging my love of words

My north star in the midnight sky,
You're my north star, my pure delight,
Stay with me and sparkle, never say goodbye.
—North Star, Lyricsmiths

PROLOGUE

September 2019

Detective Inspector Greaves squats down next to the body lying beneath the rickety-looking broken balcony at Seaview Cottage in the small village of Fraisthorpe.

He is careful not to get in the way of the crime-scene officer going methodically about her job. The single LED floodlight and the headlights of two police cars illuminate splintered wood, pooling blood, and the damaged skull of the deceased. Now that the earlier storm has subsided, the night air is sharp and salty. Waves continue to crash chaotically in the North Sea behind him.

Resting on his haunches, he looks up at the once handsome but now worse for wear art-deco-style house on the beachfront, then back down at the corpse. A kitchen knife is embedded to its hilt in the body's torso.

He stands as one of the paramedics slams the rear ambulance door shut and a few moments later the vehicle drives away, taking its unconscious passenger to Bridlington Hospital.

On initial assessment and going by what the first responding officers relayed when he arrived at the property, this looks like a fairly straightforward case, either deliberate or accidental. But still his cogs turn as he processes the scene, silently reciting the ABC mantra drummed into him by a senior colleague during the early days of his training: assume nothing, believe nobody, challenge everything. But then again, as his cocky colleague Detective Sergeant 'Hotshot' Hawkins often spouts: 'If it looks like a duck and quacks like a duck, it's a fucking duck.'

Turning, he surveys the immediate surroundings more closely, systematically, as is now ingrained in him, imagining a grid and sweeping his gaze slowly over each square in turn.

A few feet away, he spies two wooden posts sticking out of the ground, about a metre apart. Taking a couple of soggy steps closer, he realises they form the top of the handrail for the steep wooden steps descending directly to the beach.

Above, one of the retro patio doors leading from the first floor of the house to the balcony is wide open.

Near the front corner of the house, he spots what looks like deep, recent car tyre tracks, in the wet, muddy scrubland.

Straightforward or not, cases like this are rare around here, in this practically comatose east coast village, so this could be his chance to finally prove himself worthy of promotion. 'DCI Greaves' has a nice ring to it. Not wanting to appear gleefully macabre in front of the crime-scene officer, he resists grinning.

THREE WEEKS BEFORE

CHAPTER ONE

MONDAY

Carly grasps the steering wheel, squinting at the small, scruffy, bloodied orange-and-white mound in front of the wrought-iron gates. She inhales sharply as she realises the mound is a dead fox, and she sits back, the pads of her fingertips pressing firmly against her chest as she works to steady her breathing.

It wasn't there when she left this morning so it must have been hit by a car. Despite the new house not being on a busy main road, she supposes accidents happen, especially in a rural village. She shudders, hoping the animal didn't suffer.

After a moment, she snatches up the remote and points it at the gates. They open slowly, shunting the fox's stiff corpse towards the exterior grass verge.

Carly quickly drives into her wide gravelled driveway, parks in front of the left-hand garage and exits the car, leaving the gates open and the fox alone.

Letting herself into the quiet house, she checks her reflection in the mirror above the console table as she drops her keys into the bowl and her gym bag on the floor. She showered at the health club and her long blonde hair is still wet and hanging limply around her face. She tuts at what she sees, gently patting and pulling the skin around her eye sockets, moving her head this way and that, appraising the difference a nip here and a tuck there would make. Removing her fingers from her face, she sighs heavily at her un-nipped and un-tucked mirror image then makes her way upstairs.

In the bedroom, the glow from Fletcher's phone screen lights up his face as he lies in bed, his chin tucked into his chest.

'Good swim?' he asks as she crosses the room to open the curtains and blind to let the early September sunshine in. She tucks the heavy, floor-length curtains behind the cardboard boxes stacked neatly on the floor. For once, the remaining renovation mess is not at the forefront of her mind.

'There's a dead fox outside the gates,' she says, grimacing as she looks out of the window. Its snout is still just visible from this angle. She crosses her arms and tuts, not wanting to put into words what it might mean and why it bothers her, but she can't help herself. 'That's the last thing I need today – a bad omen.'

Fletcher puts his phone down, throws back the duvet and crosses the room. He stands behind his wife and frowns. 'Oh,' he says, looking out too and wrinkling his nose. 'I'll get rid of it before Eaden sees it.'

Carly nods while silently scolding herself for not considering her stepdaughter sooner, like a good mother should. She must do better. 'That was my first thought too,' she lies. 'She'd be so upset if she saw it, sensitive little thing. I knew you'd take care of it. Thank you.'

'No problem. And there's no such things as bad omens; you'll do great today.' He kisses her neck, a quick peck. 'I can't believe the kids aren't awake yet, they're usually hollering mere minutes after you leave the house. Now you're back, I'm going to push my luck and grab a shower before they're up.'

'Will you miss it after today?' she asks, still gazing outside. 'Your quality time together while I swim each morning?'

He stops in the doorway of the en suite and considers the question as he stretches upwards, holding onto the top of the door frame. 'As much as I do love breakfast time with the little munchkins, I definitely won't miss the mad morning juggle. Work's so manic I'll be glad to be up and out straight away from now on. Perry can't wait for me to be properly full time either. How are you feeling about the new job?'

Carly turns towards him and sighs dramatically. 'The new dress I ordered hasn't arrived, so God knows what I'm going to wear. I really wanted to make a good first impression and now I'm just going to look like a... what do you say here? A frump!' She moves towards the wardrobe, opens the door and puts her hands on her hips, staring into its depths, immediately frustrated by the supposed problem.

Fletcher laughs as he turns on the shower then reappears in the doorway. 'A frump? Did my mum teach you that word? You're definitely not a frump; you look good in everything.'

'You're sweet but full of it,' she says, throwing him a small smile as he takes off his boxers and grabs a clean towel from the chest of drawers. She flushes at the sight of his naked, toned, muscular body – despite being eight years older than her, he's still in great shape – and starts rifling through her clothes which are grouped by colour, scowling at and discounting items as she goes. 'Maybe before Sonny came along but now...' She assesses her Lycra-clad stomach critically and pinches barely an inch of flesh between her fingers, screwing up her face in disgust. 'And I weighed myself at the health club after I swam, and I haven't lost even one pound this week!'

A baby's sing-song chatter sounds through the monitor on the bedside table.

Fletcher groans. 'Speak of the devil, my shower will have to wait.' He moves towards his own wardrobe. 'Whatever you wear will look fine,' he says as he pulls on his favourite Lyricsmiths T-shirt and a fresh pair of boxers, turns off the shower and leaves the bedroom.

Carly hears a familiar ringtone and pauses mid-rummage. Fletcher's phone is face down on the bedside table and she stares at it for a long moment, the desire to pick it up and look at it almost visceral.

As she deliberates, Fletcher sweeps back in and swipes it up, glancing at the screen. 'Perry,' he says, holding it up. 'Told you he can't wait to spend even more time with his better-looking and better business-minded cousin.' He flashes her one of his cheeky grins.

'Tell him I said hey!' she calls automatically, and far too cheerfully, as he heads towards the sound of their son's increasingly animated babble.

CHAPTER TWO

Fletcher reaches into the baby's cot and scoops him up, planting a smacker on his rosy cheek. 'Now then, Sonny Jim. Shall we wake up Sleeping Beauty?' he asks his son, still warm from sleep. Together, they sit on the edge of Eaden's single bed. She's curled up like a croissant in the top corner of her mattress, clutching her favourite yet very worn cuddly toy, her long, red, curly hair fanned out on her pillow. Fletcher marvels at her ability to sleep so deeply despite having to temporarily share a freshly plastered, undecorated room with her little brother while they finish renovating the house. He strokes her freckled face with his finger while Sonny attempts to chatter, and she opens her eyes and looks up at him.

'Good morning, my beautiful girl,' he says. 'How about I change Sonny's nappy then make my special pancakes before school?'

'Sunshine pancakes?' she asks, stretching and smiling widely up at him.

'Of course!' he says. 'The best kind. And what other special things are happening today – can you remember?'

Like her energy switch has been flipped, she kneels up and bounces up and down. 'School!'

He laughs. 'That's right; it's back to school. What else?'

She looks at him quizzically and shrugs, upturning her palms as high as her shoulders.

'It's Polly's first day too, remember? So how about we get a move on before she gets here?'

Eaden nods vigorously and clambers off the bed. 'Will you make sunshine pancakes for Polly too, Daddy?'

He smiles at his daughter as he lays Sonny on top of the changing table underneath the window. 'I certainly will, sweetheart.'

Carly pokes a diamond earring through her lobe as she enters the kitchen wearing a navy-blue knee-length fitted dress and nude heels, her blonde hair swept up in an elegant chignon. She stands in front of the island as Fletcher finishes ladling pancake batter into a hot pan.

'Do I look okay?' she asks, running her hands down the front of her dress, over the vertical line of buttons. 'My mummy tummy's not too prominent in this, is it?' She twists her body left and right, slender hands placed across her flat belly. 'It's the best I could do seeing as the new one I ordered hasn't turned up in time. I paid extra for quicker delivery too.'

'You look great, as I knew you would,' says Fletcher, looking pointedly at her. 'Are you keeping your hair up? I think it looks gorgeous down. A bit less severe.' He flips the pancake and lets out a cheer. Eaden joins in, and Sonny emits a high-pitched squeal of his own from his highchair as Carly smooths the sides of her hair in the wake of her husband's comment, chewing her lip as the pan sizzles.

Fletcher slides the fresh pancake onto the plate beside him, then crosses to the table and serves it to Eaden, adding blobs of chocolate spread then extending them into 'sunshine rays' around it, as he usually does. Unable to wait, she dips her finger in one of the blobs then sucks the chocolate off.

'Thanks, Daddy!' she says, smiling up at him, chocolate painted on her little square front teeth.

'You're welcome, sweetheart,' he replies, grinning then licking the pads of his own fingers. He turns and reaches out to pull Carly to him.

She resists him, arms outstretched. 'Oh no you don't! There'll be no chocolate marks on this dress, thank you. In fact, I think I might go change into something else anyway; this makes me look like a whale and I'll be uncomfortable all day.'

'Hey, come on, babe,' says Fletcher, his voice softer than his expression. 'Less obsessing, more progressing, remember? This is a fresh start. It's a new country for you, and a new life for all of us. It doesn't matter what you wear; you'll be fine. There's no need to get changed.'

The doorbell chimes and Eaden looks up from her plate. 'Polly!' she shouts.

Fletcher kisses Carly on the cheek. 'Sounds like the cavalry's arrived.' He taps her on the bum.

Carly frowns and glances at the kitchen clock. It's still propped up on the counter until she decides where she wants to hang it. 'She's not due for another half an hour.'

'Good to know she's an eager beaver and better early than late. Are you going, or am I?' asks Fletcher, wiping his hands on the tea towel.

'No, I'll go, Chocolate Fingers. You're not even dressed yet. Not exactly a great first impression.'

'She saw me at her interview – I was dressed then,' he says, moving back around to the hob.

Carly tuts and quickly glances round the kitchen, which is a work-in-almost-finished-progress. She sees the bits that are still to do: tiling the splashback, putting blinds up at the windows and bi-fold doors, and painting the skirting boards. She sighs. She feels like she spends a considerable portion of her life sighing about one thing or another; life feels utterly overwhelming at times, especially as a mother. Then she remembers that Polly's here to make things easier for her and her spirits lift slightly.

Through the left-hand strip of glass in the front door, Carly spies a bright orange suitcase and catches a glimpse of long, dark, wavy hair. She checks her reflection in the mirror above the console table then opens the door to welcome their new nanny.

Polly Blake's smile is wide, showing teeth so straight and perfect they don't look real. Or maybe they're fresh out of braces. Carly tries her best to offer the same in return, but the gut punch of envy threatens to disable her, and she struggles to stifle her audible gasp. She remembers thinking Polly was attractive during their FaceTime introduction two weeks ago, despite her inexpertly applied make-up, but in real life, with apparently no make-up except a slick of lip gloss, the young woman is flawless; not a wrinkle, not a visible pore, not a blemish. Carly lifts a hand to her own face, fingers hovering over her skin, staring at Polly who looks back at her expectantly.

'Sorry,' she says, blinking rapidly, snapping herself out of it. She opens the door wider and stands aside. 'My head's not with it this morning – can I still blame baby brain eight months on? Please, come on in. It's lovely to meet you "in real life", as they say. I'm so sorry I couldn't make the formal interview in person, but I'm sure Fletcher handled it just fine. Well, he must have done because here you are!' She laughs lightly. 'Did the taxi find us okay? We're a little secluded down here so the street's not immediately obvious to everyone.' She's aware she's gabbling and forces herself to take a breath.

Polly wheels her suitcase over the threshold and hitches her rucksack back onto her shoulder. 'Yeah, all good, Mrs Lawrenson.'

'Oh, call me Carly, please. Just leave your luggage there beside my gym bag,' she says, gesturing to the hallway floor. 'Fletcher will take it up to your room for you later.'

Polly gestures outside. 'By the way, there's a dead f–'

'By the gate. Yes, we know,' interrupts Carly, nodding. 'Fletcher will deal with that too.'

'Did I hear my name?' Fletcher peeps out of the kitchen, one arm holding onto the door frame. 'Hi, Polly,' he says with a grin. 'Welcome to the madhouse.'

Polly smiles brightly again and Carly stares openly. She's wearing black leggings, a cropped vest top and a thick, oversized checked shirt with only the bottom two buttons done up, and battered Converse All Stars. Her long brown hair falls in messy waves over her shoulders and chest, almost reaching her exposed midriff. Small gold hoops adorn her earlobes, and her fingernails are painted bright pink. She looks casual yet sensational, as though she belongs in a trendy girl band.

Her skin is *pearlescent*, Carly thinks. It's mesmerising and sickening in equal measure, and she has to physically stop herself from reaching out to poke Polly's cheek, to check if the young woman is actually human or an extremely realistic cyborg. She would pay good money for an epidermis like that – and may well do once she settles in at her new job.

'Polly!' Eaden appears and crashes into Polly, hugging her legs. Polly wobbles and reaches out a hand to steady herself, placing her palm flat against the door.

'Here she is, your number one fan,' says Fletcher. 'She's been counting down the days since you met at the interview. Now, if you'll excuse me, I'll leave you in the capable hands of my wife while I grab a belated shower.' He picks up Polly's suitcase and holds out his hand for her bag, which she passes to him. Collecting Carly's gym bag too, he heads upstairs. Despite being laden down like a pack horse, he makes quick work of the ascent.

'Come on, Polly, Daddy made sunshine pancakes for

breakfast,' says Eaden, taking Polly's hand and pulling her towards the kitchen. Polly laughs and allows herself to be yanked along, Carly following behind them.

'Sorry,' says Carly again, then cringes at herself. If she's not sighing, she's apologising. She's a little taken aback by how comfortable Eaden seems to be around a relative stranger then catches herself – this 'stranger' is their new nanny and the fact that Eaden seems attached to her already is a good thing. 'She's a little excitable this morning. I think Fletcher must have been a bit too generous with the chocolate spread.'

'It's okay,' says Polly, waving and smiling enthusiastically at Sonny. He regards her with interest. 'Sorry I couldn't start yesterday, by the way. That's why I'm a bit early today – to help make your morning less stressful, especially as it's your first day too.'

'Well, I'm glad you're here. My hands are full, and I definitely need the help now I'm going back to work.' Carly glances at Sonny. 'Actually, do you mind giving him his yogurt while I finish getting ready? Fletcher started breakfast but his attention span is as bad as the kids' sometimes.' She laughs and shakes her head.

'I want Polly to sit with me,' says Eaden, pouting.

This time, Carly catches the sigh before it escapes from her. She surveys Eaden with a stern expression. 'Sonny needs Polly more than you, sweetheart. He's only a baby and you're a big girl now.'

'It's okay,' repeats Polly, smiling at Eaden. She moves over to Sonny's highchair. 'Gorgeous kitchen,' she says, gazing around the space before turning her attention to the baby, retrieving the yogurt and spoon from the island next to him and placing them down in front of him. His hand splays, little fingers dipping into the open pot.

'Yes, well, it will be – eventually,' replies Carly, casting a critical eye around the space again. Generally, she's happy with how it's coming along, and the kitchen, dining and seating zoning has worked out well spatially, considering she planned it all remotely. 'That's the problem with having a builder for a husband; your own house is never top priority. Right, if you're okay here, I'll leave you to it.'

Carly turns to move past Sonny just as his little yogurt-covered hand reaches out for her. He plonks it flat against her torso then looks up at her with a gummy smile.

'Sonny!' Carly cries, looking down at the creamy stain on her navy-blue dress. She lets out an almighty sigh and throws her eyeballs to the ceiling.

From the table Eaden laughs. Is Carly imagining it or is Polly suppressing a smile too?

'Let me help,' offers Polly, adjusting her expression and scooting around the highchair with a tea towel.

'I knew that fox was a bad omen,' says Carly under her breath, plucking at her dress. She plasters on a smile. 'If you'll excuse me, I need to go get changed.'

As she leaves the kitchen, she hears Polly and Eaden dissolving into giggles, already united.

Lips pressed together, Carly enters the bedroom and walks over to her wardrobe. She glances over to the en suite and through the crack in the door she sees the blurred outline of Fletcher behind the steamed-up shower screen. A wild idea about joining him injects itself into her mind but the thought of him seeing her naked in daylight for the first time since Sonny was born makes her anxious, plus she doesn't want to be late for work. No, there's a time and a place for all that and now that Polly's here, she hopes the times and places will increase – with flattering lingerie and lighting, obviously.

Speaking of flattering, she looks at her clothes and tries to find something else to wear. If only that new dress had arrived yesterday when it was supposed to. She thinks again about the dead fox being a bad omen and that maybe an accidental stain is the extent of it. Carly tells herself it's not a big deal; she's got enough time to change, and she'll feel better in something else. Slipping off her belt, she rolls it up and places it in the top drawer inside her wardrobe, amongst all the other accessories chucked in there. She can't wait to have fitted wardrobes, sectioned drawers and a proper dressing table. As she closes the drawer, the black velvet box catches her eye, and she picks it up. Inside contains a jumble of jewellery: her pearl wedding earrings, a delicate gold chain with a diamond studded letter 'S' attached that Fletcher bought her when Sonny was born, and a lip gloss in shade *Prick Tease* – a vibrant English mailbox red.

She stares at the contents of the box as if temporarily frozen then she hears a buzz and flicks her eyes towards the bed, to where Fletcher's phone lies casually on top of the duvet. Carly quickly snaps the box shut, puts it away and moves over to the bed, one arm outstretched, just as Fletcher emerges from the en suite in a cloud of steam with a towel wrapped around his waist.

They lock eyes and her cheeks bloom guiltily.

CHAPTER THREE

Fletcher looks from Carly to his phone on the bed. 'Were you going to look at my phone?' he asks, bending down to swipe it up.

The silence stretches between them, and she deflects by gesturing to the stain on her dress. 'I came back up to change. Sonny got yogurt on me.' She smiles and turns back to her wardrobe.

'Carly, were you going to look at my phone?' Fletcher repeats in an abrasive tone, holding it aloft, his grip tight.

She sniffs as she takes a dress out of the wardrobe and hangs it on the back of the door then begins to unbutton the dress she's wearing, refusing to look at him. Her flaming cheeks answer for her.

He sighs the weary sigh of a frustrated man and lets his arm drop. 'I thought we were past this.'

She chances a glance at him. 'It buzzed,' she whispers. 'It caught my attention. I thought it might be important, so I was going to hand it to you.'

'It'll only be Perry messaging about work,' he says. 'He can wait five minutes while I have a shower.'

'Okay.' She nods and slips out of the soiled dress, concealing most of her body behind the open wardrobe door.

'I don't get why messages from my cousin are so snoopworthy.'

She selects a cream Reiss wrap dress with three-quarter-length sleeves to wear and ties the straps against her left hip. She thinks the colour makes her looks seem washed out but the cut flatters her figure. 'I wasn't going to snoop,' she says, managing to keep the bite out of her voice. 'But you've got to admit he seems to message you constantly.'

'We *are* business partners. We need to be in touch, you know. I thought you liked Perry. You even said to say hey earlier.' He runs his free hand through his wet hair and droplets of water run down his neck and onto his bare shoulders.

'I do like him, but do you have to be in touch at all hours of the day and night? Even though you work together every day and practically every weekend too?' She pouts, already treading the well-worn path of their usual argument. Even though she doesn't want to, she hears herself spouting the next sentence in the sequence. 'And if it's not Perry messaging you, it's your mother.'

'We're running a family business together, Carly!' Fletcher repeats his stock refrain in his standard irritated tone. 'And Uncle Frank only died a few months ago – Perry's still grieving for his dad and we're trying to pick up the pieces of the company together. We've been over this a hundred times!'

She knows she's being unreasonable, that her new job nerves and her own insecurities are exacerbating her emotions, but before she has the chance to apologise, Fletcher's phone buzzes again and he automatically looks down at his screen. Carly sees him smirk and annoyance flares within her once more. She raises her eyebrows and crosses her arms, staring at her husband.

He resumes his defence. 'Perry and Mum are my family, Carly. They're Sonny and Eaden's family – you know Mum's their only grandparent – and they're your family now too.

They've welcomed you with open arms and they care about us all. A lot. Why is that such a problem for you? I thought we agreed to leave all this suspicion and paranoia behind us when we moved.'

Carly drops her head, annoyance quickly morphing into self-pity. 'Perhaps *I* should have stayed behind too!' Her lip wobbles as her words hang in the air between them, waiting for the sympathetic response they were supposed to elicit.

But instead of pacifying her as expected now that she's on the verge of tears, Carly is surprised to see Fletcher stride over to her bedside table. He takes a slimline box out of the drawer and tosses it onto the bed. 'Here, take your medication, Carly,' he says. 'You really need to calm down.'

In a fit of frustration, painfully aware she's proving him right, she snatches up the box of pills and launches it at him. He ducks and it ricochets off the door frame, bouncing all the way down the stairs.

The box comes to a stop by Polly's feet. She's standing at the open front door opposite an older woman, with Sonny on her hip and an ASOS parcel in her hand. She looks down at the hallway floor then up towards the top of the stairs. Fletcher's raised voice has now been replaced by a loaded silence.

'Well, dear, I think that's my cue to leave you to it. Remember to pass on my apologies about not bringing the parcel round earlier,' says Meryl Bennett, Fletcher and Carly's neighbour. 'And don't forget to tell them about that fox,' she stage-whispers, waving gaily as she walks back up the drive to her own house next door.

Polly places the parcel on the console table, moves Sonny to her other hip then squats down to pick up the box. She reads the label: *Mrs C Lawrenson / diazepam.*

19

'Good girl,' she says to Eaden as she returns to the kitchen to find her finishing her juice, an orange moustache on her top lip.

She places the box of pills on the island and glances at the clock which is propped up on the granite worktop that runs the length of the back wall. They've still got fifteen minutes before they have to leave for Eaden's school, but Polly doesn't want to be late on her first day. 'Now, how about you pop upstairs, brush your teeth and put your school uniform on? Can you do that by yourself, or do you need me to help you?'

'Help me!' says Eaden.

'Come on then, show me where.'

Polly waits as Eaden gets down off her chair and skips across the room then she follows her eldest charge back into the hallway and up the stairs, jiggling Sonny on her hip as she goes. She feels a thrill as her phone vibrates in her back pocket; she knows exactly who it's from and she's frustrated that she can't read it immediately. *Patience,* she reminds herself.

As she climbs the stairs slowly, mirroring Eaden's now steady pace, she gazes around the hallway. The walls are white and freshly painted but bare, devoid of family photographs or art or colour, and the wooden steps haven't yet been carpeted. Polly looks over the banister and down the length of the hallway. Except for the double glass doors through to the kitchen, all the other solid doors are closed, and all the décor – walls, floor, the few pieces of furniture she can see – is on the neutral/natural spectrum. *Fifty shades of beige,* she thinks.

As she reaches the top of the stairs, she sees straight into what she assumes must be the master bedroom, and Fletcher's toned, naked back. Her glossy lips part and she stares as he pulls a black polo shirt over his head and torso then tucks it into his combats. Sonny wriggles in her arms and emits a sound as Fletcher spins round to face them.

Having been caught ogling, Polly decides to brazen it out. She offers Fletcher a wide smile and points down the hall to where

Eaden has disappeared to. Just then, Carly emerges from the bedroom wearing a cream dress, black boots and carrying a black Chanel handbag. She looks fresh, classy and beautiful.

'Sorry,' Carly says, tucking her long hair, now released from its chignon, behind her ear. 'I'm ready now. Let me show you where the children's things are quickly.'

'Lead the way,' says Polly. As she turns to follow Carly down the hall, she glances back at the bedroom doorway, but Fletcher has moved out of sight.

CHAPTER FOUR

'Any other questions about Eaden's school?' Carly throws the question back over her shoulder to Polly as they all return to the kitchen. Carly puts her designer handbag on the island and walks over to the fridge.

'No, all good,' says Polly as Carly retrieves what must be Eaden's lunchbox. It's yellow with a rainbow on the front. 'I google-mapped the location yesterday and now I know pick up and drop off times, we'll be fine getting there and back.' She smiles down at Eaden as Carly passes her the lunchbox. 'And this one can always help me until I get to know the other mums... or rather, nannies. Private school norms and all that.'

Carly blinks – did she hear a note of judgement in Polly's voice? She shakes the thought out of her head; Polly's assumption is probably right, after all. 'Great. Sonny's stroller is in the utility room.' She points to the kitchen wall. 'The other side of here.'

'I'll go and get it now,' says Polly, advancing towards the double doors just as Fletcher sweeps in from the hallway.

'Woah.' He laughs, swerving around Polly and Sonny. Eaden laughs too, which in turn prompts a 'Ha!' from Sonny.

'Sorry, Mr Lawrenson,' says Polly, giggling.

'I told you – call me Fletcher. And actually, it's us who should be apologising to you, Polly,' he says. 'You've not had the smoothest welcome so far. I promise it's not always like this, but this morning's been a little bit more stressful than usual.' He glances over at Carly who smiles tightly.

Polly's gaze bounces between the two of them. 'No, it's fine,' she says as she hoists Sonny up higher on her hip. 'I'd rather jump in both feet first, I'm definitely an all or nothing type of girl.'

'Good to hear,' says Carly as she picks up her handbag. 'Like I said, make yourself at home and just text me if you run into any problems. You've got my number as well as Fletcher's now.'

'As long as I keep Sonny's hands away from yogurt, I'm sure everything will work out brilliantly.' Polly's eyes glisten mischievously. 'Now, how about we find your pushchair?' she asks Sonny and heads into the hallway.

Carly's tight smile makes another appearance and she and Fletcher lock eyes.

'Ready?' he asks her.

'I'm ready, Daddy!' shouts Eaden.

'So you are, munchkin,' he replies, matching his daughter's enthusiasm and lifting her into his arms. He kisses her noisily on the cheek. 'Have a great day, Eades, and Daddy will see you later. Be a good girl for Polly on her first day.' He taps her on the nose with his finger. 'And who else's first day is it?' he asks.

Eaden looks over at Carly and then back at Fletcher. 'Carly's,' she replies after a moment.

'That's right. Shall we wish Carly good luck for her first day at her new job?'

Eaden pouts at her father as he nods his encouragement. She turns to look at her stepmother. 'Good luck,' she says, her voice barely more than a whisper.

'Good girl,' says Fletcher, placing Eaden back down and then ladening her with her schoolbag and lunchbox, like a Buckaroo donkey.

'Thank you, sweetheart. I hope you have a good day too,' says Carly as she picks up her handbag. As she does, she notices her diazepam tablets next to the sink. She plucks them up, drops them into her bag and follows her husband and stepdaughter out to the hallway.

As Polly emerges from the utility room with Sonny strapped into his Bugaboo pushchair, Carly notices the ASOS parcel on the console table and points at it. 'Where did that come from?'

'Oh, your neighbour brought it round when you were...' She gestures upstairs and grimaces. 'It arrived yesterday, apparently. She says sorry for not bringing it earlier.'

Carly tuts and rolls her eyes. 'That'll be the dress I wanted to wear today. Better late than never, I suppose.' She clutches the parcel and turns to face the others in the hallway. 'I'll just run upstairs and get changed now. It'll give you time to move that *f-o-x* in the driveway,' she says, and hurries upstairs, her heels hammering on the bare treads.

'Carly, you look fine as you are,' calls Fletcher as his wife reaches the landing. 'Perry's waiting!' He throws his hands up in exasperation and rolls his eyes at Polly.

'Two minutes!' shouts Carly from upstairs.

Smirking, Polly shrugs back at him and steers the pushchair towards the front door.

He looks at her and extends his forefinger into the air. 'Christ, this feels like the longest morning ever. Will you wait one minute while I just deal with...' He angles his finger towards the door, and the animal carcass beyond it. 'Before this one sees it,' he whispers and angles his finger again, towards his daughter.

'No problem,' she says and squats down next to Eaden. 'Shall we double-check we've got everything?'

Fletcher returns a few minutes later, and pushes the front door open wide as Polly takes hold of the pushchair once more.

'All clear. Oh, before I forget, I got a spare set of keys cut for you.' He opens the drawer of the console table and passes them to her. The letter 'P' dangles off the gold keychain.

'Thanks,' says Polly, looking down at her initial. 'That's really kind of you.' She slides the keys into her overshirt pocket and releases the brake on the pushchair.

'Bye, Daddy.' Eaden waves up at him awkwardly, both hands still full, as he stands by the door, holding it open for them all.

'Bye family, have a good day,' he sing-songs cheerfully.

He closes the door and shakes his head as he paces the tiled floor waiting for his wife. A minute later his phone buzzes, and he takes it out of his pocket. He looks down at the screen, reads the message and grins.

CHAPTER FIVE

Carly gazes out of the car window as they pass all the other luxury houses in their village. In the shadow of the Humber Bridge, Swanland is peppered with beautiful properties, most of them like theirs: high-walled, gated and set back from the road, concealed by tall evergreens or thick laurel hedges, and surrounded by the wolds and woodland. It's idyllic.

She knows she's lucky. She knows she's got a lot to be thankful for, grateful for, but she can't seem to snap herself out of the headspace she's been in lately. The headspace she's been trapped in for months, growing more and more claustrophobic with each passing day.

She remembers a time when she felt light and carefree and *thin*. She thinks that feeling thin is the best feeling there is because thin equals desirable, which equals youth and beauty. It also equalled a great career in her late teens and twenties when she worked as a model. Not a *supermodel*, obviously, but she always had steady work – fashion spreads in mid-priced women's magazines, fitness advertising campaigns, a bit of mid-range designer runway work here and there. But now she feels *baggy* and *saggy*. Eye bags. Bingo wings. A revolting kangaroo pouch of a belly since having Sonny. It disgusts her. Her own body, which once felt so deliciously svelte and streamlined, now feels like a fat suit. Her life, which once felt so free and fun, now feels so complicated and stressful.

She feels Fletcher's strong, workman's hand slide onto her leg and looks down at it, his wedding ring glinting in the morning sunlight. That's something else that feels stranger these days; her husband's hands on her. But it's different for men, isn't it? They can father children with hordes of different women and still be considered 'fit' and sexually attractive. The rise of the 'dad bod' is testament to that. Not that Fletcher has a 'dad bod'; he's still very much in the 'fit' category, in all senses of the word.

'I doubt she would have heard much,' he says, giving her knee a little squeeze before moving his hand back to the gear stick.

'Hmmm?' Carly looks over at him blankly as she tunes back into the here and now.

'Polly,' he says, glancing at her. 'I doubt she would have heard us arguing this morning, not from downstairs. Don't worry about it.'

'I wasn't even thinking about it – it's already forgotten,' says Carly with a small smile before looking back out of the window.

'Well, anyway, I'm sorry we argued, especially before your first day at your new job.'

'How old is she?' she asks, side-stepping his apology.

'Who? Polly?'

Carly turns to him again and nods.

'Erm... early twenties, I think?' He phrases it as a question then shrugs. 'It's on her paperwork. I'll check it later.'

'Are you sure? She looks even younger today than she did when we FaceTimed, like she's barely out of school. Her skin is flawless.' Carly brings her fingers to her own face. Not wanting to smudge her carefully applied make-up, she smooths them down her neck instead.

'As I already told you, I checked all her credentials and

references and she's perfectly qualified and experienced. She comes highly recommended too,' Fletcher confirms. 'But obviously you're welcome to double-check.' He glances over at her.

She meets his eyes briefly and smiles. 'No, I trust you.'

He returns his focus to the road. 'Well, she seems to have taken to Eaden and Sonny straight away, and they've taken to her instantly too, which is the main thing.'

Carly nods as she lifts her designer bag onto her lap and flips down the visor above her. As they enter Hessle, she scrutinises her face in the inset mirror then takes powder and lipstick out of her bag and reapplies them.

'You look great. And that new dress will definitely make a good impression.' He pulls up outside *Image Aesthetic Clinic* and idles the car.

Carly pushes the visor back up, stows her make-up back in her bag and lets out a long, slow breath as she surveys her new workplace. The clinic is the end unit within an upmarket parade of shops, featuring a hairdresser, a café, a florist and a woman's clothing boutique, near Hessle's main shopping square. Sitting outside the café is a homeless man with an empty takeaway coffee cup positioned in front of him next to a cardboard sign asking for spare change.

'He ruins the posh shop vibe a bit,' says Fletcher scornfully, nodding towards the man.

Carly frowns at his judgemental comment but chooses not to challenge it. It's not the first time he's shown a lack of empathy for those less fortunate than himself and it's a side of him she doesn't want to actively encourage. She often wonders what he'd say if he knew that her parents were actually alive and well but living in trailerville USA. Were it not for her modelling break at seventeen, she could easily have ended up homeless at one point too.

Not wanting to think about any of that today, or ever, she

turns to face him. 'Thank you for waiting for me to get changed. I feel much more confident in this dress than the cream one, and you were right about my hair looking better loose.' She pauses. 'And I'm sorry too. I know Perry's had a tough time of it lately – you all have – and I'm not trying to cause problems or be the "opinionated American".' She makes air quotes and rolls her eyes as she says the words. 'I just–'

He doesn't wait for her to finish before clamping his hand back on her knee. 'Hey, it's okay,' he says. 'We've had some big life changes recently; it's been quite the ride. And I know Perry's needed a lot of hand-holding lately but things will get better as we get into a rhythm of working together again. We've come a long way since we were kids, skivvying up ladders and mixing cement for Dad and Uncle Frank, and it's good to be back at it, no matter the hard graft we're going to have put in to fully revive the business. But now Polly's here to help with the kids it means we'll both be able to focus on work more.'

He gives her a peck on the cheek and smiles. 'Speaking of work, I'd better get going to quote that new job round the corner before I go to the Chestnut Avenue house. I don't want to leave Perry on his own for too long. You know how he gets without me there to take the lead.'

She looks at him, frustrated that he interrupted her before she could speak about her feelings, but soothed by his words, nonetheless. She knows she has a tendency to overthink everything, and he does always seem to be able to bring everything back into perspective.

'Okay. Well, thanks for playing chauffeur. I know it's on your way anyway but I appreciate having one less thing to worry about this morning.' She opens the car door and steps out onto the pavement, smoothing down her Karen Millen utility midi dress.

He leans across and looks up at her through the open door. 'Have a great first day, babe.' He flashes her his trademark megawatt smile as she closes the door then pulls the car back out into the stream of rush-hour traffic.

For once, Carly doesn't give herself time to hesitate or worry or let nerves get the better of her; she walks purposefully to the glass door of the clinic, stealing another quick sympathetic glance at the homeless man, then takes hold of the long silver handle and steps straight inside. The spacious reception area is decorated in light blues, greens and greys and smells fresh and clean. The modern reception desk is positioned in front of the back wall underneath a large, illuminated *Image Aesthetic Clinic* sign.

There's a closed, frosted glass door to the left of the desk and Carly sees the shadow of someone behind it. They open the door and walk through, and Carly recognises her new boss Gavin Elliott from her Zoom interview. His sharp features morph into a smile, instantly softening his angular face, as soon as he sees her.

'Hello, Carly!' he says enthusiastically, offering her his hand to shake.

'Hey there, Gavin,' she says, taking his hand, her American accent sounding so pronounced to her own ears.

'Perfect timing, I was just about to get an espresso from the machine. Would you like one?' he asks.

'Thanks, but no thanks. I only drink water and herbal teas – no caffeine for me. You go right ahead though.'

He turns towards the futuristic-looking coffee machine atop a glossy white sideboard on the left-hand side of the reception area, places a cup under the spout and presses a button.

'Only water and herbal teas, huh?' he asks as the coffee drips into the white cup.

'Yeah. I have enough other vices to be getting on with.' She laughs a bit too loudly at her own joke.

He laughs too as he picks up his cup. 'So, it's great to meet you in the flesh, so to speak. When Marilyn, my last receptionist, told me she was pregnant, I wasn't sure how I was going to replace her as she'd been with me since the start. Thank God Fletcher got in touch when he saw my Facebook post and suggested you. The thought of trawling through applicants was too much to bear.'

'Well, there's absolutely no chance I'll be leaving to have another baby any time soon so I'm here for as long as you'll have me,' says Carly.

'It was very serendipitous for us all, what with you moving back to the UK. How's Fletcher doing after everything that happened?' Gavin takes a sip of his coffee and closes his eyes briefly, appreciating the taste.

'He's good, thanks. As you know, one of the reasons we came back was so he could take over his Uncle Frank's building company after he died, along with his cousin Perry. Their dads used to run it together back in the day, so Fletcher and Perry feel like they're stepping into their shoes by taking over the family business. I don't think Perry could have coped by himself; he's definitely not as business savvy as Fletcher.' She stops and laughs again. 'God, listen to me blurting everything out. I probably told you all this already in my interview. Typical American!'

'No, it's good to know they're doing well. I remember Perry, even though he was a couple of years below us. Fletcher and I were really good mates all through school and college, all of...' He looks to the ceiling and squints his eyes, mentally calculating. 'Twenty-odd years ago now. Wow, I feel old.' He takes another small mouthful of his espresso.

'Tell me about it,' says Carly. 'But at least you're in the right business for helping people not feel, and look, so old.'

He smiles. 'I am indeed.'

Gavin looks past Carly and raises a hand in greeting to someone outside. She twists round just in time to see the homeless man from earlier passing the sign-written logo on the large window, returning Gavin's wave with a wide smile. She gauges his age around thirty – a few years younger than herself. His clothes are crumpled yet look relatively clean and although he's lean, he's not overly skinny. She notices a cleft lip through his short, patchy beard.

'That's Benny,' explains Gavin. 'He helps all of us shop owners out with odd jobs now and again in exchange for food and drink, and sometimes cash. In fact, I've asked him to deliver some flyers for us ready for our new Saturday clinics, so you'll meet him properly soon enough.'

'Oh, okay. How long has he been–' she searches for the most appropriate word but can't find one, '–around here?' she finishes lamely.

'A good while. A few months at least now. Jeanette in the hairdresser's gives him the occasional free hair wash and Rocco who owns the café often lets him have his pick of the unsold sandwiches. We don't like to pry but we heard he sank into a severe downward spiral after his wife had an affair and took his baby son away.'

'Wow, how awful.'

'Mmm,' agrees Gavin. 'Yet despite his hardships, he's become a friendly face around here. Always willing to help.'

Carly nods, absorbing Benny's sad story, thinking about how easily anyone's life can take a turn for the worse at any time due to any number of bad things happening.

'And speaking of faces, you're going to be the face of *Image Aesthetic Clinic* now, the first one people see as they walk through the door. I agree with Fletcher – I think you'll make an excellent first impression and you're a great fit for the business due to your background in modelling.'

'Really?' Carly brings her hand to her face as if to check it's definitely the one he's referring to, before basking in the welcome compliment. 'Well, I certainly hope so.'

'And if you ever feel like you need a bit of touching up yourself, just let me know.'

His words hang in the air between them, inflating in the

space, pushing her back. She recoils, a mask of shock on her flushed face.

His eyes widen as he realises how inappropriate his offer sounded. 'No... God, I'm sorry, that didn't come out right.' He shakes his free hand as if he's trying to wash the words clean. 'I'm so sorry, Carly. I didn't mean... it wasn't an innuendo... or that you needed...' He trails off and looks at her straight in the eye. 'I'm sorry. That was not the impression I wanted to give you on your first day.'

She clutches her bag strap with both hands, twisting it slightly, a nervous tic. 'It's fine,' she says, smiling tightly. 'Right, how about you show me around then?'

CHAPTER SIX

Polly is slicing an apple for Eaden's after-school snack when the little girl comes running back into the kitchen holding a big book. She slides it onto the table and clambers along the built-in upholstered bench seat with a huge grin on her face.

'What's this?' Polly asks as she places the small bowl of sliced apple and satsuma segments next to the book and leans on the table. She glances over at Sonny, still asleep in his pushchair after the walk home from Eaden's school.

'My special scrapbook!' says Eaden, clearly delighted to show Polly her prized possession, still fizzing with energy even after her first day back in the classroom.

'Wow!' says Polly, genuinely admiring the cover. It's covered with lilac velvet fabric and Eaden's name is sewn neatly onto it, each letter a different colour of the rainbow. A wide pale pink ribbon is tied in a bow along the thick spine. It's clear a lot of love and care has gone into creating it.

'Can I look inside?' Polly asks and Eaden nods enthusiastically. She gestures for the little girl to scoot along the bench and sits down next to her. They turn the front cover over together and Polly sees *My Bedroom Project* written in fancy lettering in the centre. The next page is a mood board containing scraps of colourful material, paint-colour cards and pictures cut from magazines of scalloped paint effects, bed canopies, rainbow rugs, cushioned window seats and candy-striped beach huts. Polly doesn't need to exaggerate her admiration for the scrapbook; it's professional interior-design project quality. 'This is amazing, Eaden. Did you do this all by yourself?'

Eaden laughs with delight. 'No, Granny helped me.'

'Is this what you want your new bedroom to be like?'

Eaden nods as she carefully turns the thick pages with delicate fingers, eyes dancing over the contents.

'You must be very excited.'

'Daddy says I can have whatever I want, and I want it to look like the beach.'

'Do you love the beach?' asks Polly.

'Yes. We go there sometimes.'

'You do? When you go on holiday, you mean?'

Eaden nods. 'Or weekends. Daddy drives us.'

'Oh, you mean a beach near here?' asks Polly, surprised. Her northern geography is sketchy.

'Yes,' says Eaden. 'Daddy calls it our seaside house.'

'Wow, how lucky you are to have another house near the beach!' says Polly as enthusiastically as she can without disturbing Sonny.

Eaden turns another page. A faded Polaroid photograph of a laughing woman holding a baby aloft, the sun behind giving her a halo, takes pride of place. It's backed onto floral paper and surrounded by a border of pressed flowers that have been carefully stuck in, creating a frame. It looks so lovingly crafted.

'Who's this?' asks Polly, pointing at the photo, suspecting who it might be and watching Eaden's reaction closely.

'My mummy,' says Eaden.

Polly nods. 'She's very beautiful. Is this you?' She taps the baby in the image.

'Baby Eaden,' she whispers, staring at the picture.

'What a lovely photograph and a precious memory,' says Polly, stroking Eaden's curly hair. 'Thank you for showing me.'

Eaden turns to a double-page spread featuring a beach hut created from card and stuck down across the centre fold. The page itself is blue at the top and yellow at the bottom: sky and sand. There's a sun and a stripy kite in the sky and the bottom looks textured, as though actual sand has been sprinkled over it. It's obvious a child has coloured in the planks of wood, but the double doors fold open to show the drawn, incredibly detailed interior. Clearly Granny is a creative crafter.

'What a very special book this is,' says Polly, taking it all in as Eaden traces her little fingers across the page as though she's reading Braille. 'Don't forget about your snack.' She pulls the bowl closer to the scrapbook and passes her young charge a slice of apple.

Eaden takes the apple and munches on it, humming to herself while she does. Polly's heart swells with affection for this little girl who has already been through so much, and for Fletcher who has suffered a great loss too.

Polly's phone vibrates in her back pocket and she pulls it out to check the message on the screen. She grins at the words, and texts back a few choice emojis before noticing the battery is running low. She looks at Eaden who is still mesmerised by her scrapbook and intermittently bringing fruit to her mouth in smooth robotic movements.

'I'm just going to run upstairs to get my phone charger,' she says. 'Will you be all right here for one minute?' She holds up a finger as she stands and glances over at a still sleeping Sonny.

Eaden glances at her and nods.

'Good girl.' Polly leaves the kitchen, takes the stairs two at a time then hurries to the back bedroom: her new domain. It's slightly smaller than the room Eaden and Sonny currently share but still a good size. It houses a double bed, two bedside tables, a chest of drawers and a wardrobe, all pure white with T-bar gold handles.

The walls, woodwork, tufted rug and heavy, floor-length curtains are all off-white; a 'stylish colour palette' according to Carly earlier, or a seemingly soulless gallery space according to Polly now. Surely a house decorated in a neutral palette is futile when children live there too, and what's wrong with a bit of colour anyway?

However, it has its own en suite and Polly is extremely grateful not to be sharing the main family bathroom with Eaden and Sonny. Thanks to Fletcher bringing it up earlier, her lone orange suitcase stands beside the bed – she travels light – and her bag sits on top.

She unzips the bag, retrieves her phone charger from the inside pocket and leaves the room. As she's about to descend the stairs, she glances over at Fletcher and Carly's bedroom door, which is ajar. She hesitates for a split second, if that, then as though magnetised, finds herself pushing the door open and stepping inside.

The first thing she notices is the pleasant smell; fresh yet subtly perfumed like one of those excruciatingly expensive scented designer candles that Teddy sometimes bought her.

Her eyes roam quickly around the space, hungrily taking in as many details as she can, feeling slightly jarred by the many contrasting elements: walls stripped of paper but crisp white sheets on the king-sized bed; bare, unpolished wooden floorboards but a large, thick-pile Persian rug laid in front of the deep bay window; piles of cardboard boxes and baskets pushed against walls but a tall, ornate, gilt-edged, freestanding mirror positioned in the corner; a rickety pair of art-deco-style double wardrobes that have seen better days either side of a beautiful, tiled fireplace with a marble surround.

Polly can't help herself – she moves to one of the wardrobes, opening the doors and peeking inside. It's Carly's. She runs her fingers along the collection of expensive-looking clothes, all varying shades of charcoal, navy, white, cream and brown, and marvels at the many boxes of shoes stacked beneath, all Perspex and transparent so their contents can be easily seen and selected. Something about them makes a connection in Polly's mind to the many heads of Princess Mombi in *Return to Oz* and she shudders. She closes the doors carefully and moves to the nearest bedside table, throwing her charger onto the luxury sheets. She pulls open the single drawer and freezes, suddenly sensing she has company.

'Polly?'

Eaden is standing in the doorway watching her. Polly feels her face prickle with guilt, but she stands slowly and smiles, closing the drawer as she does. She picks up her charger from the bed.

'I couldn't find my charger so I'm going to borrow this one of your mum's,' she lies, holding it aloft. 'I'll put it back before she even realises it's gone, I promise.'

Eaden stares at her, a complicated expression on her face. 'Carly's not my mum.'

Polly winces. 'Oh, of course, I'm so sorry, silly me.' She holds her breath as she waits for Eaden to say something else then she hears an already familiar squeal from downstairs and realises Sonny must be awake. She crosses over to the doorway and kneels down in front of Eaden. 'I really am very sorry, Eaden. That was my mistake and I won't ever make it again. I hope you can forgive me. And shall we keep me borrowing Carly's charger a secret for now, just between us?'

Eaden regards her solemnly for a moment then nods.

Polly exhales. 'Thank you. Now, how about we go back downstairs and check on your baby brother?' She stands and holds out her free hand for Eaden to take, which she does. Polly twists back and pulls the bedroom door closed, relief washing over her.

Heading into the kitchen, Polly is shocked to see a well-dressed, white-haired woman wearing pearls holding Sonny. She is sure she locked the front door behind them when they got back from school. Frozen to the floor while her heart hammers, she frantically scans her surroundings for other glamorous intruders.

'Granny!' shouts Eaden, letting go of Polly's hand and running towards her grandmother's outstretched free arm. Polly huffs out a relieved laugh, panic instantly allayed, glad she hadn't been forced to fight the formidable-looking old woman to save the baby.

'Hello, my darling girl!' The older woman bends down to kiss the top of Eaden's head as Eaden attaches herself to her grandmother's trouser-clad leg like a koala. 'Did you have a good first day at school? How can you be in year two already?'

As her heart rate returns to normal, Polly takes a moment to admire the woman's stylish grey and white attire and bright pink lipstick. Her pearl earrings match her necklace, and her short hair has been beautifully styled, silver highlights practically sparkling under the kitchen spotlights.

'Miss Coles said my reading was very good, Granny!' Eaden reports proudly.

'Well, how wonderful. But I'm not at all surprised – you're a genius!' She strokes Eaden's hair and looks up. 'Hello. You must be the nanny,' she says to Polly.

CHAPTER SEVEN

'Yes,' confirms Polly. 'I'm so sorry. Sonny was asleep, and Eaden and I were just upstairs for a few minutes.' She holds up the phone charger, lamely justifying her temporary irresponsibility.

The older woman shakes her head and smiles warmly. 'No apology necessary. He was just stirring as I walked in, so I had the pleasure of being the first one he saw when he opened his eyes. Didn't I?' She repeats the question twice to her grandson before kissing his flushed cheek. Sonny gurgles happily. 'I'm Stella Lawrenson, by the way. Lovely to meet you. Fletcher has told me all about you. He's very happy you're here to help out with these two.' She pauses. 'And Carly, obviously.'

'I'm Polly and I'm very happy to be here too,' says Polly, still squirming.

'I'm sorry if I gave you a scare just now. Your face was a picture! I let myself in through the bi-fold doors with my key.' She looks down at Eaden. 'Now, little lady, can Granny please have her leg back so she can go and change your brother's nappy?'

'Oh, I can do that.' Polly steps towards Stella, offering to take

Sonny from her.

'Nonsense. You make us a lovely cup of tea and I'll be back in two ticks. I need to make up for lost time and nothing gives me greater pleasure than looking after my precious family.'

'Well, if you insist, be my guest. Thank you.' Polly smiles her gratitude and moves towards the island, setting the charger down.

Stella leaves the kitchen with Sonny and Eaden returns to her scrapbook at the table as Polly tries to find which of the many cupboards contains the cups. As she's opening and closing doors, she hears Eaden's voice: 'cold.' She smiles to herself. She moves along to the next cupboard and hears 'warmer.' She bends down to the cupboard below and hears 'colder.' She reaches up to the next cupboard and is greeted with a collection of cups and mugs. 'Hot!' shouts Eaden from the table, giggling with delight.

Polly laughs too. As well as selecting two china cups, she finds and fills the teapot and a milk jug and places them on the kitchen table, along with a beaker of juice for Eaden and a sippy cup for Sonny.

'How very civilised!' Stella acknowledges Polly's efforts as she returns from changing her grandson a few minutes later. She places him in the highchair that Polly has already moved to the head of the table.

'Eaden just told me you don't take sugar, but do you want biscuits – if I can sniff them out?' Polly winks at Eaden whose eyes crease as she takes a glug of her juice.

'You won't find any biscuits in this house.' Stella stirs the contents of the teapot then pours out two cups of tea. 'Carly doesn't allow the children to have refined sugar as a rule. In fact, my daughter-in-law has many strict rules, as I'm sure you'll discover in due course.' She purses her lips as she holds up the milk jug. Curiosity piqued, Polly nods, noticing Stella's hardened expression as she adds milk to both cups before stirring them and passing one across the table.

Before Polly can ask for examples of the supposed 'strict rules' she's referring to, Stella changes the subject, her tone lightening.

'I see my granddaughter has been showing off her special scrapbook.'

'She has; it's amazing.' Polly smiles.

'We love it, don't we, poppet?' Stella asks Eaden as she strokes the cover gently. She looks back up at Polly. 'Fletcher promised her she could have anything she wanted for her new bedroom and I'm sure you know by now she wants a seaside theme. We've been gathering ideas and inspiration ever since she decided and it's become something of a passion project, for both of us.'

'Can we do some more now please, Granny?' asks Eaden.

'Not just now, my darling, but we will – very soon! I've been collecting a few more pictures and treasures and bits and bobs in my big craft box to show you and before you know it, Daddy will have your new bedroom all ready for painting.' Stella touches the tip of her manicured finger to Eaden's nose and Eaden giggles.

Polly passes Sonny his juice bottle and takes a sip of her tea. Considering how stunned she felt when she first saw Stella holding Sonny earlier, she feels very comfortable with her now. Whatever disharmony there might be between Stella and Carly, Polly decides she likes the older woman.

'Now, I'm not one to pry, and like I said, Fletcher's already told me a few general details, but I'd love to hear them directly from you, Polly – what brought you to my son's family?' Stella takes a sip of tea and Polly notes the proprietary phrase: 'my son's family'. If she stands a chance of being accepted into this household long term, as she needs and wants to be, she must get Stella to like her too.

'Well, I've been nannying for a few years now and my last post was abroad, in America–'

'America?' interrupts Stella. 'Whereabouts?'

'New York,' confirms Polly.

'Fletcher didn't tell me that! He lived in Brooklyn for a while. What a coincidence!'

'Well, it's a big place but I know, right?' Polly laughs. 'I come home and end up nannying for a family who have just moved back to the UK too.'

'Meant to be,' says Stella sagely, putting her cup down and patting Polly's arm. 'You don't have an accent. Mind you, Fletcher and Eaden didn't pick one up either, despite Carly being a native.'

'I wasn't there that long,' says Polly. 'It was just a one year contract. I was really homesick the whole time anyway, so I decided to come back rather than find a new family to nanny for out there. Although it's great looking after children all day, and I do love the job, it can be lonely, especially if there's only one child and the parents work long hours. Fletcher told me he and Carly needed a nanny so they could create a healthy work-life balance, which is win-win all round.'

'Did you already have family of your own in New York? Is that why you decided to move there in the first place?' asks Stella.

'No, I moved there on a reckless whim after the nannying job I had before that ended.' Polly shrugs and laughs. 'I wanted to do something spontaneous and exciting while I was young.'

'How old were you when you went, if you don't mind me asking?'

'I was twenty-two. I'm twenty-four now.'

Stella pats Polly's arm again and smiles. 'You've obviously got great genes; I would have guessed younger.' Sonny shrieks as though in agreement with his grandmother.

Polly ignores the compliment as she takes another sip of tea. 'I'm ready to settle down now though, here in the UK. I think this job will give me stability and hopefully I can help to provide some stability for Carly and Fletcher too. I know they've been through a lot.'

Stella looks over at Eaden turning the pages of her scrapbook. She knits her brows together and nods. 'They have. And what

43

you said about providing stability is music to my ears. They need it now more than ever. It's wonderful that Carly has got a new job, and I truly hope it fulfils her as much as she hopes it will, but what's wrong with being a stay-at-home mum anyway? It seems like a dirty phrase these days. I stayed at home with Fletcher, and he's grown into a wonderful family man who loves and respects his mother, wife and children. Some women just don't realise how lucky they are to have a family.'

Stella purses her lips again, seemingly mulling over her next words. Polly waits. After a moment she continues, 'I don't want to speak out of turn or give you another scare – good lord no – but "disjointed" is the word I'd use to describe the state of affairs in this household right now. You have every right to know that now that you're living here too.'

'What does disjointed mean, Granny?' asks Eaden.

Stella looks affectionately at her granddaughter. 'No idea, big ears!' She smiles cheekily. 'It means not joined up, sweetheart.'

Eaden tilts her head to one side. 'Like handwriting?'

Stella laughs. 'Yes, in a way, clever girl. Anyway, I've already said too much.' She mimes zipping her lips shut, locking them and throwing an invisible key over her shoulder.

Eaden mimics her, making Polly and Stella dissolve into giggles, and Sonny joins in, banging his palms forcefully on the highchair's wooden tray-top. As their laughter echoes loudly around the spacious kitchen, Polly feels she fits in perfectly to this home and family, as though she truly belongs. For real, this time. She won't ever let what happened before happen again.

'Well, I must be going.' Stella sighs, pushes her chair back and stands up, a hand over her heart. 'It was so lovely to meet you, Polly, and thank you for the tea. I thoroughly enjoyed spending time with you and my gorgeous grandchildren. I hope we can do it again soon.'

'Anytime,' replies Polly as her giggles subside, pleased they've already forged a sturdy connection.

CHAPTER EIGHT

Once Stella has left, Polly decides to take the children out to the garden to make the most of the early September afternoon sun.

She opens the bi-fold doors fully and surveys the professionally landscaped garden with its elegant outdoor furniture and tall heat lamps, all protected with custom-made covers.

The large lush lawn is dotted with and surrounded by mature trees and flowering plants and is not overlooked by any houses beyond. It's absolutely stunning and clearly not used regularly by Eaden and Sonny. The only evidence of children living here at all is a wooden playhouse in the back corner, painted yellow with a white roof and door. *It's fancier than some New York studio apartments, and probably bigger too*, muses Polly.

She lays Sonny's playmat on the grass in the shade of the Japanese maple tree and places a few of his cuddly and wooden toys on top.

Then, as Eaden skips along the stone path to the playhouse, she picks Sonny up from his highchair, takes his sun hat from the basket under his pushchair, places it on his head and walks out onto the lawn.

'Coo-ee!' Polly hears a voice and sees a hand pop up over the wall. Meryl's head appears a moment later. 'I just wanted to confirm that the mistress of the house got her parcel, along with my apologies.'

Polly checks that Eaden is happily playing then moves towards Meryl. She gives her a small wave. 'Hi again. Yes, she did. Thank you.'

'How are you settling in, dear?'

'Good so far,' she says, then gives a little laugh. 'I think so, anyway.'

'Well, you look right at home anyway. How are the renovations coming along? I haven't heard as much banging or drilling lately.'

'Um, from what I can tell, I think all the major stuff has been done, including the décor. There are just the kids' bedrooms and the master left to finish.'

'Neutral tones throughout, am I right?'

Polly smirks. 'How did you guess?'

Meryl looks over at the house, shielding her eyes from the sun. 'I thought as much. I've never seen Carly wear or carry anything that's patterned or colourful – quite the opposite to myself, as you can tell.' She gestures towards her worn floral flannel shirt and burgundy corduroy trousers.

'I'm the same,' admits Polly. 'Bold choices all the way. If this was my house, I'd repaint every single room.'

Meryl nods her agreement. 'I'm not surprised they wanted a full refresh though; out with the old and in with the new in all senses of the phrase.'

'What do you mean by that?' Polly looks at the older woman quizzically.

The older woman considers her for a moment. 'Well, I just mean that Fletcher used to live here with his first wife, Pippa, then it was let out for a year to husband-and-wife author friends of Stella's after Fletcher ran off to America with the little one. No judgement,' she adds, holding her palms up to offset her judgemental comment.

'Ran off?' asks Polly.

'Yes. Well, flew off, anyway. Gosh, Stella was in bits. Her heart broke for them after the accident and Pippa's death. Terrible business.' Meryl gives a slight shake of her head. 'All she wanted to do was keep them close, comfort them, but he decided a fresh start was what they needed. Became fixated on it, apparently. A change of scenery, away from the memories. He told Eaden to point to somewhere on the globe and that's where they went – just packed up and jetted off halfway across the world right before Christmas! Apparently, it was only going to be for a few weeks but then he told Stella he'd met someone – who now we know was Carly – and that they were getting married. A fresh start indeed! He instructed Stella to rent out the house and said he'd live off the income.'

Meryl tuts and shakes her head. 'She begged him to come home, that Eaden – who was only four years old at the time, little poppet – needed stability, her family around her, and so did he, but he wouldn't be persuaded. Stella said she'd never heard him sound so flat and bleak, despite his supposed happy news.' Meryl shudders slightly despite the sun. 'She knew it was the grief talking, that he'd come back eventually, but he certainly put her through the wringer for a while.'

Polly blinks rapidly as Sonny tugs on her hair, processing Meryl's gossipy synopsis of the situation. She hadn't known any of this extended backstory until now. She knew Fletcher's first wife had died but she'd been under the impression he originally moved to America for work in a rational, planned fashion. No wonder she sensed Stella's frostiness towards her new daughter-in-law earlier; her son's second marriage screamed rebound. 'Well, they seem like a great family now,' she lies, not wanting to say anything that might get back to Stella, Fletcher or Carly.

Meryl makes a noncommittal sound. 'Appearances can be deceptive, dear.' She gestures around the garden, making a circling motion with her hand. 'This, here, what you're doing on your *first day*, I've never seen Carly do, not once since they came back in July. The only time I've seen her out here is when she's exercising, alone. Yoga and skipping. And she swims every day at the local health club, apparently. Obsessive, if you ask me. If she was as interested in those children as she is in exercise and her appearance and clothes – today's parcel was one of many I've taken in since they've moved in – then perhaps they wouldn't have any need for a nanny.' She sniffs. 'No offence, dear.'

'None taken.' Polly untangles her hair from Sonny's palm and jiggles him up and down, quite enjoying Meryl's unfiltered vitriol.

'And *him* – Fletcher? Well, I know grief materialises in many different ways but to wrench your child away from her loving extended family, fly her thousands of miles away, marry an American woman, then have a baby with that woman before your first wife is cold in her grave? Quite frankly, it's a lot. All I'll say is keep your wits about you. I can't put my finger on it but something's not quite right with this family. I don't care what Stella says about him – it's mother's bias.' Meryl lets out a long breath, evidently exhausted from all her unsolicited tattling.

Polly watches Eaden through the open door of her playhouse, moving toys about and talking to herself. 'Do Fletcher and Carly often fight?' she asks Meryl.

Meryl scrunches up her mouth and blinks before answering. 'You've witnessed it already?'

Polly hesitates then nods.

Meryl shakes her head and tuts. 'I don't mean to scare you, but they're a fiery couple.'

Polly thinks about Stella using the word 'scare' too earlier and wonders whether the older women's assessments of the Lawrensons' marriage is being judged too harshly through their generation's outdated filter. She can't believe for a second that she needs to be *scared* of them.

Meryl corrects herself, 'Or perhaps a smouldering couple might be a better description; no brutal blazing rows as such but there always seem to be the promise of flames despite no apparent warmth between them, if that makes sense? It's just a feeling I get based on what I've observed, and from what Stella's told me. Of course, you're welcome to form your own opinion, dear.'

'Well, I don't scare easily,' states Polly, 'and I really want this job so I'm just going to have to tough it out.'

CHAPTER NINE

Carly hears laughter as she walks through the door and, for a moment, wonders if she's in the right house. She realises, with a pang of sadness, that she barely heard the sound in stereo while she was responsible for looking after the children. She drops her house keys in the bowl on the console table and hooks her bag over the newel post feeling a familiar annoyance that the cloakroom isn't finished yet. She believes in the 'tidy house, tidy mind' ethos and the longer they live in an ongoing renovation and not the calm, clean, clutter-free home she envisaged, the more uptight she feels.

She takes off her heels and carries them upstairs to find Polly bathing Eaden and Sonny in the family bathroom. She watches them from the hallway, simultaneously envious of Polly's seemingly carefree attitude and easy interactions with the children, and utterly relieved that she doesn't have to do this task herself every evening anymore. She wonders whether other mothers feel the same way or if she's abnormal. She hasn't felt like her 'normal' self since before Sonny was born.

She shifts and Polly jolts with surprise.

'Oh hi.' Polly blinks. 'You made me jump skulking around out there.'

Carly feels like a guest in her own home as she sits down on the closed toilet after placing her shoes on the landing. Sonny splashes in delight.

'How was your day?' she asks.

'We've had a great day, haven't we?' Polly asks Eaden and Sonny enthusiastically.

'Yes!' Eaden cheers and Sonny squeals in response.

'How was yours?' asks Polly, rinsing bubbles off Eaden's hair, her own long locks almost dipping in the water.

'It was good, thank you. It was nice to feel like myself again… to think about other things.' Carly looks over at the children in the bath and twists her wedding ring around her finger.

'Is Fletcher not with you?' asks Polly.

'No, he's working late. Again. I got an Uber home. Did you find everywhere and everything okay?'

'No problems with school drop-off and pick-up and I think I'm finding my way around the kitchen, thanks to help from this one.' She plonks a blob of bubbles on Eaden's nose and Eaden laughs loudly.

'Granny helped too!' she shouts.

'Stella was here? When?' asks Carly, instantly stiffening.

'After we got home from school,' confirms Polly, glancing back over her shoulder. 'She popped round to see the children. Stayed for a quick cup of tea. She was very welcoming.'

Carly pouts. 'I bet she was – to you. It's okay to not let her in, you know, if she turns up again unannounced and you're too busy to sit and chat with her. I've asked her not to disrupt the children's routine unnecessarily. We'll schedule plenty of time with her on the weekends and in the holidays now Eaden's back at school.'

'Oh, I didn't let her in; she used the bi-fold door key that Fletcher gave her,' says Polly.

Carly's lips part and she raises her perfectly shaped eyebrows. 'He's given her a key, has he?'

Carly has worked herself into an emotional state by the time Fletcher gets home from work; even later than he said he'd be, which has only aggravated her further. She's a boiling pot of bubbling liquid, lid clattering, struggling to keep the lava-like contents contained.

She sits on their bed in the dark in her workout gear and listens to him moving around downstairs. Then she hears his heavy work boots on the uncarpeted steps. She's lost count of how many times she's asked him to take them off in the hallway, to prevent dragging dirt further into the house. He's missed the children's bedtime again, but she's not surprised; she knows that his logic will be that Polly's here now to help Carly with that so there's no need for him to be. She was hoping that Polly being here would mean more time for them as a couple but if today's anything to go by, nothing's going to change on that score, certainly not as quickly as she expected it to.

She looks through the gap in the doorway as he comes into view. He's moving slowly, his attention absorbed by his phone, seemingly amused by something on the screen. He pushes open the bedroom door fully, turns on the bare-bulbed ceiling light and starts as he sees Carly sitting on his side of the bed.

'Christ!' he exclaims. 'Why are you sitting in the dark?' he asks, recovering his composure quickly and sliding his phone into his back pocket.

Carly sniffs. 'Waiting for you.'

He looks at her. 'Well, here I am.' He bends down to kiss her cheek, but she turns her tear-soaked face away. He takes a step back and sighs. 'What's wrong? I told you I'd be late.'

'I didn't think you'd be this late. Just because Polly's here now it doesn't mean you can wash your hands of all your responsibilities,' she retorts as she turns on the bedside light, turns off the main light, peeks out into the hallway, closes the door and turns back to face him, arms crossed.

He shakes his head. 'I'm not trying to wash my hands of any responsibilities; I wanted to be home earlier, but we can't just leave a wall half plastered, Carly. And then the client wanted to chat through some changes. It's my *business*,' he hisses.

'Yes, and this is your *family*,' she hisses back.

'A family I provide a very good life for thanks to the business.' He tilts his head back and puts his hand on his hips.

'I'm providing now too!'

He chuckles and shakes his head again. Sitting down on the bed, he takes his phone out of his back pocket and puts it on the bedside table.

'What's so funny? My job is menial in comparison to yours?' Carly's nostrils flare.

He yanks off one of his boots. 'No, not at all. If going back to work so soon after having our son makes you happy, that's great. But your wages just about cover the nanny's wages so you're effectively working to pay someone else to look after our children.'

She gapes at him. 'You encouraged me to go back to work!'

'I supported you in your decision,' he says, tugging off his other boot and looking up at her. 'Your mind was already made up. You made it quite clear you didn't want to be a stay-at-home mum once we moved here, and that's okay. I get it. You want your own identity, you don't want to be a 1950s housewife blah-blah-blah. Just don't pretend you're doing it to help provide for your family when you're really doing it for purely selfish reasons.'

Tears well in her eyes again. He always knows exactly what to say, how to verbally hit her where it hurts. She swipes an overflowing tear from her cheek, re-crosses her arms and promptly switches tack to a safer topic. 'Your mother was here today,' she says.

He shrugs. 'So?'

'She let herself in with the key you gave her. Ambushed Polly.'

He takes a deep breath and rubs his knuckles along his jaw, clearly wondering how best to respond. Evidently opting to tread the path of peace, he apologises. 'I'm sorry, I should have asked you first, but I thought, what with you going back to work, it might be a good idea for Mum to have her own key, just until Polly settles in properly.'

'You said she had excellent credentials. Is she not capable of looking after two children alone? Or are you saying you don't trust her alone with them; that you want Stella to keep an eye on her?'

'No, nothing like that.' Sighing, he stands and prises open her arms, taking her hands in his. 'Look, babe, all Mum wants to do is help. She wants to be involved in the children's lives–'

'And you both thought that I can't object if I'm out of the way at work,' she states, interrupting him. 'You've been conspiring behind my back.'

'No, we haven't.' He pauses. 'But one of the main reasons we moved back here was to benefit from family support while I built the business back up and you focused on a new career. How are we supposed to do those things with no help? You know what they say – it takes a village to raise kids, apparently.'

'But that's what Polly's here for!' Carly pulls her hands away and jabs a finger in the direction of Polly's bedroom.

'Yes, day-to-day, but why not accept the extra help Mum's offering too? She adores the kids. She just wants to be a good grandmother and she promised she wouldn't be free and easy with the key.' He looks at her dolefully. 'I'll take it back if she abuses the privilege but can't you just give her a chance to prove herself, please?'

The question hangs in the air over their battlefield as Carly considers allowing his words to soothe her maudlin mood. She sighs and feels an ebb of relief that the argument might be fizzling out when his phone buzzes. She glances over at it but only sees his lock-screen photo of Sonny and Eaden. He's obviously got it set so his messages don't display as banners.

'That's probably your mother. I bet she's bugged the house and is listening in!' She meant it to sound light-hearted but even to her own ears her tone is harsh and spiteful.

He leans down, snatches up his phone and moves his face inches from hers. 'Don't be so fucking ridiculous!' he snarls with fury in his eyes.

Carly recoils and he shoves past her, strides to the en suite and slams the door.

CHAPTER TEN

Polly steps out of the shower in her en suite and hears Fletcher's raised voice. She wraps a towel around herself and presses her ear against the back of her bedroom door, but the house falls silent again. She's glad the children haven't woken; it took a while to settle Sonny earlier. *Is he so used to his parents fighting he just sleeps through it?* she wonders.

She dries herself and yanks her pyjamas on then waits at the door again, running a comb absentmindedly through her long dark hair as she listens. She's thirsty but she doesn't want to walk past Fletcher and Carly's bedroom when they're having an argument, or, worse, risk getting embroiled in the frosty aftermath should one of them exit as she's sneaking down the stairs.

She waits ten more minutes then decides the silence means the coast is clear. Besides, she doesn't want to feel like a prisoner here; it's her home now too and she's allowed to get a drink when she wants!

In the dark kitchen, Polly opens the fridge. She gets out a carton of organic juice and sets it down on the island. As she begins looking for a glass, she notices a light on outside and wonders briefly if Stella has dropped by again. She walks slowly towards the triple bi-fold doors and looks out. Carly is on the patio, skipping. Polly deliberates whether to go outside to speak to her. She decides she probably should and takes a bottle of Evian from the fridge for her.

'You must be wondering what you've walked into,' says Carly without preamble as she approaches. She's barely out of breath despite the quickness of her jumps.

'Judgement-free zone here,' replies Polly.

'Two arguments in one day is actually good going for us lately, although the second one could have been avoided if I didn't have such an interfering mother-in-law or a mummy's boy husband.' Carly stops skipping and checks the digital display on the rope's handles. She seems satisfied with the number of calories she's burned off.

Carly takes the bottle of water Polly hands her. She nods her thanks, opens it and takes a few mouthfuls.

'Do you want to talk about it?' Polly asks. She senses Carly needs to vent and she's interested in listening to what goes on behind the scenes in the tension-filled Lawrenson household. Forewarned is forearmed.

'I think Fletcher cheated on me in America, not long after Sonny was born,' she shares boldly. 'It nearly destroyed me.' She takes another sip of water then replaces the cap. 'I think he's doing it again now. All the signs are there. And why wouldn't he? That's his pattern!'

Polly tries her best not to look shocked at the unexpected overshare. She doesn't want to ask the obvious question, but she can't help herself. She's a magnet for gossip today, it seems. She coughs and swallows. 'What signs?'

'Just little things.' Carly pauses, clearly consulting the formulated list in her head. 'Permanent voicemail whenever I ring him, yet he answers the phone to everyone else; work "emergencies" practically every weekend; new projects to quote all of a sudden; and not forgetting the mysterious *Prick Tease.*'

Polly laughs nervously, all too aware she's opened a can of worms now. She feels she must ask. 'Prick tease?'

Carly nods. 'It's a lip gloss – shade *Prick Tease.* I found it in his car. It was used so it's unlikely to be a gift and I don't wear lip gloss, especially not whore red by a cheap brand. It was under the corner of the passenger seat. I haven't asked him about it because frankly, I'm afraid of the answer. I moved here for him, for our family, for the promise of a fresh start and a better life, and this is how he repays me!'

Polly widens her eyes and presses her lips together, her whole body itching with discomfort. Carly resumes skipping at a slower pace as Polly takes a seat on the low wall adjacent to the patio, unsure about how to respond. She doesn't need to; the other woman continues, barely missing a beat.

'We only met twenty months ago, and we've been married just over a year. I fell pregnant within three months of meeting him, and I was three months pregnant when we got married. Talk about whirlwind!' Carly laughs without mirth. 'And we've been here in the UK since July. Fletcher wanted to move back even earlier as Stella was pressuring him to take over the family business after Frank's death, but I wanted to completely revamp the house before I moved in, so it felt like our family home rather than just his old house or worse – Pippa's mausoleum. Fletcher flew back a couple of times for business stuff, and your interview, obviously, while I orchestrated the renovation from the States.'

'How did you do it all from so far away?' asks Polly, relieved to be able to redirect the conversation. She looks up at the house. It's such a handsome property, even from the back garden.

'I knew exactly the style I wanted so I sent floorplans, Pinterest boards and sketches of my own to the builders Fletcher lined up – his cousin Perry and a few of his Uncle Frank's contacts. It wasn't the easiest with a newborn!'

'It must have been pretty stressful,' says Polly. 'Looking after a newborn is difficult regardless, never mind managing a renovation and preparing to emigrate.'

'It was a bit of a blur most of the time, but I did enjoy having a project to work on. Thank God the house turned out okay, for the most part. Of course it's not finished yet.' She rolls her eyes. 'I lost count of all the night-feed FaceTimes I had with the builders checking on progress. I was grateful for the time difference.'

'I bet Fletcher was a big help though, wasn't he?' asks Polly.

'He tried his best, but he was busy with Perry and Stella, sorting out the transfer of the business. He looked after Eaden a lot though. I just didn't have the time or energy for her too, especially as Sonny was such a fussy baby. Or maybe it's me.' She stops skipping and shrugs. 'Maybe I'm not meant to be a mother, or a stepmother. I know Eaden resents me, and I don't really blame her. She must see me as a cuckoo in her and Fletcher's nest.'

Polly pulls down the corners of her mouth, considering Carly's words. 'I'm sure it's tough being a mother and a stepmother, and a wife for that matter. Having three people making demands on you must feel like a lot of pressure sometimes.'

Carly nods fervently. 'You said it. I feel like the pressure is crushing me at times. I mean, I try to stay as attractive as possible but I'm just an ageing ex-model, past her best and definitely not a patch on perfect Pippa – Fletcher's first wife.' She screws her face up as she says the phrase *perfect Pippa*. 'The dead are always elevated to superior status, you know? And she was an interior designer.'

'Oh?' says Polly, surprised at the change of subject – she can barely keep up. Carly's like a wind-up toy with new batteries, oversharing relentlessly and inappropriately.

'Yes, she had her own business. This was way before Fletcher took over his dad and Frank's business, obviously. If she were here now though, he'd be taking care of the construction side of things and then recommending her design services once the houses were done. Dream partnership.' She rolls her eyes again, but as she moves the light from the kitchen briefly illuminates how watery they are. 'That's why I really insisted on the renovation – I couldn't bear to see her thoughts and ideas and designs everywhere I looked. It was bad enough knowing they were, and always will be, in Fletcher's head.'

'You shouldn't torture yourself like this,' says Polly sympathetically. 'Sonny's a happy baby, you've done a great job on the house, and you've just started a brand-new career.'

'Yeah, I guess so…' Carly trails off, batteries finally draining. 'God, I'm so sorry for oversharing. It's not in your job description to listen to me and all my neuroses. I thought the skipping would de-stress me, but I think a long hot soak in the tub might be in order instead.' She touches Polly's shoulder. 'Thank you for listening but please just ignore me. I'm just being paranoid. No need to mention any of this to anyone.' She looks at Polly pointedly in the soft halo of light.

'My lips are sealed.' Polly mimes zipping her lips, just like Stella did earlier, locking more secrets inside.

CHAPTER ELEVEN

TUESDAY

The next morning, Carly returns from her swim to a calm, pleasant kitchen; a completely different atmosphere to when she managed, or rather mismanaged, breakfast times alone when they lived in the States, and when they first moved to this house in Swanland. Polly is feeding Sonny and Fletcher is sitting with Eaden. Eaden's scrapbook is open between her and her father on the table and they're looking through it as they eat their respective breakfasts.

'Good morning, everyone,' she says as she strolls over to the sink. She makes herself a cup of herbal tea using the newly installed instant hot water tap that still thrills her.

'Good morning, Mummy,' replies Polly, on behalf of Sonny.

'Good swim?' asks Fletcher.

Carly nods and gives him a tight smile before blowing on her steaming tea. 'Sorry I'm back a bit later than usual, I thought I'd dry my hair there today.'

'Not a problem,' he says, before finishing off his toast.

'Daddy, how long until my new bedroom's ready?' asks Eaden.

'Not long now, munchkin. How about we go for a walk

around the shops at the weekend and you can choose some new things?' he suggests.

'Won't you be working this weekend?' Carly asks Fletcher, surprised.

'Hopefully only Saturday morning. We can go on Saturday afternoon. What do you say, Eades?'

'Yay!' she cheers and Fletcher beams at his daughter's obvious delight.

Carly forces a smile to disguise her disappointment at not being invited along. She worries that Eaden will never fully take to her if Fletcher doesn't bother to include her in things like this too. But now is not the time to voice her concern, especially after their heated exchange last night. She'll wait until she can broach the subject privately and sensitively.

'Oh, I saw Mallory at the health club. She's one of the mums at Eaden's school,' Carly says, directing her words towards Polly. The nanny has her long hair styled in a French plait today and Carly is momentarily taken aback by how much younger she looks with it off her face, even younger than yesterday. 'Her daughter Celeste is having a birthday party in a couple of weeks. She says she'll give you Eaden's invitation at school drop-off or pick-up sometime next week.'

'Okay,' says Polly. 'I'll look out for her.'

'Wow, another party!' exclaims Fletcher to Eaden, ruffling her hair. 'You've got a better social life than me, kid.'

She tilts her head to the side, regarding him. 'What's a social life, Daddy?'

He laughs, pulling his phone out of his pocket and checking it. 'You know what? I can't even remember. Right, I'd better make a move.'

'So soon?' asks Carly.

'Yeah, Perry's already on his way to Chestnut Avenue. Lots to get done today. See you later, alligator.' He kisses Eaden, picks up his empty plate and leaves the table. He puts the plate in the sink then bends to kiss Sonny too. 'See you later, ladies,' he says, smiling at Polly before giving Carly a chaste peck on the cheek on his way out.

Sonny squeals in response and Carly jumps at the sound. She feels unusually edgy this morning and puts it down to the guilt she feels about gossiping to Polly last night. It was so unprofessional of her. She picks Fletcher's plate out of the sink and loads it into the dishwasher before turning towards the younger woman and gesturing for her to cross over to the island. Polly gives Sonny his spoon, glances at Eaden, and complies.

'I'm so sorry again about offloading onto you last night.' Carly's voice is a low whisper. 'I don't want you to think I'm some insufferable American...' she casts around for the phrase she wants, 'verbal vomiter or something, because I'm not. I don't know what came over me, and I'm sorry for subjecting you to that, especially on your first night. And Fletcher's always been adamant he's never been unfaithful, and I do believe him, so I'm probably just being hormonal or premenstrual or something. It won't happen again.'

'No need to apologise, really,' Polly assures her, crossing her arms. 'I'm glad you trust me. Is there anything practical I can do to help? Pump him for a confession, perhaps?' She laughs and Carly frowns. Whether made in jest or not, she considers it a strange, crude offer. But, she reasons, it's still early days and they'll soon understand each other's sense of humour better.

Carly quickly rearranges her frown into a smile. 'No, you just being here is help enough. And I've had words with Fletcher about Stella just dropping by whenever she feels like a snoop. It's not on. The children need to get used to their routine and I need to feel like she's not checking up on us all, and by "all" I mean me – and you. I know she disapproves of me going back to work so soon and I wouldn't put it past her to be compiling a dossier of evidence of how negatively it's affecting Sonny and Eaden.' Carly stops and squeezes her eyes shut. 'God, listen to me going on again! I'll shut up now and go get ready for work. You're okay here, yes?'

Without waiting for a reply, she picks up her cup of tea and heads out the kitchen and up the stairs.

———

At work, Carly feels agitated. Gavin is with a client in the treatment room, and she's meant to be familiarising herself with the whole range of treatments available at the clinic, and their prices, but instead, her mind keeps replaying the conversations she had with Polly last night and earlier this morning.

She feels embarrassed that she has already shared so much, and that she and Fletcher fought twice while Polly was in the house yesterday. She doesn't want Polly to leave because then what? Would they be able to find another nanny straight away? Would Carly have to leave her job or agree to – God forbid – Stella stepping into the breach while they found a replacement, which then wouldn't happen because Stella would just take over permanently and phase Carly out altogether?

Once again, she wonders if she should have just refused to leave Brooklyn and given Fletcher an ultimatum: either move back to his old house in the UK with just Eaden or they all stay in the States and make their new, blended family work as best they could. But their marriage was hanging by a thread as it was, and he was fervent with promises of a better life, a fresh start, help with the children, renovating and decorating the house however she wanted, eradicating all traces of Pippa, making time for them as a couple as well as a family, and supporting her in a new career of her choice.

But now she suspects he was just telling her what she wanted to hear while she was worn down with the responsibility of a newborn and the hatred for her post-pregnancy pudgy body. All so he could fly high in the family business, a business that he hopes to one day pass down to Sonny, and she knows he also harbours the notion that Eaden might grow up to be an interior designer like Pippa. Where does she fit into this future vision?

She needs immediate reassurance to decelerate the escalating thoughts in her head. Plucking her phone out of her bag, she WhatsApps Fletcher, apologising again for their argument last night. Surely that's something he's likely to respond to. Two ticks appear, letting her know that the message has been delivered. She waits for them to turn blue. When they don't, she gets up to refill her water bottle from the water cooler next to the fancy coffee machine and stares at her phone from afar.

She sits back down at the reception desk and checks the ticks again. Still grey. Tutting, she puts the phone back in her bag and pushes her bag under the desk with her foot just as Gavin and his clearly happy client return to reception. Carly plasters on a smile, wishing that she could rejuvenate her marriage as easily as Gavin's needles rejuvenate women's faces.

CHAPTER TWELVE

By the time Carly leaves work at 5pm, the WhatsApp message ticks are still grey. She is fizzing with insecurity and her thoughts are like beetles, burrowing around inside her brain. They've reached the deepest, darkest layer by the time she parks across the road from the house Fletcher is currently working on, in Chestnut Avenue. It's adjacent to a main road, on a corner, so she's got a good view of the front and side gates, which are both wide open for access in and out. Perry's van is in the driveway beside an almost full skip, and both its back doors are wide open too.

Turning off the engine, Carly leans forward as Perry appears, carrying materials to the van. It looks like he's packing up, so she scans for Fletcher but he's nowhere to be seen. She leans back and waits.

After a while her phone vibrates on the seat next to her and she snatches it up in anticipatory relief that Fletcher has replied to her earlier message, but it's just Polly sending a cute picture of the children. Too distracted to properly take it in, she throws the phone back down. Although she's sure Polly means well, the stab of 'mum guilt' that she hasn't gone straight home to see Sonny and Eaden is an almost physical sensation, but she needs to focus on her husband right now. She watches Perry make another two trips from the house to the van, and then he slams the back doors closed. A couple of minutes later he reverses the van onto the road then drives away. Carly frowns; the gates are still open, but she can't see any movement inside, or Fletcher's car anywhere.

After a few more excruciating minutes, Fletcher finally makes an appearance just as a white BMW pulls up outside the gates and a red-headed woman emerges. Carly's stomach drops as she watches them greet each other, and judging by Fletcher's body language, the woman is familiar to him. She snatches up her phone and leans forwards to watch their exchange while opening the camera and pressing record.

Carly's still awake at 1am, pretending she isn't. Fletcher is facing away from her, but his phone screen is emitting a soft glow from beneath the duvet. She lies there, as stiff as a mannequin while his tiny movements create seismic shifts in her psyche. He still hasn't replied to her WhatsApp apology, nor mentioned it since he got home, but now he's busy on his phone in the early hours.

She thinks back to one terrible night in America, right after Sonny was born, when he would only sleep if he was resting on her chest. She recalls how intensely suffocating that feeling was, not only the weight of the baby himself but the difficult choice she constantly faced: disturb her sleeping son and cope with him screaming all night or surreptitiously check her new husband's phone for evidence he was already cheating on her and then spend the night screaming at him. She wonders what she would find on his phone tonight – messages from the woman she saw him with earlier?

They had chatted for a while on the pavement of Chestnut Avenue, smiling and laughing, while Carly filmed them from her vantage point across the road. Then Fletcher wallked back towards the house, shutting the side gates behind him, as the woman drove away. Nothing physical happened between them at all – and Carly has watched the video about fifty times to be sure – but she suspects Fletcher is too sneaky to be that obvious in public.

Is that the supposed client he's working for or is she someone else, someone more meaningful? Are they really carrying out building work on that house or has Fletcher arranged for Perry to pop by occasionally just in case she starts getting suspicious? Has Fletcher bought the house just so he has somewhere in plain sight to conduct his affairs? Or is he a bigamist and that woman is his wife too and they are renovating the house ready for his other secret family? Is the house actually an upmarket, suburban brothel that Fletcher and Perry frequent on a regular basis?

Carly knows her thoughts are spiralling ridiculously, and she needs to calm herself down. It doesn't help that in the early days of their relationship, when they were intoxicated with each other, Fletcher faux-ashamedly admitted he'd cheated on an ex-girlfriend – pre-Pippa – with a client of his dad's and Uncle Frank's, back in the days when he and Perry used to labour for them on evenings and weekends if jobs overran. Fletcher described the client as 'a classic bored housewife who wanted a bit of fun with a teenage toyboy' and that it had just happened one day, without any prompting on his part. And then it kept happening until they finished working on the house.

He had passed it off as nothing more than an extra but enjoyable task at the end of his shift. He said he and Perry laughed about it, that Perry called him 'jammy' for hooking up with a 'cougar'. Carly remembers thinking that she wasn't surprised; what woman wouldn't want him now but especially then? And it wasn't as if he was married, he was just a nineteen-year-old kid at the time. But now she sneers at her own naivety, at her own smugness back then.

She closes her eyes and focuses on her breathing, as silently as she can, echoing Sonny's tiny breaths through the baby monitor. When she opens her eyes again Fletcher's phone's glow has gone. She risks looking over at him and he's as still as a corpse. After a while she hears his breathing deepen, become even and rhythmic, and she finally lets out her own breath fully. She lifts the duvet, puts on her cream silk robe and exits the bedroom, carefully avoiding the creaky floorboards before closing the door softly behind her.

Downstairs, in the cloakroom off the utility, she weighs herself and the number on the scales, which is lower than the last time she checked, instantly makes her feel marginally better. She goes into the kitchen, makes herself a herbal tea and takes it into the lounge, where she sits cross-legged on the Persian rug against the sumptuous stone-coloured sofa. Placing the cup on the low, wooden, antique apothecary coffee table that she bought on Etsy but was assured was sourced from Morocco, she reaches for her laptop and logs into Facebook where she navigates to Fletcher's business page: *Lawrenson Building Company Ltd*. Scrolling down to the latest post, she sees it's populated with a few pictures. She clicks through them quickly and confirms it's the Chestnut Avenue house she stalked today.

She allows herself a small sigh of relief that it is a real project they're working on but then she sees *her* – the woman Fletcher was looking cosy with earlier. It's only showing a side profile but it's definitely her. Scrutinising the image closely, Carly realises with a jolt who the woman reminds her of – Fletcher's first wife, Pippa. Her hair is the same shade of red. The same as Eaden's too. Carly's chest constricts painfully as she checks to see if the photo has been tagged, but it hasn't.

Frustrated not to be granted access to a deeper layer of information, she focuses in on the woman in the image and begins to critically compare herself to her, a form of self-flagellation. While her untouched tea goes cold, she simply sits and stares and seethes, obsessively assessing the freckled face and the petite frame of the homewrecker she is sure is secretly fucking her husband, and she vows to find hard evidence to prove she's right.

CHAPTER THIRTEEN

WEDNESDAY

The next morning, Carly returns from the health club and heads upstairs after popping into the kitchen to check on Polly and the children.

Fletcher exits the en suite as she enters the bedroom. 'Good swim?' He places his phone on the bedside table, throws the wet towel on the bed and pulls on his pants and combat trousers, before opening his wardrobe and taking out a fresh polo shirt.

She follows his lead, pretending everything's fine, pretending that he wasn't on his phone in the early hours, pretending that she didn't fall asleep downstairs after forensically sifting through his Facebook business page as well as his and Perry's personal pages. 'Fifty laps,' she boasts. 'Got to banish this baby weight somehow.'

'What baby weight? You look great.' He pulls his shirt over his head, runs his hand through his still damp hair and gives her a quick kiss on the cheek. Picking up his phone he heads for the door. 'I'm off.' He stops, shaking his phone twice as though he's remembering something. He turns back to her. 'I might be late again tonight but only because Perry needs to leave early. I promise, though, as soon as we break the back of this first big job, things will get a bit easier. Thank God for Polly though, eh? For giving us a bit of freedom and flexibility. At least you're not tied to a finish time now either.'

Carly knows exactly what he's doing but she plays along. 'True,' she agrees, keeping her expression impassive. An idea comes to her and she swallows, wanting to make sure her tone's just right. 'Hey, if Perry's leaving early, why don't you have half an hour off before him and meet me for a quick bite to eat at lunchtime?' She forces a smile as he fails to hide his obvious surprise and confusion.

'Nice offer, but no can do. Too busy today. Sorry. And since when did you start eating lunch?' he throws over his shoulder as he leaves.

'Didn't you bring anything to eat?' Gavin is sipping an espresso in the small but stylish staff area at lunchtime, looking like a man with no worries in the world.

Carly wonders if he does have anything to worry about but as it's only her third day, she refrains from asking him the probing personal questions that are on her mind. She wants to ask if he's married, and if so, if he's ever cheated on his wife, or even considered cheating on his wife. Is cheating at the forefront of all men's minds, or just her husband's? What's that saying: once a cheater, always a cheater?

But Fletcher didn't cheat on Pippa; Pippa *died*. Yes, he moved on quite quickly, but Pippa couldn't un-*die*, could she? What would have been the point in him torturing himself in her memory forever? Nine months was a perfectly acceptable amount of time in which to meet and marry someone new, in Carly's opinion. At least, it was back then, when it worked in her favour, she acknowledges guiltily. What's that other saying: marry in haste, repent at leisure?

Carly heaves a deep sigh before she realises Gavin is looking at her expectantly. His question finally makes its way to her ears. 'Sorry, miles away. No, I didn't have time to prepare anything. Too busy sorting everyone else in the family out, you know how it is,' she says, then instantly feels like an idiot. What if Gavin doesn't know how it is, what if he doesn't have a family but wants one, and here she is rubbing his face in it?

Never mind, she's got bigger worries to deal with. 'You know what? I might just pop out for lunch, if that's okay? Grab something off-site. Maybe at the café a few doors down.' She cringes at the phrase 'off-site', but she's said it now. She hooks her bag over her arm. 'Won't be long.'

As she walks quickly to her car parked down a side street, past the café, she makes brief eye contact with Benny, the homeless man, who is sitting outside on a folded up sleeping bag, his paper cup and sign at his feet. He's holding a battered paperback – the cover suggests it's a crime novel. Sympathy surges through her and she returns his smile, reminding herself to start bringing spare change to work from now on.

Less than ten minutes later she's back outside the Chestnut Avenue house. She feels better equipped to cope with whatever she sees today because instead of sprouting wildly, her worries are more contained now that she has some concrete answers to yesterday's pressing questions. All she wants today is one thing: to catch him red-handed with the red-haired woman in the Facebook photo so she can step back from the edge and find a new way forward. Maybe even back to Brooklyn, she thinks wildly. Hard evidence is handy leverage for myriad positive separation or divorce outcomes. It's not what she wants, but she has to think practically.

Desperate to see something worthwhile, Carly can't believe her luck when Fletcher and Perry appear in the open doorway of the house after just a few minutes. They speak to each other briefly before Perry disappears back inside and Fletcher walks briskly down the front path and out through the wrought-iron gate.

For a second Carly thinks he's going to spot her car parked opposite, but he looks left and heads down the street. Tracking his progress, she watches him stop at a car that's not his – the white BMW again – and pull open the passenger door. As he gets in, she cranes her neck, squinting to see the driver through the windscreen and is surprised to see that it's not the woman from yesterday, the Pippa lookalike, but another woman entirely with blonde curly hair and vibrant red lips. Is she *Prick Tease?*

Despite her shock, she remembers she needs evidence. Grabbing her phone, she zooms in and snaps a few photos of them talking and laughing for a minute or two. The woman even reaches over and pushes Fletcher's shoulder playfully before they drive away.

With shaking fingers, Carly rings her husband, squeezing her eyes shut as she whispers, 'Pick up, pick up, pick up', but after three rings it goes to voicemail. She feels the heat of humiliation and drops the phone onto her lap as though it has burned her. He's rejected the call. He's rejected her.

For the rest of the afternoon, with time to fret while Gavin is in the treatment room with clients, Carly continues to fixate on Fletcher and the blonde woman, constructing imaginary scenarios in her head. More than once she takes out her diazepam pills and more than once she puts them back in her bag. The side effects put her off, and she refuses to eat just to take pills on a full stomach.

As soon as she gets home, she changes into her exercise gear then rushes into the kitchen where Polly and the children are eating. 'I'm going to catch the 6pm yoga class at the health club – destress a bit. You'll be okay here?'

Polly looks up at Carly, brows raised. 'Oh, you don't want to stick around for a while before bedtime?'

Carly's ears prick up at what she's sure is a hint of judgement in her nanny's voice and the bubbling emotions inside her threaten to reach boiling point. She gestures for Polly to follow her out of the kitchen into the hallway.

'Is there a problem?' she asks curtly, crossing her arms and tapping her trainer-clad foot on the patterned Amtico flooring.

Polly shakes her head, seemingly perplexed. 'What do you mean?'

'Was that your way of saying I haven't spent enough time with my children today?' Carly snaps at her, cheeks flushed.

Polly laughs innocently. 'No. I just thought you might want to sit and relax with your family for a few minutes after a busy day at work, that's all.'

Carly regards her with narrowed eyes. 'Because I get enough of that kind of judgement from my mother-in-law. Wait, has she dropped by unannounced again today?'

'No, and I'm sorry, I wasn't judging you. I wouldn't do that, no matter what Stella says.' Polly smiles as she holds her employer's gaze.

Carly's jaw drops. 'So she *has* said something scathing about me?'

'No, but if she did, I wouldn't believe it anyway.' Polly reaches out and briefly squeezes Carly's arm.

After a moment Carly's shoulders sag. She uncrosses her arms and looks over at the children. Eaden passes Sonny his spoon, which he grasps with his little fingers.

'I'm sorry.' She sighs. 'I didn't mean to snap. This is why I need yoga!'

'Are you okay?' Polly asks. 'Do you need to vent about anything else?'

Carly shakes her head and blows out a breath. 'I've done enough of that already; you don't want to hear more of the same.'

She slides her phone out of her yoga pants' pocket and looks at the time. 'Listen, I need to go if I'm going to get to the class on time. If you could start bathtime, I'll finish off when I get back.'

'No problem. What time will Fletcher be home?'

Carly sighs. 'God knows.' She shrugs. 'Whenever he's finished with his fancy woman, I suppose.' The words are out before she can stop them.

Polly's eyes widen. 'What do you mean?' she asks, repeating her question from earlier.

Carly grimaces at yet another verbal vomit and shakes her head again. 'Forget it. I shouldn't have said anything.'

'Has something happened?' Polly persists, her brow furrowing.

Carly presses her lips together in an attempt to keep the words on the tip of her tongue inside, but a second later they spill out of her anyway. 'I caught him today, looking far too flirty with some blonde woman. And I saw him yesterday, with a red-head. He's such a fucking player.' The anguish is clear in her voice.

'Where did you see him?' asks Polly.

'At the house he's working on. I think one of the women lives there but I don't know about the one today. She picked him up outside at lunchtime and they drove off together in her car despite him saying he was too busy to have lunch with me.'

Polly's face is a mask of shock and Carly feels a twisted satisfaction that her husband's infidelity can elicit such obvious sympathy for her; it really must be as bad as she thinks it is.

Encouraged by her nanny's response, Carly shows her the pictures she took on her phone at lunchtime of Fletcher and the woman in the car. Polly swipes through them with interest, flicking back and forth and even enlarging some of the images as Carly reiterates that he's always messaging someone, claiming it's his mother or Perry.

'But who messages their mother at 1am?' she asks. 'And why would he be messaging Perry at that time when they work together all day every day? No, it's the perfect cover: new country, new business, new woman.'

Carly feels herself deflate as though punctured when Polly hands the phone back. Her face flames with embarrassment. 'I've done it again, haven't I? Offloaded inappropriately. What is *wrong* with me?' She presses her palm to her forehead and closes her eyes.

'No, you haven't. Honestly,' Polly reassures her. Then she touches Carly's arm again lightly. 'I know exactly what you should do.'

Carly looks up. 'What?'

Polly grins. 'You should find those women and confront them, face to face. You deserve to know the truth.'

CHAPTER FOURTEEN

THURSDAY

Taking a deep breath, Carly rings the doorbell of the house on Chestnut Avenue. It's lunchtime. She listens to the muffled chimes resounding inside, still audible over the noise of drilling and banging.

As she waits, she replays Polly's words from last night: 'You deserve to know the truth.'

'But what if I'm wrong? What if it's just my overactive imagination?' she had worried.

'Do you think you're wrong?' Polly had asked. 'Based on the photos and what you've seen with your own eyes so far?'

'No,' Carly had whispered. 'I really don't.'

Now she's here she feels nervous yet justified in her actions. She's a wife and a mother; she has a right to investigate potential threats to her marriage and her family. She's doing the right thing.

The door opens and the woman with the long red hair appears, the Pippa lookalike from the Facebook photo.

'Hi, can I help you?' She smiles, her face open and unsuspecting.

Carly feels like she knows her after spending so much time

scrutinising her image. She looks slightly older and less like Pippa in the flesh, with tiny lines around her green eyes and an uneven skin tone beneath the freckles. But she's still extremely attractive, and probably a similar age to Carly herself. Bizarrely, she considers telling the woman to make an appointment at *Image Aesthetic Clinic* if she wants to combat her crow's feet. Instead, with steel in her voice, she juts her chin out and says, 'I'm Fletcher's wife.'

The woman's brows knit together in confusion at Carly's stony expression then her smile returns. 'Oh, do you need me to get him?' she asks, pointing behind her into the noisy belly of the house.

'No,' begins Carly, glaring at her, harnessing her courage. 'I do not need you to get him, I need you to stay away from him.' Her voice is low and urgent.

The woman gives an abrupt bark of laughter, tucking her hair behind her left ear. Her mouth conveys amusement, but her eyes are wary. 'Sorry?' It's a question rather than an apology. 'What's this about? I think you've made a mistake.'

'There's no mistake.' Carly shakes her head. 'Look, I'll cut to the chase – I saw you. With him. And if you think you're the only one he's sleeping with then you're even more stupid than he thinks I am.' She fizzes with adrenaline, with righteousness, as she spits out the words she's been desperate to expel.

'Carly?' Perry appears behind the woman, and frowns. 'What's going on?'

'I don't know… She thinks…' The woman answers first, gesturing towards Carly, unable or unwilling to articulate the accusation.

'I don't *think*, I know,' Carly clarifies, ignoring Perry, annoyed but not surprised he's got himself a ringside seat. She jabs her finger towards the woman. 'I saw you and Fletcher looking very cosy on Tuesday and then I saw him driving off with a blonde yesterday. He's playing you too.'

'Carly, what the fuck? As if!' Perry raises his hands to his head and stares at her with wide eyes like a cartoon figure drawn to convey utter insanity.

'Stay out of this, Perry,' Carly warns, with more bravado than she feels. She really should have waited until this evening, but she was bolstered by Polly's encouragement and she couldn't bear the extra hours of brooding about it.

'Yesterday?' The woman frowns. 'Do you mean with Petra, my wife? They went to collect our tile delivery at lunchtime. And as for "carrying on", well...' A laugh bursts from her. 'I think perhaps your imagination has run away with you on that score. We're happily married.' She crosses her arms across her chest as she makes her statement, her diamond-encrusted wedding ring clearly visible.

Time slows down as Carly stares at the woman and then Fletcher steps into view in the hallway, and she feels like she might faint. She's got this all horribly wrong. Again.

'Mate, you need to hear what she's accusing you of!' Perry puts a hand on his cousin's shoulder.

'I already did.' He looks at his client. 'Rachael, I'm so sorry about this. I promise I'll explain but could you please excuse us for a few minutes first? Perry, can you...' He gestures vaguely to the interior of the house.

Without looking at Carly, Fletcher steps out of the house and steers her down the front path and out into the street. 'Where's your car?' he asks.

She points to the right and they head towards it in silence. Once inside, she expects him to instantly explode but he just sits and stares out of the windscreen for a few moments, as though in a stupor.

'Fletcher, I–'

'Shut up, Carly,' he says, slicing the end of her sentence off before she can even speak it. He finally looks at her and his eyes blaze with fury and embarrassment. His jaw pulses the way it always does when he's beyond angry and he clenches his fists in his lap. 'We'll talk about this properly later. But first, let me just say this: if you ever pull a stunt like that again, try to jeopardise not only my business but my reputation, I will *deport* you.' He stares his threat into her. 'Do you understand?'

Her body shakes but she nods vigorously as her eyes overflow and tears roll down her cheeks.

'Good. Now go. I'll see you at home tonight.'

A few hours later they face each other in their almost finished, expensively renovated kitchen. The granite worktop, hard edges and numerous existing snags mirror the current state of their marriage: cold, sharp and with a few unresolved issues.

Fletcher seems calm and controlled but Carly knows she's pushed him further than she's ever pushed him before, maybe too far this time. Polly has taken the children out for tea, at Fletcher's request, so they can be alone to have this out. Carly was too ashamed to fill her in on what happened and stayed in their bedroom until Fletcher got home, like a chastised child, feigning a migraine. She looks at him now through puffy eyes.

'So, please, explain.' He unclasps his hands and rests them, palms up, on the table.

She wants to reach out and hold them, slip her hands inside his, feel his strength supporting her rather than potentially threatening her. He holds the power here and they both know it.

She knows grovelling won't work but she doesn't know how to explain what she did today without sounding paranoid, irrational, delusional. And although she doesn't want to inflame the situation further, she needs him to understand that he's played a part in all this too. She pulls out an object from her pocket and places it on the table between them.

He sits up straighter and clasps his hands again. 'What's this?' he asks, looking at the tube of lip gloss.

'I found it in your car last weekend.' She looks at him, waiting for a response, but he only shakes his head in confusion. 'It's not mine and it's been used so it couldn't be a gift. I thought... the worst.' She pauses again but he just gazes blankly at her, giving a slight hitch of his shoulders. She licks her lips. 'The worst being that it belonged to a woman you were having an affair with.'

Now he reacts – a scoffing sound – but he still doesn't speak so she lets her words run out.

'And that coupled with all the phone calls and messages you take from and send to other people yet ignore mine, and being on your phone in the early hours, and giving your mother a back-door key without consulting me, and the fact we haven't had sex since before Sonny was born...'

She takes a breath and tears well in her swollen eyes. 'I got worried and suspicious, and my confidence got lower and lower, and I guess I started looking for evidence that everything I imagined was happening was actually happening, which is why I spied on you at work and saw what I thought I saw with you and your clients. I'd always rather know the truth than live a lie.' She wipes a tear away and sits back against the upholstered bench seat.

He rubs his thumb across his forehead and sighs, his hostility receding fractionally. 'Okay. Firstly, this might be a client's or Eaden might have picked it up from school or a friend's house, or one of Perry's girlfriends might have dropped it – he has that bloody many and he borrows the car sometimes. But I don't remember ever seeing it before. You could have just asked me about it when you found it rather than constructing wild theories in your head.'

Carly nods, the lip gloss blurred through her watery vision.

'Secondly, I answer all phone calls and messages that are *business*-related in a timely manner. I don't know how many more times I can explain or justify this. Perry and I run a company together, a very busy company that requires us to constantly communicate with clients and potential clients and suppliers and other trades and the bank and probably a hundred other people. And that's why I'm still awake in the early hours scrolling my phone because I've got a million things going round my mind and I don't want to miss or forget anything important. And as for Mum... I shouldn't even have to explain why I gave her a back-door key – she's my *mother*. She owns thirty per cent of the business, she and Dad gave me this house, and she's a loving grandmother to our children.'

'I know. Fletcher, I–'

'Thirdly,' he interrupts, 'when you saw me – *spied* on me – chatting with my clients, we were talking about ideas for Eaden's bedroom. Rachael and Petra have just set up an interior design agency and kindly offered their help if we needed it, but you've fucked that up now. Thankfully, I think I managed to smooth things over, but you really embarrassed me today, Carly. How dare you just turn up and confront Rachael like that?'

Shame takes hold of Carly's neck and threatens to strangle her once more. 'I'm so sorry. I've been struggling but I shouldn't have let everything build up...' She covers her face with her hands and chokes out a sob.

He sighs. 'It's all in your head, Carly. All of it.' He taps his fingertip against his temple a few times. 'This ridiculous paranoia is such a turn-off. But we haven't had sex since before Sonny was born because of your issues, not mine. I pay you compliments, I show you affection, I give you free rein with designing and decorating the house, I work hard for our family, and this is the thanks I get? Accusations, stalking and confrontations? I thought your pills were supposed to help you feel better. Do they take a while to kick in or what?'

She puts her hands back on the table but doesn't look up. 'I haven't been taking them.'

He looks at her incredulously. 'Why the fuck not?'

'Because one of the possible side effects is weight gain and I didn't want to risk that happening,' she whispers.

'So, you'd rather put your physical appearance – which is absolutely fine, by the way, as I have said a thousand times – over your mental health and ruin our marriage in the process?' He tuts. 'So much for our fucking fresh start!' He stands, snatches up the lip gloss from the table and turns to leave.

'Wait,' she pleads, her hand outstretched, 'I'll start taking my medication. I really will. Tomorrow morning, I promise. I'm sorry. Now we've had this out, let's just put it behind us. Please. I'll be better.'

He looks back over his shoulder. 'This shit needs to stop. Right now.'

'It will.'

He closes his eyes and sighs, then nods and leaves the room.

CHAPTER FIFTEEN

FRIDAY

Carly returns from her usual morning swim as Polly is making breakfast for the children. Eaden has her scrapbook open on the table and Carly remembers what Fletcher said about scuppering the chance of his clients' interior designer agency helping out with Eaden's new bedroom. Another wave of shame washes over her as she thinks about her appalling actions yesterday, but then a brilliant idea bounces into her brain: she'll order some fabric samples and accessories for Eaden to choose from herself. They'll be able to go through them together, perhaps even add a new page to her scrapbook. It'll bond them, finally.

'You're back early,' says Polly, glancing at the clock.

'I've come home to shower today. Has Fletcher left already?' Carly asks.

'No, I haven't seen him yet this morning. He must still be upstairs. I've been up since just after you left with this one.' She nods towards the baby. 'Thought I'd let the man of the house sleep in.'

'Okay, thanks. I'll head up.'

'Hey, how did it go yesterday with... you know what?' Polly asks. She yawns as she hands a fractious Sonny a slice of banana.

'Oh, I'd just got myself worked up over nothing, as usual. We had a good chat yesterday and everything's fine now. More than fine. In fact, that's why I'm home early – so we can have a bit more time together before work, if you know what I mean.' Carly bites her lip coquettishly.

Polly raises her eyebrows. 'Wow. Good for you. You're more forgiving than I would be in your situation.'

'He's done nothing I need to forgive; I got it wrong,' states Carly crisply.

'Sure,' replies Polly, refilling Eaden's cup of juice. She's so absorbed in her scrapbook she doesn't even notice.

Sonny reaches for Carly, and she picks up another slice of banana from his bowl and holds it in her palm for him to take, which he does. She smiles at Sonny then winks at Polly before leaving the kitchen.

Upstairs, Carly enters the bedroom just as Fletcher exits the en suite with a towel wrapped round his waist, droplets of water still on his skin.

'Good swim?' he asks, and although she detects a lingering frostiness in his tone, she's relieved to hear his usual question, hopeful that it means they really can move on from yesterday.

'Great swim!' she replies over-enthusiastically. 'I weighed myself at the health club and I've lost another two pounds. I feel good today.' He simply nods and grabs a pair of clean boxer shorts from the drawer. 'Hey, I was thinking about ordering some fabric samples and a few accessories for Eaden's bedroom project, you know, to get things moving with that sooner rather than later, and for Sonny's new room too. Perhaps Eaden and I can go through a few ideas together?'

He considers it, pulling the corners of his mouth down. 'Okay,' he agrees as he pulls the boxers on. 'Nice idea.'

'Great, I'll order everything on my lunch-break today with

next-day delivery so we'll have it all to look at over the weekend, after you get back from your shopping trip.' She's aware she's overcompensating, babbling, but she feels like she needs to show him she's trying.

She steps close to him as he reaches for his combats. 'Right, I'll jump in the shower then.' She tentatively places her palm against his warm, damp, bare chest and meets his eyes. It feels nice to touch his naked skin for the first time in a long time. There have been moments recently when she wondered if she ever would again. 'Fancy washing my back for me?'

He gazes at her for a moment then places his own hand over hers and gently moves it away. 'I appreciate what you're trying to do, Carly, but things are still a little bit raw for me after yesterday's events, and I need to get to work. So do you.'

'I thought we were putting it all behind us,' says Carly evenly, trying not to sound too wounded by his rejection.

'We are, and we will, but not right this minute. I can't be late to Chestnut Avenue, especially not after yesterday.' He pauses. 'Have you taken your medication yet this morning?'

'Not yet but I will.'

He waits.

'Now?' she asks as he stares at her.

He nods.

She crosses over to her bedside table and retrieves the box of pills. She takes one out then swallows it down.

'Good girl. Maybe put a reminder on your phone so you don't forget again.' He moves towards her and kisses her quickly on the cheek. 'I'll see you tonight and we'll have a nice family weekend. Things will be fine.'

'Perhaps we could eat together tonight, spend a bit of time alone? I could pick something up on my way home from work?' she suggests.

'Sure. Sounds good.' His phone buzzes in his hand but instead of looking at it he looks at Carly.

Knowing she no longer has the right to question him about anything, she simply smiles and heads into the en suite, an image of breeziness.

Downstairs, Polly has already strapped Sonny into his pushchair and is helping Eaden into her blazer when Carly reappears.

'Could you do me a favour and pick up a couple of things from the supermarket after you've dropped Eaden off at school, please, Polly? I'm going to cook for Fletcher later – we're having a date night.' She grins girlishly.

'Oh, okay.' Polly hands Eaden her lunchbox. 'Things went well this morning then?'

'Fletcher had to rush off to work, which is why we're making up for it tonight.'

'Great. I'm pleased it all worked out.' Polly smiles tightly.

'And if I could ask you to stay upstairs after you've bathed the children later... to give us some privacy? Take any food and drink you want to your room, of course.'

'Sure. You're the boss,' Polly replies sharply, leaning down to wipe Sonny's runny nose. She doesn't want to hear or think about Carly trying to revive her pathetic sex life. Nevertheless, she adjusts her tone as she tends to the baby. 'He's got a bit of a snuffle today, poor little man.'

Carly looks down at her son and sticks her bottom lip out. 'Oh no. There's some Calpol in the bathroom cabinet if you think he needs it.' She turns her attention to Eaden. 'Have a great day at school, sweetheart. I've got a surprise coming for you tomorrow that I think you're going to love!'

Through sharp, squinted eyes, Polly stares at Carly while she softly strokes Sonny's downy fair hair, wondering whether her employer has been body-snatched. Eaden seems to be equally surprised and holds onto Polly's leg, regarding Carly warily.

'Well, I'll be off then,' says Carly, as she finishes checking her reflection in the mirror beside the door. 'No rest for the wicked! I'll message you what to get from the shop as soon as I've decided what meal we're having.'

'No problem.' Polly's smile slides from her face as Carly leaves. 'Happy to help,' she says to herself, bitterly, as Sonny begins to cry.

CHAPTER SIXTEEN

Fletcher enters the silent house and locks the door behind him. He carefully places his car keys in the bowl on the console table and glances into the empty kitchen before quickly ascending the stairs. He can faintly hear a shower running at the back of the house – the one in Polly's en suite. Rounding the landing, he heads to his children's bedroom at the front of the house where he finds Sonny sleeping in his cot. He reaches down and softly strokes his rosy cheek, smooths back a few damp wisps of hair, listens to his heavier than usual breathing.

'The Calpol's knocked him out.'

He hears Polly's voice behind him but doesn't turn around, watching his son's chest rise and fall. 'The sleep will do him good. Thanks for letting me know he isn't well.'

'No problem. He was not a happy bunny earlier. Puked his breakfast all over me, hence the shower.' She laughs and leans against the door frame. 'I'll have to apologise to your wife though.'

Fletcher frowns. 'What for?'

'I think it's best if Sonny and I stay in the house today so I won't be picking up her shopping for your date night now. Sorry,' she says, insincerely.

He turns around and looks at her. Her long dark hair is wet and she's wearing a short black robe. It's clinging to the curves of her still-damp body in places. 'She asked you to do that?' He tuts. 'She said she was going herself on her way home from work.'

'It's okay. I can't do it now anyway.' She shrugs.

'No, it's not okay, Polly; you're not our maid.'

She looks at him and her full lips form a smirk. 'I can be a maid, if that's what you want.'

He stares at her, biting his tongue between his front teeth, Sonny's snuffling breaths the only sound in the room.

'Or would you prefer me to be a cheerleader again?' She cocks her head to the side. 'Get my pom-poms out and put my hair in pigtails for you to pull on?'

He reaches into his pocket, retrieves the *Prick Tease* lip gloss and holds it up. 'I think I'd prefer you wearing just this today. Carly found it in the car – it must have fallen out of your bag or pocket during our last rendezvous.' He moves towards her and slowly traces her lips with the tube before pushing its tip gently inside her mouth. She lets him. 'Don't lose it again.'

She salutes and sucks on the tube suggestively.

Smiling, he slowly unties her robe and opens the silky material, exposing her still-damp naked skin. He leans down and kisses the soft delve above her collarbone, up her neck and then her ear, enjoying hearing her breath catch and quicken. 'You smell incredible,' he tells her.

She moves one of his hands down her body. Lower, then lower still. Soon his fingers are touching her, playing with her just how she likes it, as she takes the lip gloss out of her mouth and snakes her arms around his neck, grabbing his hair, gasping with pleasure in between kisses frantic and deep. She moans into him as he makes her come, cheeks flushed, and eyes shut tight, intense pleasure engulfing her.

'God, I needed that,' she whispers as the shuddering subsides and she catches her breath. 'It's been torture this week not being able to kiss you or touch you or taste you.'

'Tell me about it,' he agrees. Leaving the sleeping baby, he tugs her through to her bedroom. She throws the lip gloss onto the bedside table as he turns to face her. 'You're so fucking beautiful,' he tells her earnestly before slipping off her robe completely and pushing her back on the bed. He rakes his eyes over her hungrily, enjoying the sight of her nubile, naked body, whilst undoing his combats. She waits for his instruction, letting him lead, letting him take control as usual.

He signals what he wants her to do. She obliges, kneeling before him, taking his penis fully in her mouth as he throws his head back in ecstasy. He wraps her wet hair around his fist and watches her sucking and licking him, enjoying the show she puts on for him, before pulling her up to kiss her passionately again. On the bed he opens her legs wide and pushes into her slowly, lowering himself onto her, congratulating himself on what a clever boy he's been.

CHAPTER SEVENTEEN

SATURDAY

Carly climbs out of the car in the driveway just as the delivery driver pulls up outside the gates. 'Perfect timing,' she says, smiling as she takes the large box containing the fabric samples and accessories for Eaden's bedroom from him.

Inside, she sets it on the hallway floor and walks into the kitchen. 'Is Eaden still asleep?' she asks.

'Miraculously, yes,' replies Polly as she tries to persuade a grizzling Sonny to eat some breakfast. 'This one's sniffles are getting worse. Fletcher just changed him, but I said I'd bring him down here with me while he gets ready for work and to let Eaden have a Saturday morning lie-in.'

Carly's hand hovers over her son's head but she stops short of actually touching him. He pushes away the spoon Polly's holding, his red and blotchy face contorting. 'Have you given him any Calpol this morning?'

'Not yet, but I will. I thought it'd be better to try to feed him first as he didn't eat much yesterday either.' Polly frowns as Sonny continues to refuse the fruit purée she's offering.

'Good thinking. I'm sure he'll perk up later and I'll be home this afternoon to take over.' She crosses the kitchen and gets herself a glass of organic juice then stands at the island. 'Meanwhile, Eaden's got a soft play birthday party this morning then Fletcher's taking her shopping for bits for her new room when he's done at work.'

'Oh, is this Celeste's party – I thought that was in a couple of weeks?'

'Celeste's party *is* in a couple of weeks. Her mother Mallory will give you Eaden's invitation for that one, remember?' Carly smiles. 'Today's party has been in the diary for a while, since before you arrived.'

'Mallory, yes, I remember. I still haven't met her yet. Do I need to take Eaden to this party today?' asks Polly as Sonny sneezes.

'Thank you but no. Stella's taking her – it's all arranged. Probably just as well with Sonny being a bit under the weather. Don't say anything to Eaden but I've ordered a few extra special surprises for her bedroom too, hopefully win her round a bit.'

'Well, kids usually do respond well to bribery.' Polly attempts to wipe Sonny's snotty nose while he does his best to prevent her from doing so by jerking his head from side to side.

Carly briefly scrunches her brows together then decides not to read into Polly's abrasive tone and lets the comment slide. She drinks her juice and puts the empty glass in the dishwasher. 'We'll hopefully start designing her room properly tomorrow. It'll be good to spend some time together, just us girls – it's long overdue. And now that Fletcher and I are back on track, life is good!' She raises her eyebrows and grins.

'Back on track?' asks Polly, lifting Sonny out of his highchair as he lets out a cry of protest.

Carly can't hide her glee. 'Date night was a roaring success. I ordered in from Fletcher's favourite takeaway seeing as the baby kept you busy all day, and let's just say I was the dessert!'

Polly draws in a sharp breath while trying to jiggle a writhing Sonny on her hip.

Carly detects an awkward shift in atmosphere and realises it was another overshare too far. She mentally kicks herself and deflects. 'Anyway, I bet you're looking forward to your well-deserved time off after a crazy first week! Do you have any plans for this afternoon and tomorrow?'

'Well, as I don't know the area yet, I thought I'd just get my bearings. Maybe get a bus into town and catch a film at the cinema.' Polly shrugs.

'A bus?' Carly scrunches up her nose. 'Save yourself the ordeal – you're more than welcome to borrow my car as Fletcher will be taking Eaden out in his. I'm sure he said he'd already put you as a named driver on the insurance. And if you want a guest day pass to my health club anytime, please just ask.'

'Great. Thanks,' says Polly, trying and failing to get Sonny to take his dummy.

'Don't mention it,' replies Carly as she leaves the kitchen. 'What's mine is yours.'

Carly reaches the landing carrying the box that was delivered at the same time as Fletcher appears carrying a yawning Eaden out of her bedroom. The little girl's curly red hair is wild from sleep.

'Morning,' says Fletcher. 'Just depositing this one downstairs then I'm heading to work. Sonny's still a bit off this morning.'

'I know, poor thing. Polly's got it all under control though and I'll be home by lunchtime.'

'Hopefully I will be too,' he says.

'What's that?' asks Eaden, pointing to the box.

Carly smiles. 'It's that surprise I told you about! For later,' she says with jollity.

'Come on then, you,' Fletcher says to Eaden. 'Let's go get you some breakfast before Granny collects you for your party. How much fun are you going to have today?'

'Lots, Daddy!' shouts Eaden raising both arms in the air.

As Fletcher and Eaden make their way downstairs, Carly takes the large box to the children's room. She can't wait any longer to look inside. Placing the box on the chest of drawers next to the cot, she retrieves the nail scissors from the family bathroom cabinet to slice it open, then lifts the box's flaps and gasps at the gorgeousness within. Fabric sample books, velvet cushions, a pastel-coloured peg shelf, a patterned rug; all beautiful, quality items. She takes two sample books out and flips through the different materials, running her fingers over the soft textures, absorbed in the ideas running through her head, anticipating Eaden's excitement and by extension, Fletcher's approval.

'Bye, family!' Fletcher's voice followed by the front door closing interrupts her and she checks her phone. Time to get ready for work herself. She leaves everything on the chest of drawers to go through properly later and heads to her own bedroom to change.

After dressing for work in grey tailored trousers, a baby-pink silk blouse and an AllSaints fitted cream blazer, she sends Fletcher a quick WhatsApp message, telling him how much she enjoyed last night. It feels good to be sending him these sorts of messages again, and it feels even better that they have finally ended their drought. It wasn't the most satisfying sex they've ever had but it was only the first time they'd done it since the baby arrived eight months ago. She feels relieved she was able to perform the act without any residual trauma, and thankful that her body seems to have healed well enough following Sonny's harrowing birth. Baby steps indeed.

She looks at her reflection in the mirror, smoothing her hands over her slim hips and twisting her body this way and that to scrutinise her figure, and allows herself to admire what she sees for the first time in a very long time.

Her skin looks fresh and glowing (maybe due in part to last

night's sex!) and the relentless swimming and skipping and restricted eating regime is slowly starting to pay off. She's finally somewhere near where she used to be before she met Fletcher, at least externally. Not as slim and stunning as she was when she was scraping a meagre living modelling in her teens and twenties – not eating because of the job but also because she just couldn't afford to – but perhaps not bad for her early thirties. As long as she sticks to it.

In her opinion, there's nothing worse than a married woman, especially a mother, who has 'let herself go'. It might have been acceptable for her own mother, who seemed to revel in abusing her body with excessive alcohol and cannabis and calories, but Carly cannot imagine a worse fate for herself.

Fletcher replies to her message before she leaves the house. It's just a smiley face emoji and one kiss but that in itself reassures her even more. No agonising over ignored messages today. She instinctively feels that they're in a better place now and that there's no need for her to worry anymore. She hopes not anyway. Last night proved that he still considers her attractive and desirable despite her own negative fixations. She congratulates herself on suggesting the date night in the first place – it was exactly what they needed to resuscitate their marriage.

As she drives away from the house, she passes Stella driving in, on her way to pick up Eaden for her party, and for once, her immediate reaction isn't irritation. *Yes,* she muses, *things are definitely looking up.*

Carly arrives at work fifteen minutes early. *Image Aesthetic Clinic* opens for only three hours every Saturday, from 9.30am to 12.30pm, and Carly is expected to work one or two of those per month, which she's more than happy to do.

Today and every other Saturday is an open day for clients to ask Gavin questions about treatments in between pre-booked mini-consultation slots. Carly feels buoyant; this is what she hopes to become one day – an aesthetics practitioner. She's fascinated with the concept of anti- and reverse-ageing treatments and plans to stay looking – and feeling – as young and desirable as possible for as long as possible, whatever it takes. Her strict exercise and diet routine is helping her feel better about herself for now, but she's already learnt a lot about the range of treatments Gavin offers in his clinic, and she's earmarked a few she'd like to try. Become the face of the business, in all senses of the phrase.

'Morning, Gavin,' calls Carly as she settles herself behind the reception desk, which already feels like a second home. The door between the reception area and the small hallway leading to the two treatment rooms and staffroom is open to encourage clients to wander around freely. Gavin prides himself on being as transparent in his practices as possible.

'Morning.' Gavin pops his head round the door, smiling warmly at her. 'All set for your first open day?'

Carly nods. 'Yes, I'm really looking forward to it. I've been memorising all the treatments during my morning swims, and I've read all the literature you've given me, as well as those websites you recommended. I know I've still got a lot to learn but I think I can comfortably answer any general questions today while you're doing the consultations.'

'Excellent. Well, I've got six fifteen-minute consultations booked in, but I could squeeze in a couple more if anyone wants one, maybe even for you if you want to hang around when we're done?'

'Oh, I'd love one but I can't stay late today unfortunately – Sonny isn't feeling well and the nanny's off this afternoon.'

'Well, if you ever want my professional opinion, you're more than welcome to it, anytime.'

She stands up and crosses her arms. 'Go on then, give me a thirty-second consultation. You've seen my face practically all day every day for a week, what would you recommend?' She smiles broadly at him.

'Carly, you're a beautiful woman. I would recommend taking a good look in the mirror and realising that,' he says with sincerity. 'I know I'm running a business, but I call it how I see it and will never try to convince women – or men – to have work done that they don't actually need yet.'

She holds a hand up, insistent. 'No, don't flatter me, Gavin. I'm in my thirties now and however much I wish I was, I'm not immune to the cruel ravages of time. Go on, I genuinely want your professional opinion. Be honest.' She lets her arm drop to her side and nods her encouragement.

'Well, if you're sure.' He concedes, smiling and moving closer to her, raising his hands up to her face. 'May I?' She nods and he gently places his fingers on her skin, pressing in some areas and pulling in others, moving quickly but methodically around her features, practised in his process. He makes his recommendations as he works: 'I'd suggest fillers to minimise your nasolabial folds and add extra definition to your jowl line; and Botox – just a couple of units to keep your platysmal neck bands at bay, and also to shape and lift your brow.'

'That much?' Carly recoils and reverses, the backs of her knees banging into her chair.

'Not that you need it urgently, like I said.' He evidently hasn't picked up on her alarmed tone as he continues to scan her features. 'Merely prevention suggestions if you want to magic a few years off.' He waggles his fingers as he says the word 'magic' and smiles.

At that moment, the door opens and Benny, the homeless man from outside the parade of shops, peers shyly into the clinic. Gavin turns away from Carly to welcome him and Carly plasters a shaky smile on her own clearly haggard face, the little confidence she had begun to recultivate in her appearance earlier now completely eradicated.

'Now then, my good man,' her boss greets Benny, sweeping around the desk and swiping up a pile of flyers advertising their open days.

Benny steps inside to shake Gavin's hand, ducking his head politely at Carly too. She listens as Gavin lists the more upmarket areas in Hessle he'd like Benny to target with the flyers as she surreptitiously takes in the homeless man's appearance: sad hazel eyes with extraordinarily long lashes, slightly pallid, dry skin, and the cleft lip she noticed previously visible through his unkempt beard. He's wearing a frayed T-shirt and jeans with a worn, green, partially zipped-up utility jacket, and she wrinkles her nose slightly as his stale body odour reaches her nostrils.

A wave of sympathy washes over her, followed by guilt for frequently forgetting that there are people in the world with much worse worries than her. Her heart swells with gratitude for her own beautiful family and her secure luxurious home and she resolves to try to stop sabotaging her own happiness from now on. She really is her own worst enemy sometimes.

CHAPTER EIGHTEEN

'Hey.' Fletcher whispers the greeting from the children's bedroom doorway an hour after he left the house on the pretence of going to work. Polly is leaning over Sonny's cot, and he joins her, running his fingers gently up and down her back. 'How is he?'

'Not great but he's finally gone down for his morning nap,' she says, her tone crisp.

'Poor little kid.' He strokes his son's mottled cheek tenderly. 'Anyway,' he says after a few moments, 'talking of going down…' He tugs on her French plait then twists her round and presses her against the chest of drawers next to the cot, sliding his hand up to her breast and smirking. 'You know I love it when you wear your hair like this… it makes me want to coil it in my fist and–'

'Wow,' Polly interrupts, pushing his hand away. 'First of all, gross segue to go from talking about Sonny to that.' He opens his mouth to speak but she gets there first. 'And second of all, I'm not sure you deserve to do anything with me after last night.'

'Last night?' His dark brows knit together.

'Carly took great pleasure in telling me that she was dessert after your date night.' She pouts and leans back against the drawers, moving Carly's box to the side and hooking her hands over the lipped front.

Fletcher sighs heavily and runs a hand through his hair. 'Not here,' he says, gesturing for her to follow him. Polly sighs too, pushes herself off the drawers, picks up the baby monitor and leaves the room. They resume their conversation in her bedroom.

'Listen, I can explain,' he says, dragging a hand down his face, puppy-dog eyes already activated.

She places the baby monitor down on her bedside table and crosses her arms, currently immune to his charms. 'Let's hear it then.'

'It wasn't a date night.' He makes air quotes around the phrase 'date night'. 'It was a takeaway and a quick, meaningless shag at bedtime. I was thinking about you the whole time.'

She scoffs and turns her head away, repulsed.

He instantly realises his mistake. 'No, I didn't mean it like that! Fuck! I'm sorry, okay? Look, I need to make sure she doesn't suspect anything, don't I, just for a while?'

Tears well in Polly's eyes but her mouth is a hard line as she turns back to him. 'Did you really have to have sex with her?'

He clenches his jaw and throws his hands up in the air. 'I'm sorry. I didn't want to, I swear.'

'But you stepped up for the greater good?' She blinks and her tears slink down her cheeks.

He holds her by the upper arms, squeezing gently. 'It wasn't like that! Come on, don't give me a hard time about this, not when things are going to plan.'

She shrugs him off. 'Are they going to plan, Fletcher? Was it in the plan for you to be fucking her again within a week of me being here? You said she was practically frigid, that you hadn't slept together since before we met, yet she took immense delight in regaling me with the news this morning while I was feeding your poorly son his breakfast. She didn't even show any concern or try to soothe him at all, she was more interested in sharing the details of your sex life!'

'But that also proves what a shitty mother she is!' he says with fervour. 'And things *are* going to plan – even better than we hoped, in fact. Thanks to you planting the idea in her head, she confronted Rachael at the Chestnut Avenue house and made a huge fool of herself, which Perry saw too, so that's two witnesses to her crazy behaviour. Mum's already got her concerns about Carly's parenting, so she'll be on our side as well, and you and I get this quality time together while she's at work.' He lowers his voice. 'All this progress and you've not even been here a full week yet. Things *are* going to plan,' he repeats and cups her cheek in his palm.

She searches his face and sees nothing but sincerity. Or is that what he wants her to see? How well does she know him, really, outside of a bedroom? But she loves him, she's sure of that. She nods and finally allows him to embrace her, sighing heavily against his chest.

'I love you, baby, that's all you need to remember,' he says, his chin resting on top of her head.

She pulls away and looks up at him, wiping her cheeks with her fingers. 'Oh yeah?' She manages a playful smile. 'Come on then, show me how much.'

Twelve minutes later, Fletcher pulls out of Polly and lies back on her bed, panting heavily.

'You okay there, old man?' she teases, despite being quite breathless herself. They always manage to work up a sweat.

'Oi, less of the old,' he manages to reply. 'I might be just past forty, but I still manage to satisfy you.'

She leans over and kisses him hard on the lips. 'You certainly do. You got the moves,' she says, laughing.

He grins back, catching his breath. 'Oh, did Mum say she was dropping Eaden back off here after the party or do I need to collect her?'

Polly flops back down again. 'She said she'll bring her back here after lunch, ready for your shopping afternoon.'

He looks over at her forlorn expression and props himself up on one elbow. 'You don't know how much I wish I was spending the afternoon with you and both the kids instead.'

She pouts at the ceiling and twists her hair around her fingers. 'Me too.'

'One day soon. I promise.' He reaches for her hand and kisses it.

She sniffs, puts a brave face on and gives him a gentle shove. 'You'd better make yourself scarce again before your mother or your wife come home and find you in my bed and scupper *the plan*.'

'Yes, ma'am.' He salutes. 'I'll just jump in the shower first.'

'I'll check on Sonny. I haven't heard a peep out of him though; he must finally be sleeping soundly.'

He sits up and holds her face in his hands. 'Long game, remember?' he says and pulls her in for a passionate kiss.

'Long game,' she repeats when they break apart again.

He gets out of bed, gathers up his clothes and heads across the hallway.

Polly gets dressed, brushes her hair and smooths the bedsheets before leaving the bedroom. She can hear the shower running in Fletcher and Carly's en suite and smiles to herself at the thought of Fletcher naked and soapy. It won't be long before they can take showers together whenever they want.

'Long game,' she whispers again to herself, reinforcing his words, as she walks down the hallway towards the children's bedroom. She enters the room, approaches the cot and looks down at the sleeping baby. She frowns, not immediately understanding what she's seeing but instantly feeling a full body blow of absolute fear. Her vision swims and her head pounds.

'Fletcher!' she screams.

CHAPTER NINETEEN

C arly pushes past the huddle of people hanging around Hull Royal Infirmary's entrance and scans the signs, searching for the children's accident and emergency department. Panic pounds in her ears and tears obscure her vision and she can't make sense of all the words and arrows and colours.

She spins around, blinking rapidly, looking for someone to point her in the right direction. She's surprised to make eye contact with Benny, the homeless man, who raises his hand in greeting from the doorway but she's too distracted to respond, and simply turns and rushes off, conscious that precious seconds are ticking by.

'What happened? Where's Sonny?' Carly calls as she finally catches sight of Fletcher within the labyrinth of corridors, her heels clicking loudly on the sheet vinyl floor.

'He's fine now, he's been checked over and he's on a breathing monitor,' says Fletcher, his face pale but his expression dark.

'A breathing monitor? What happened?' she asks again. She clutches her bag to her body as though it can provide some comfort.

He runs his hand through his hair and glares at her. 'Polly

found him with a book of fabric samples over his face, not breathing. And there were some nail scissors in his cot too. Did you leave them on the chest of drawers next to where he sleeps? Don't you realise how dangerous that is?'

Carly catches her breath, realising that she plonked the scissors and the samples on top of the drawers after opening the box this morning, then just left them there to sort through later. She hadn't given them a second thought.

'But... I...' She swallows, the sorry scene projected in her mind's eye. 'Didn't Polly see them and move them when she put Sonny down for his nap?' she asks after a moment, her logical brain overtaking her emotional response.

'Obviously not. And anyway, she's not the maid, Carly, it's not her job to tidy your mess away. It's her job to keep our son safe and if she hadn't checked on him when she did, well...' He scowls and rubs his thumb against his lip as though to contain the unspeakable remaining words.

Carly simply nods, still in shock at not only receiving a call from Fletcher to tell her that Sonny had been rushed to hospital, but also at the powerful, maternal emotions she's finally feeling after all these months. The mere thought of anything bad happening to her baby is enough to make her feel nauseous and light-headed.

The doctor opens the door next to them and motions for them to enter the room. Sonny is asleep in a transparent cot, oblivious to everything going on around him. They gather around him as the doctor addresses them. Carly reaches for Fletcher's hand, but he moves away slightly and puts his hand in his pocket. The lump in Carly's throat grows. She tries to gulp it down.

'Sonny experienced an apnoea episode, or a breathing pause,' the doctor explains. 'This caused bradycardia, which means his heart slowed down and he turned a bluish colour as a result. I believe your nanny found him and performed infant CPR?'

'Yes,' Fletcher confirms.

'What caused the apnoea?' asks Carly.

'Apnoea may come on quickly and without warning, especially during times of stress or infection. I notice Sonny has the sniffles and–'

'We've given him Calpol,' interrupts Carly.

'Yes, your nanny informed us of that. The sniffles are a contributory factor but has there been anything at home that could be causing Sonny some stress?' She looks between Carly and Fletcher, waiting for one of them to respond. Fletcher clears his throat but doesn't speak.

'I've only just returned to work after having Sonny, and our nanny's new to our family,' Carly says, staring down at the baby. She looks at the doctor, suddenly stricken. 'Does that mean this is my fault?'

'It's nobody's fault,' the doctor says, and Carly is grateful for her kind and reassuring tone. 'Just something to be aware of. We'd like to observe your son for a while longer, to be on the safe side, then you can take him home. I'll be back later to discharge him.'

'Thank you,' says Fletcher. The doctor nods and leaves them alone, clicking the door closed behind her.

'Why didn't you mention the fabric samples and scissors?' Carly asks.

'You heard the doctor – it was an apnoea episode. Do you want me to tell her there were foreign objects in his cot too? Because you know what will happen if I do. Do you really want social services sniffing around? Do you want to risk Sonny being taken away? Actually, don't answer that.' His eyes blaze with fury.

'Fletcher! How could you even think I would do something to deliberately hurt him? It was an oversight, an accident! I opened the box with the scissors and took the samples out but then I had to get ready for work. It was a one-off. I'm sorry!' She collapses in anguished tears.

He listens to her sob for a few minutes, her fingers clutching the edge of the cot their little boy is lying in, and relents. He places his hand on her back. 'No, I'm sorry. I'm so stressed. It's a mistake anyone could have made, and the doctor didn't seem to think there were any other contributing factors, so it was just an unlucky coincidence. I just can't believe we nearly lost him.'

Carly wipes tears from her cheeks with shaking hands and turns her gaze to Fletcher.

'Why didn't Polly hear him stop breathing on the monitor?' she asks after taking a few deep breaths.

Fletcher mirrors her frown. 'What?'

'You said "If she hadn't checked on him when she did" but wouldn't she have rushed to him as soon as she couldn't hear him breathing anymore?'

At that moment Polly appears through the doorway. Carly observes her red-rimmed eyes, blotchy skin and terrified expression but she turns away from her, anger forming a fist in her stomach.

'How is he now?' Polly asks, her voice a faint whisper.

'The doctor says he's going to be fine,' Fletcher says.

'Carly, I'm so sorry... I really am... I should have got to him sooner...'

'Hey, come on now, it's–' Fletcher reaches out an arm but doesn't make contact with her.

Carly interrupts him. 'Why didn't you?' she asks Polly.

Polly gapes at Carly then at Fletcher, wide-eyed, fresh tears threatening to spill. She shakes her head. 'I...'

'She saved him. That's all that matters. We can all do better from now on.' Fletcher looks at Carly pointedly. She turns back to Sonny.

'Just go, please, Polly. This is a time for family only,' says Carly.

Polly nods. 'I'll wait outside,' she says in a small voice. 'I really am so sorry, Carly.' She shuffles from the room, closing the door quietly behind her.

Fletcher sighs heavily. 'I'll take Polly home. I've rung Mum and told her what's happened. She's frantic, as you can imagine, but she's taking Eaden back to our house as planned and she'll stay with her as long as we need her to. I'll make sure they're okay then come straight back to be with you and Sonny until he's discharged.'

Carly nods once. 'Fine.'

Fletcher pulls into the driveway and turns off the car's engine. He looks over at Polly who has been openly sobbing for the whole twenty-minute drive home from the hospital. He puts his hand on her thigh, but she roughly pushes it off.

'I'm going to pack my things and leave. Today.' She tries to open the passenger side door, but he grips her arm and forcefully wrenches her back to face him.

'Polly, calm down!' he commands. 'Think of the bigger picture here... This could work well for us.'

She stares at him, her mouth slack. 'What do you mean?'

'Listen,' he says, twisting towards her and taking her trembling hands. 'Carly's the one who left scissors and fabric samples right next to her baby's cot – yes, it was awful that they ended up in there and it might have had something to do with Sonny stopping breathing, or it might have been a terrible coincidence, but he's going to be okay. And he's going to be okay because *you* checked on him when you did.'

'But I would have checked on him sooner if we weren't so busy fucking! And it was *our* fault those things ended up in his cot in the first place – I moved them aside when you pushed me against the drawers, remember? We did a terrible thing. We're

terrible people, Fletcher! How can you spin this any other way?'
she cries.

'Because I have to. My son could have died today, Polly, but he
didn't, thanks to you. Do you understand how grateful I am to
you for that? Carly is only suddenly pretending she's a loving
mother because she feels guilty for her part in this. And yes,
perhaps it's manipulative to make more of it, to shift the blame
towards her, but this will help us with the plan. Now she's
grateful to me for not saying anything to the doctor, we won't
have social services interfering, and we can use this to our
advantage to get rid of her. Long game, remember?'

Polly looks at him through puffy eyes then hangs her head,
uses the heels of her shaking hands to smear the tears from her
cheeks.

'Come on now, let's go inside,' he suggests softly. 'Leave Mum
to me, I'll explain everything. Go straight upstairs and have a bath
and then get some sleep. It is supposed to be your afternoon off,
after all. I'm going to go back to the hospital and wait for them to
discharge Sonny but, please, don't worry about any of it anymore.'

Inside, a worried-looking Stella rushes to greet them before
Fletcher has even closed the front door behind them.

'Oh Fletcher, my goodness, what a trauma! How are you?' she
asks, her voice full of anguish.

'I'm fine thanks, Mum.' He puts an arm around her shoulders
and gives her a reassuring squeeze as she leans into him, shaking
her head.

'And how are you, dear?' she asks Polly, but continues without
waiting for an answer. 'Thank heavens you found little Sonny in
time. I dread to think.' Stella twists her pearl necklace, concern
etched all over her face.

'Is Eaden all right, Mum?' asks Fletcher, stepping towards the
kitchen.

'Yes, she's fine, she's playing with her party bag favours. I haven't said a word to her about this, but I've been on my nerves ever since you phoned, torturing myself by imagining the worst. Do you know any more about what actually happened now?'

Fletcher turns back to his mother and speaks softly. 'The doctor said he had an apnoea episode and stopped breathing, but he's stable now. I'm going back to the hospital to wait with Carly, but they said he could come home soon.'

'An apnoea episode?' Stella repeats at volume. 'But what on earth caused that?'

Fletcher flicks a conspiratorial look over at Polly before answering. 'They don't know definitively but it might have had something to do with a book of fabric samples that fell into the cot and covered his face.'

'Fabric samples?' Stella frowns. 'How did they get there?'

'Carly ordered them for Eaden's new bedroom, opened the box with a pair of scissors, then put the scissors and the samples on the chest of drawers next to Sonny's cot. They must have been too near the edge and fell in,' explains Fletcher.

'Scissors too? Goodness me!' Stella gapes at Fletcher, incredulity flashing in her eyes. 'How irresponsible! How... how thoughtless!' She puts a hand to her forehead and shakes her head. 'I'll have a few choice words to say to Carly once Sonny is home safe and sound.'

'No, Mum, please don't do that,' says Fletcher sternly. 'She feels terrible enough as it is and all that matters is that Sonny's okay. Let's just forgive and forget and move on.'

Stella huffs and tuts. 'You're *too* forgiving, Fletcher. And I may forgive,' she says, wagging a finger at him, 'but I certainly won't forget.'

She marches into the kitchen and back to Eaden.

Fletcher looks at Polly who still seems shell-shocked after their harrowing afternoon. 'Are you okay?' he asks.

'No. I just want to be on my own. I need time to get my head round all this.' She looks at him with vacant eyes.

He nods and steals a look through the kitchen doorway. Stella is sitting on the sofa by the bi-fold doors with Eaden. They've both got their heads down, engrossed in a storybook on Stella's knee. He risks stroking Polly's cheek with his thumb then drops his arm by his side. 'Things will work out, I promise,' he says.

Fresh tears well in Polly's eyes. 'Don't make promises you can't keep.' She pushes past him and heads upstairs, leaving him alone in the hallway.

CHAPTER TWENTY

It's nearly midnight by the time Fletcher and Carly arrive home with Sonny. Fletcher carries his sleeping son in from the car, but Carly takes him as soon as they're in the house.

'I'm going to sleep in Eaden's bed tonight. I want to stay close to him,' she says.

Fletcher relents, partly due to amazement, partly due to guilt, partly due to exhaustion. He called Stella from the hospital earlier, once it became apparent they would be home very late, and she has taken Eaden back to her house overnight to give everyone some space and Eaden an undisturbed night's sleep. He thought Polly would appreciate the time alone too.

He and Carly part ways on the landing without another word to each other. Just before he heads into their bedroom, Fletcher steals a glance at Polly's door, but it's firmly closed. He closes his own door behind him, ready to collapse straight into bed.

In the children's bedroom, Carly settles Sonny into his cot and stands back to look at him. She's utterly spent, a hollowed-out shell of the person she was this morning. The books of fabric samples are stacked on top of the chest of drawers, the scissors on top, next to the box she opened. Fletcher or Polly must have moved them back out of the cot. Carly puts the samples and scissors in the box and then slides the box on top of the wardrobe out of harm's way, as she should have done earlier.

She thinks back to her chipper mood before she left for work, ashamed of gloating about her and Fletcher's sex life rather than paying her baby son more attention. She's a wretched mother, or at least she has been until now. She vowed at the hospital to do and be better, and she quietly repeats that vow to Sonny again now. She will be more present, more focused on Sonny – and Eaden – than wrapped up in herself. Perhaps even leave her job and devote herself to the children and Fletcher and the house. Take Stella's advice. Sack Polly as there would be no need for her anymore.

A random thought suddenly occurs to her, and she crosses the hallway to the master bedroom, clutching the baby monitor in her hand. Fletcher's already in bed but his bedside lamp is still on.

'Everything okay?' he asks, dropping his phone screen down onto the duvet.

'Why did Polly ring you and not me when she found Sonny not breathing?'

'What?' A ghost of a frown crosses his face, gone as quickly as it appeared.

'You can't say it's because I was at work because you were at work too. So why did she ring you and not me?'

'I don't know,' he says, hitching his shoulders. 'She was probably too panicked to make a conscious choice. What exactly are you asking? Because Polly's actions, in whatever order they occurred, saved him today.'

'So, you haven't ever told her to ring you first if anything ever happened with Sonny?'

He sighs and sits up. 'No. Nor Eaden, for what it's worth. Polly knows she can ring either of us in a medical emergency.'

'Okay.' Carly nods, thinking. 'And did you come home and go with them in the ambulance or go straight to the hospital?' she asks next.

He lifts his hands then brings them down onto the duvet again, a gesture of exasperation. 'I came straight home,' he says.

She frowns. 'But how did you get here so quickly, before the ambulance? Chestnut Avenue is about a fifteen-minute drive, maybe longer in busy Saturday lunchtime traffic.'

'I was on my way back from picking up supplies nearby. I was five minutes away, luckily. Where's all this coming from, Carly? Are you accusing me of something?' He scrunches his face up and glares at her.

'No, I just want you to answer me honestly!' she hisses.

He sits up. 'So, you don't think I'm being honest now? Are we back to this, already? What exactly do you think I'm lying about? Because may I remind you that the only lie I've told today – or rather, the only time I've omitted the truth – was to cover your arse at the hospital!'

'You think I'm a bad mother, don't you?' She nods, agreeing with her own supposition.

'No, I don't. But you're emotional and paranoid and trying to bait me into saying something so you can accuse me of God knows what!' he retorts.

'Actions speak louder than words, Fletcher.' Carly crosses her arms across her body, the baby monitor beneath her elbow.

He closes his eyes, takes a deep breath. When he opens them again, he fixes her with a steady, hate-filled glare. 'My actions have protected you, and us as a family, from a social services investigation. Can't you see that? And yes, you're right – actions do speak louder than words, and right now, you're still more concerned with confronting me with your cock-a-doodle thoughts than being with Sonny, even after everything that's happened today. You should go to bed, Carly.'

'There it is – the truth of what you really think! I feel wretched about what's happened today. I will torment myself forever!'

'Will you? Or will you slide back into your default detached settings once all this has blown over?'

'You're a bastard!' she cries, eyes shining with hurt and fury. 'Post-natal depression is a real – and common – condition!'

'I know!' he shoots back. 'But inventing scenarios, making accusations, confronting clients over imaginary affairs and questioning your own nanny's motives isn't common – those behaviours are all thanks to paranoid delusions.'

'I knew you'd bring all that up again,' she says, her bottom lip wobbling as she stares at him, exposed and attacked.

'You're giving me no choice, Carly. I'm struggling to understand you lately and, quite frankly, I've had just about as much as I can take. I'm going to sleep.' He slams his phone down on the bedside table, turns off his lamp and plunges them both into darkness.

Carly lies awake in Eaden's single bed, opposite Sonny's cot. The bare plaster walls give the room a cell-like quality and she feels that it reflects where she perhaps deserves to be – a cell, either padded or prison. Her body is exhausted, but her mind refuses to shut down. She keeps playing the events of the day over and over again, pausing and analysing selected frames, not even sure what she's looking for.

A shadow appears in the hallway and Carly hears a soft tap on the door. Polly pushes it open slightly and peeks around it. Carly can just about make out her worried expression in the glow from Sonny's night light and is again struck by how young she looks.

'Can't sleep either?' Polly whispers.

Carly sighs, her anger towards her nanny almost dissipated. 'No. I was just thinking about making some herbal tea. Do you want one too?'

Polly nods.

Downstairs in the kitchen, in the small hours of the morning, the two women sit opposite each other at the table, Sonny's baby monitor in between them. His breathing is rhythmic and peaceful.

Polly reaches out and lightly touches Carly's arm. 'Carly, I'm so sorry about Sonny, I really am. If I could rewind time...'

Carly shakes her head and clucks her tongue. 'I'm in no position to judge. I'm hardly in the running for mother of the year.'

'Don't say that. Being a parent is such hard work. I'm sure you've done the best you can,' Polly says.

'I haven't,' Carly admits plainly. 'I didn't nourish my body enough during pregnancy and we didn't bond after he was born. I can categorically state that his difficult birth was the most horrific and traumatising experience of my entire life, worse than my worst imaginings.' She shudders at the flash of memory that she usually tries so hard to suppress. 'Subsequently, I had post-natal depression. *Have* post-natal depression,' she corrects herself. 'And then I nearly had a breakdown after convincing myself that Fletcher was cheating on me in the days and weeks after Sonny arrived. I'm amazed he didn't leave me. I pushed him too far then and I've pushed him too far again now. I'm going to end up pushing him away completely.'

Polly's lips form a small smile, but it doesn't reach her eyes. 'It sounds like you've been under a ton of stress. And I feel like I've caused you even more. If you can't forgive me for what happened today, just tell me and I'll leave.'

'No, Fletcher's right – you saved him,' says Carly. 'And you've given me a wake-up call. I want to be a better mother, for Sonny and for Eaden, but I need to work on myself too. I need to break this vicious cycle once and for all, and I need help to do that. I can't do it alone.' She smiles. 'No, I don't want you to go, Polly. We'll get past this hiccup.'

'Thank you,' says Polly with a nod.

Carly stands and picks up both cups, turning to place them on the island. As she does, her robe falls open exposing a bruise on her collarbone, a deep purple watercolour of a mark, loud and vivid against her pale skin.

Polly notices it. 'Wow, that looks sore.'

Carly tugs her robe back into place quickly and tightens the belt. 'Oh, I slipped in the shower at the health club. I felt so light-headed and just... bashed it against the faucet. Anyway, come on, let's go back to bed and try and get some sleep. Put this godawful day behind us.'

CHAPTER TWENTY-ONE

SUNDAY

The next morning, Fletcher knocks on Polly's bedroom door. He's holding Sonny who is sucking his dummy contentedly, his cheeks rosy and eyes alert.

'Can we come in?' He gives her one of his impossible to resist smiles.

Polly nods and sits up in bed, pulling a pillow behind her to lean against. She feels tired but chatting to Carly last night loosened the noose of guilt slightly, about Sonny at least. She's even starting to feel a speck of sympathy for the other woman now that she's getting to know her better.

'Where's Carly?' she asks.

'Swimming of course,' replies Fletcher, sitting on the bed.

'Oh, I thought she might not go today. We were up quite late last night, or should I say early this morning.'

'You and Carly?' he asks, a chime of surprise in his voice.

'Yeah, I apologised again and–'

He interrupts her. 'You've got nothing to apologise for. I told you. The little man's fine – look.' Fletcher demonstrates the fact by jiggling Sonny up and down then sits him on the bed between him and Polly, propping him up against his leg.

'I know but I still feel awful, Fletcher. Not only about what we did yesterday but what we're doing to Carly now too – she thinks what happened to Sonny was her fault, but it was ours.'

He reaches for her hand but she moves it away so he squeezes her leg. 'We're being cruel to be kind. Everything will work out for the best for everyone in the end.' When she doesn't reply he asks, 'What did you talk about last night?'

Polly shrugs and leans forwards to gently stroke Sonny's bare foot. 'I asked her if she wanted me to leave, and she said no; that we'll get past this.'

'See, I knew she would come round. She needs you, Pol.'

'She also said she's still got post-natal depression. She needs professional help too.'

He tuts and rolls his eyes. 'Her issues are way bigger than post-natal depression. She's got an eating disorder and probably body dysmorphia too – I've read up on it all. But she refuses to accept she has these problems.'

Polly shakes her head gently. 'I think she does know she has them, and she wants to try to get over them.'

'It sounds like you two had a very cosy chinwag. Whose side are you on anyway? You were all for us bringing her down last week,' he says, a firm edge to his voice.

Polly flicks a wary look at him; it's not a tone he usually uses with her. 'It's not about sides, Fletcher. Yesterday was a lot. I'm still trying to process it all.'

He softens, sighs, strokes Sonny's head. 'I know. Me too.'

'She had a bruise. Carly did. Here.' Polly touches her left collarbone with her right hand.

'That'll be exercise related,' says Fletcher, not missing a beat. 'She pushes herself too far. I mean, this morning's a prime example – even after swearing to be a better mother to Sonny after what happened yesterday, she's still straight down the health club, prioritising herself, punishing her body.'

'Maybe she needs to do it for her mental health, in order to *be* a better mother?' suggests Polly.

'Well, it's not helping, is it? She's draining the energy out of me, Pol, and all I want is for us to be together, properly.' He cuddles Sonny closer to him and looks at her dolefully over the top of the baby's head.

'How long, until we can be? I need to know this is going to end sooner rather than later, Fletcher. I can't live in this twisted little threesome arrangement much longer.'

'You won't have to, I promise. She'll trip up again and then probably again and then this will end, and if we play our cards right it'll end with her leaving of her own free will. Alone. Hopefully back to America. Or, if she does decide to fight me for custody of Sonny, she'll definitely lose. It'll be what's best for everyone, including her.'

Polly sighs, expelling a huge lungful of air. She's still frustrated but Fletcher has pacified her, again, for now.

'Hey, I've got an idea,' he says with a smile. 'How do you fancy spending today by the sea with Sonny? The fresh air will do him the world of good after his trauma. I've got a small house up the coast in Fraisthorpe, which Perry and I are going to renovate this winter, and seeing as it'll be yours too soon enough, you get a say in how you'd like to decorate it.'

'I wondered when you were going to tell me about that – Eaden mentioned it the other day.' She smiles for the first time since before she found Sonny unconscious. 'Wait, though, what's the catch?'

'Well, I'm going to suggest to Carly that she goes too. It'll mean I'll be able to spend some time with Eaden, have a daddy-daughter day to make up for not taking her shopping yesterday afternoon.'

She pouts. 'I'd rather spend the day with *you* and Sonny but...' She grins and claps her hands childishly. 'I do love the idea of pimping up our future holiday home, even if it's only in my imagination for now!'

He laughs as he stands up, holding Sonny. 'I thought that might cheer you up. Right, I'm going to get myself and Sonny Jim here washed and dressed before Carly gets back. See you downstairs, gorgeous.' He leans down as she rises to welcome his kiss.

Carly heads straight into the kitchen when she gets home. Fletcher is sitting on the sofa in front of the bi-fold doors and Sonny is in his bouncer on the rug at his feet. Fletcher looks over at her then back at the baby and she wonders if he's still cross with her after their argument last night.

'Good swim?' he asks, and she breathes a small sigh of relief. She walks over to her husband and son and sits on the edge of the L-shaped sofa. Long fingers of Sunday morning sunshine reach through the bi-fold doors and are warm on her skin.

'I'm sorry about last night,' she says. 'I was–'

Fletcher waves a hand to cut her off. 'Apology accepted. Emotions were high yesterday. Today's a new day, okay?'

'Okay,' she agrees instantly. She shifts to kneel on the rug next to the baby and holds up one of his soft toys, wiggling it from side to side. His blue eyes gaze at it in wonder.

'I was thinking,' begins Fletcher, 'how about you take our little man to the Fraisthorpe house today to make up for his day in hospital yesterday? Plus we need to start getting everything prepped so Perry and I can renovate over winter when work's less manic. Then we can enjoy it properly next summer in between renting it out. Earn extra funds for this nice lifestyle we've become accustomed to.' He smiles at her encouragingly.

She presses her lips together as she considers it. 'I'd forgotten all about that house.'

'Well, now I've reminded you. The sea air will be good for Sonny, and it'd leave me free to collect Eaden from Mum's and spend the rest of the day together, seeing as she missed out on our shopping trip yesterday. You could ask Polly to go with you, it'll give you a chance to re-bond as well as spend some quality time with the baby. Win-win,' he says, like a game-show host.

'But it's Polly's first full day off,' counters Carly. 'She might have something else planned, especially as yesterday went so... awry.'

'I bet she'll be only too happy to go. I think she's awake, why don't you go up and ask her?' he suggests.

'All right,' she says decisively, putting Sonny's toy down and standing up, relieved to have moved past yesterday's difficulties. 'I will.'

CHAPTER TWENTY-TWO

'Wow, impressive!' Polly heads straight towards the large picture window on the open-plan first floor of the upside-down house. The layout is designed to make the most of the view. It's one of only four small detached art-deco style flat-roofed dwellings all backing onto the long stretch of Fraisthorpe beach, which can be accessed by steep narrow wooden steps inlaid in the cliffside. Approaching the properties from the front, the Lawrensons' 'seaside house' is at the end of the row on the right.

Polly looks out towards the North Sea beyond the almost deserted beach, already indulging in daydreams of herself encouraging barefoot toddler Sonny to take a few sunny sandy steps while Fletcher and Eaden enthusiastically build an impressive sandcastle next summer. Maybe she'll have a burgeoning baby bump to complete the picture-perfect fantasy...

'It needs even more work than the pictures showed.' Carly interrupts Polly's reverie, her expression divulging her distaste.

'You've never been here?' asks Polly, surprised.

'No, Fletcher's shown me photos, but I've never seen it with my own eyes. He brought the children a couple of weeks after we moved to Swanland but I stayed home to take delivery of the new couch.' Carly's phone vibrates and she pulls it out and checks the screen. 'Oh, that's my medication reminder. Time to pop a pill!' She hands Sonny to Polly while she goes over to the grimy kitchen area to get a glass of water. Finding no glasses, she grabs one of the few mugs in the cupboard above the sink and rinses it out.

As Carly gets her tablets out of her bag, Polly wanders around the space, carrying Sonny on her hip, taking it all in. It needs a lot of updating but she can see what it could become. The large main room comprises of a small U-shaped kitchen area in the corner nearest the door, a circular wooden table and chairs beside the sliding patio doors, and a chintzy two-seater sofa and armchair in front of the naked picture window, facing out to the sea. The patio doors on the far exterior wall lead out onto an empty, narrow, rectangular side balcony enclosed by a rickety picket-fence-style barrier, just big enough for a bistro table and chairs, although it's currently empty.

Polly's imagination again races ahead to the future – leisurely weekends and impromptu balmy evenings straight after school pick-ups, each conjured scene nothing short of blissful. It's the kind of life she wants, and it looks like it's the kind of life she's going to have. 'Long game,' she whispers to herself.

'Polly?'

Polly whirls around to face Carly, so caught up in her visions that she'd momentarily forgotten the other woman was even there.

'Sorry, what did you say?' she asks, noticing Carly's pale face and shaking hands.

'I was just saying that I feel a bit woozy all of a sudden. Would you mind watching Sonny while I rest in the bedroom downstairs for a bit?'

'No, of course not. Have you eaten anything? Aren't you supposed to take some tablets with food?'

'No, I'll be fine. It's probably just stress, the past few weeks catching up with me. What with the move, my new job and yesterday's drama.'

'Are you sure that's all it is, after what you said last night? You can talk to me, you know.'

'I know, and thank you, I appreciate that. But I'm sure I'll be okay again after a quick nap,' Carly says, attempting a smile.

'Okay. Shall I wake you for some lunch?'

'No, I just need to rest. You sort yourselves out.' She leaves and goes down the narrow staircase to one of the two ground-floor bedrooms the property contains.

Polly looks at Sonny. 'Well, I guess it's just you and me then, little guy.' She jiggles him and plants a noisy kiss on his plump cheek.

Carly opens her eyes and feels disorientated for a second, then remembers she's at the Fraisthorpe house. She turns over on the candlewick bedspread to face the window and although she can't see the sea from this position on the ground floor, it's comforting to hear it. She closes her eyes again and just listens, gauging whether she still feels drowsy or not. She decides not. As well as the sound of the sea, she can hear an animated voice, punctuated with gleeful laughs. She smiles, thinking Polly must be chattering away to Sonny, and swings her legs over the side of the bed.

She takes a long drink from the mug of water she brought down with her before checking her reflection in the dusty mirror above the chest of drawers. Her hair's a bit ruffled but she finds she doesn't mind, and besides, Fletcher's not here to pass comment on it; she'll neaten it before they head home.

She goes out to the small hallway, squeezes past Sonny's

pushchair, and climbs the stairs. Although this modest house is probably not even one third of the size of their home, she feels relaxed here, and grateful to Fletcher for suggesting the trip today, even if all she's done is sleep since they arrived.

Carly steps into the main living area off the landing and sees that Polly is standing on the balcony but she's not chatting to Sonny, as she thought. The baby is asleep on the sofa, cocooned in cushions, and Polly is giggling with someone on the phone.

Carly pauses, feeling like she's intruding on a private conversation. Perhaps Polly has a boyfriend, or even a girlfriend, she hasn't mentioned. Irrational annoyance flares in her as she twists her letter 'S' necklace that she's taken to wearing again, that her nanny isn't watching her son more closely after yesterday's events, even though he's clearly contentedly sleeping. She quickly catches and extinguishes the thought, remembering that it's supposed to be Polly's day off and she's doing her a favour, and that she herself hasn't exactly been attentive to him today. How quickly promises can be forgotten.

Carly is about to take another step into the room when Polly turns on the balcony and her voice becomes clearer, floating in through the open patio door.

'...one of those punny by-the-beach house names like *After Dune Delight* or *Sandy Bottom* rather than just *Seaview Cottage*. I mean, it isn't even a cottage... I bet you would... on this very balcony, huh? Well, you'd better fix it up then, mister.'

Polly grins goofily into the phone then she notices Carly and her cheeks flush. She turns away. 'Gotta go, talk later,' she says before hastily ending the call and shoving her phone into her pocket. She steps back into the room from the balcony, sliding the patio door closed behind her, and gestures to Sonny. 'Out like a light after a quick walk to the shop,' she says. 'I got some herbal tea bags. You want one? I found a kettle and washed a couple of mugs – everything's so dirty!'

'Yes, please,' answers Carly, eyes narrowed, taking in Polly's sudden upshift in demeanour. As Polly rounds the kitchen peninsula, Carly points to the patio doors. 'Fletcher said the balcony needs repairing so be careful out there. The last thing we need is another hospital dash.'

Polly flicks the kettle on and looks over at Carly, her face still rosy. 'Okay, thanks, I will.'

TWO WEEKS BEFORE

CHAPTER TWENTY-THREE

MONDAY

It's such a busy morning at *Image Aesthetic Clinic* that Carly doesn't have time to check her phone until lunchtime. She sees a missed call from an unknown number, with a voicemail. She presses play and puts the phone to her ear. A woman from social services with an efficient-sounding voice asks her to call back as soon as possible and Carly feels herself trembling as she listens.

She immediately messages Fletcher, asking him what to do. Thankfully, he replies within a few minutes, telling her to call them back but not to worry; he's sure it's just procedure.

Carly calls the number and is greeted with the same voice who left the message – Suzanne Beckwith. Carly gives her own name as confidently as she can and asks why she has been contacted.

'Mrs Lawrenson, I understand that your son, Sonny James Lawrenson, was treated in A & E on Saturday?' Suzanne's inflection makes it more of a question than a statement.

'Yes, but he was discharged on the same day. He's fine. What's this about?' asks Carly again.

'I'm glad to hear he's fine now, but every child who visits

hospital accident and emergency departments or has out-of-hours GP consultations must be logged in a national database. This came into effect in 2015. The child protection information system is designed to help doctors and nurses spot children who are suffering from abuse or neglect.'

Suzanne's smooth explanation sounds well-trodden to Carly's ears, which she feels slightly reassured by; Fletcher's right – it's just a routine follow-up.

'Okay, well, I can assure you that my son isn't being abused or neglected,' she feels compelled to state regardless, trying to keep the defensive tone from her voice.

'I'm sure you understand I'm just doing my job, Mrs Lawrenson, for Sonny's benefit. I'm also here to offer support to you and your family in order to prevent further incidents from occurring. May I just ask a few questions, please?'

Carly purses her lips, knowing it would be futile to say no. 'Okay, yes, go ahead.'

Suzanne asks Carly to confirm Sonny's birthdate and then asks her to explain, in her own words, about the events leading up to Sonny's hospitalisation.

'I wasn't actually there,' says Carly. 'You'll have to speak to my nanny; she was looking after him while I was at work. She'll be able to tell you first-hand what happened.'

'Your nanny is Polly Blake, correct?'

'That's right.' Carly is impressed yet slightly unnerved by Suzanne's evident thoroughness.

'Yes, we will be talking to her, and to your husband, Fletcher. I believe he was the one who called the ambulance for Sonny?'

Carly frowns. 'No, Polly called the ambulance, but my husband was working close by, and he managed to get back home before it arrived.' There's a pause and Carly hears papers shuffling.

'I've got the transcript of the 999 call here, Mrs Lawrenson, and it was definitely your husband who made the call,' states Suzanne.

Carly shakes her head against the phone. 'But that doesn't make any sense. He wasn't there when it happened.'

'Mrs Lawrenson, I think it may be best if I pop round and speak to you and Mr Lawrenson and Miss Blake in person,' says Suzanne after a pause. 'And meet Sonny, of course. I'm on annual leave next week but I can do the week after?'

After agreeing to a home visit in two weeks' time, Carly hangs up, stunned. If Fletcher called the ambulance, that means he was at home when Sonny stopped breathing. Why did he lie about only being five minutes away due to picking up supplies? And if he was at home and not at work as he should have been, how come both he and Polly weren't paying attention to the baby monitor?

Her phone vibrates in her hand. A message from Fletcher.

> How did it go with social services?

She stares down at it while sparks of realisation start flashing in her head, jigsaw pieces slotting smoothly into place in slow motion.

I bet you would... on this very balcony, huh? Well, you better fix it up then, mister. Polly grinning goofily into the phone at the Fraisthorpe house. Hastily hanging up.

Carly replies to her husband.

> They need to do a home visit and speak to all of us but it's just standard practice.

Fletcher's next messages pops up within seconds.

> Told you not to worry. Forgot to charge my phone and battery about to die so see you at home later.

His words dance before her eyes and she drops the phone onto her lap, head whirling.

A few minutes later, cutting her lunch-break short, Carly returns to the reception area and unlocks the main door ready to receive clients again. She needs to keep busy rather than sitting and stewing in the staffroom on her own. She's been manning the clinic alone for the past couple of hours as Gavin's not due back from a meeting until later. On autopilot she opens the door, suddenly desperate for fresh air to clear her head. Can she trust her own thoughts – do they even make sense?

'Hello.' The word permeates despite the loud pounding of her heartbeat in her ears. Benny is standing a few steps away, his body language apologetic. They're far enough apart that she can't smell him today, or maybe it's just less pronounced outside.

Somehow, despite her inner turmoil, she manages a smile. 'Hi,' she replies.

'I wanted to check you were okay… after Saturday,' he says.

'Saturday?' she questions.

He lifts his chin, stands a bit straighter. 'I saw you… at the hospital.'

'Oh yes.' She nods, remembering catching a glimpse of him when she arrived. 'My baby son was…' She frowns, not wanting to discuss it here and now, and especially not with a stranger. But he's looking at her so kindly. 'He gave us quite the scare but he's fine now.'

'Little fighter, eh?' asks Benny.

Carly remembers what Gavin told her about Benny losing his own son following his wife's affair and her heart aches for him. What depths of despair must he have been through since then to end up like this? 'Little fighter,' she agrees, her smile genuine this time. 'Why were you there? Are you okay?' she asks in return.

'Yeah. Just helping a mate. He hurt himself. Some people will do anything for a bed for the night.' He huffs out a soft laugh at his own joke, but she can see the worry in his eyes. 'Anyway, I'll let you get on.' He gestures towards the interior of the clinic. 'Nice to chat,' he says as he heads back to his sleeping bag.

'Nice to chat to you too,' calls Carly, meaning it.

She returns to her desk in the empty clinic, and without anyone or anything else to distract her, the suspicious thoughts about her husband and her nanny pick up pace again in her brain, whirling and twisting and gathering more and more terrible titbits until they have formed a tornado of evidence. One thought in particular flies free with force, nearly knocking her out. 'Prick Tease,' she whispers to herself as she starts to tremble.

Carly drives along her street after locking up and leaving the clinic. It's still technically her lunch-break, though she'll have some explaining to do if Gavin gets back before she does. But she can't think about that right now.

As she approaches the house, she's not surprised to find the gates open and Fletcher's car in the driveway, and sadness surges through her. She parks the car on the road and walks quickly along the paved path between the boundary wall and the garages, heading for the back garden.

As she rounds the corner, something in the one remaining yet-to-be-filled flowerbed catches her attention and she deviates from her route to get a closer look. She squints down at the ground, trying to make sense of what she's seeing then recoils in horror as she realises it's the rotting body of the dead fox from the front of the house, its snout, teeth and one ear partially exposed, the soil around it disturbed. Fletcher must not have dug its grave deep enough and a cat or another fox must have been scratting at it. Carly swallows down nausea and turns back towards the house.

She creeps past the utility room door and window and then peeps through the bi-fold doors into the kitchen. It's empty and she screws her face up in immediate frustration. She'd hoped to see something – enough – straight away without having to witness the full spectacle. She doesn't want to go inside but she must; she came here for confirmation of her suspicion, and she needs to get it.

Carly quietly tries the back door, but it's locked. She takes her keys out of her pocket, unlocks it as quietly as she can and enters the house. The internal utility room door is ajar but the hallway beyond is empty. She tiptoes out and listens, straining her ears for any sounds. Then she hears it. A steady, rhythmic thump. As she climbs the stairs the thumping gets quicker, layered below heavy breaths and recognisable grunts. Pausing on the landing, Carly realises she's shaking and takes a moment to steady herself. The master-bedroom door is wide open, and the bed is exactly as she left it with the quilted throw folded over the bottom and the pillows and decorative cushions plumped and arranged just so.

Before moving towards Polly's bedroom door, she casts a glance over at the children's bedroom and glimpses Sonny asleep in his cot. She doesn't go in.

Taking shallow breaths, she places one foot in front of the other along the landing until she reaches Polly's doorway. The door is half open and from where she's standing, Carly has a clear view of the bed. Barely able to comprehend it at first, she sees Polly and Fletcher naked and moving together, both pink-faced with intense passion, oblivious to anyone and anything else. The sight of them is utterly grotesque to her, yet now burned on her retinas for ever. Clamping a hand over her mouth to stop herself shouting or screaming or crying, she backs away silently, turns around, goes downstairs and back out the same way she came in.

Once inside the confines of her car, she sits for a minute, overwhelmed yet suddenly exhausted. She feels vindicated that her suspicions were not foolish, paranoid notions that Fletcher made her believe they were, yet disgusted that she's married to an adept, manipulative liar. She breaks down, screaming and banging her palms then arms down on the steering wheel, slapping her own cheeks, pinching and punching her thighs. Once she has released all of her anger she calms, sitting like a puppet with cut strings, staring at her idiotic reflection in the rear-view mirror.

An hour later, Fletcher slaps Perry on the back and looks around at his cousin's quality plastering work. 'Everything all right, mate? You've done a good job with this.'

Perry throws him a glance and mimes looking at his watch. 'You took your time. I could have done with a hand.'

'Ah, sorry, the potential clients kept asking me to quote for more and more work, couldn't get away,' he lies.

'Let's hope they book us then,' says Perry. 'Make it worth our while.' He puts the plastering trowel down and wipes his hands on the back of his combats. 'I was just going to stop for a brew. You want one?'

'Sure. Actually, there's something I want to talk to you about.'

'What's this, you need some famous Perry wisdom?' He winks.

Fletcher runs his hand down his jaw. 'Bit more than wisdom, mate. Come on, let's get that cuppa and we'll have a chat.'

A few minutes later they sit down amongst all the building paraphernalia within the freshly plastered mud-like walls, Perry on a folding metal platform and Fletcher on a stack of upturned plastic crates.

'What's going on then?' asks Perry.

Fletcher sighs and looks down at his coffee. 'I know it's a bit of an ask, but would you mind documenting everything that happened with Carly last week, when she accused Rachael and me of carrying on?'

'What do you mean by documenting?' Perry frowns as he raises his mug to his lips and takes a sip.

'Writing it down officially. Things have taken even more of a nosedive since then and I might need some proof of her erratic behaviour so I can get her the help she needs.'

'I know what happened with Sonny was gutwrenching but are things really that bad with you and Carly?'

Fletcher rubs the back of his neck with his free hand and nods. 'I think they're heading that way, yeah.'

Perry puffs out a long breath and widens his eyes. 'Wow, I didn't realise, mate. You should have said something. A problem shared and all that.'

Fletcher shakes his head. 'I think I've been in denial.'

'Yeah, but it's not like you're heading towards divorce or anything, are you? You've only been back in the country five minutes.'

Fletcher shrugs. 'I honestly don't know. It's been going on for months and she might force my hand if she continues acting like she is. It's fucking worrying. Eaden might seem like she's doing well but underneath it all she's still fragile after Pippa's death. She needs some stability after that as well as two big moves. And there's Sonny to think about, especially after what happened at the weekend. The kids have to come first.' He glances at his cousin. 'So you'll write it all down, just in case, as soon as you can?'

Perry nods. 'Yeah. Sure, mate, I'll do it later today. Whatever you need.'

'I knew I'd be able to count on you. Thanks, cuz,' says Fletcher with a smile.

CHAPTER TWENTY-FOUR

TUESDAY

The next morning, from her vantage point on the stairs, Carly peers through the banister spindles into the kitchen as soon as she hears the front door close after Fletcher leaves for work. Polly is sitting at the table with Eaden and Sonny is in his highchair, which is positioned next to them. She needs to be quick. She races to the linen cupboard on the landing then to Polly's bedroom, pushing the door almost closed behind her and dropping the clean bedsheets on the bed. They're her reason for being in here, should Polly or Eaden venture upstairs.

Carly works quickly but methodically as she snoops, starting with the drawers in the bedside table, and when she finds nothing incriminating or of any interest in them, she moves to the tall chest of drawers opposite the bed. Nothing there either. Opening the wardrobe doors, she quickly shoves her hands into any pockets she can find – of which there are few as Polly's entire wardrobe seems to consist only of fast-fashion leggings, crop tops and a few oversized shirts and hoodies – before kneeling on the floor and looking below the hanging clothes. There are four shoeboxes, not the Perspex kind like hers, just ordinary, non-designer cardboard boxes. She lifts the lids off two at once to find a pair of high-tops and a pair of ballet pumps, two sizes smaller than she wears. She then looks inside the remaining two boxes and although one of them contains a pair of heels, the other contains what looks like cards and photos. Bingo.

Pulling it towards her with shaking hands, she quickly rifles through it, not sure what she's looking for – maybe that goddamn *Prick Tease* lip gloss? She's fizzing with adrenaline. She wants to take the shoebox back to her bedroom to look through its contents properly, but she can't risk it, and besides, she can't wait even a second longer; she needs to do this right now.

There aren't many photos and Carly doesn't recognise any of the faces in the ones she flicks through but there are a lot of mementos – ticket stubs and cards and even pressed flowers. No lip gloss anywhere yet though; maybe she was wrong about that, after all. Or maybe it belongs to yet another whore in Fletcher's harem?

Tucking that troubling thought aside, she digs a bit deeper and pulls out a few pieces of paper at random. A child's drawing depicting a mommy, daddy, a child called Talia and what looks like a dog named Jet. Polly is in the middle between Mommy and Talia.

Underneath, Carly finds a piece of folded thick white paper. Opening it, she sees the header: *T³ Design Studio* above an address in New York. Then she reads the scrawled handwritten words beneath:

I'm sorry. I'll always love you. Teddy. xxx

Despite having lived in Brooklyn, she hasn't heard of the design studio. She wonders what the note writer – Teddy – is apologising for and how it connects to Polly. Maybe he's another poor woman's husband who couldn't keep his dirty dick in his pants. She makes a mental note to look the place up online.

As she stuffs the papers back into the box, a red envelope catches her attention. A large heart has been drawn on the front with the initial 'P' inside surrounded by lots of kisses. Just like how Fletcher addresses the cards he gives to her. She turns it over and lifts the now unstuck flap to reveal a 'to my girlfriend' card. She steals a glance at the doorway and strains her ears for sounds of anyone coming up the stairs but all she can hear is faint chatter floating up from the kitchen. She takes the card fully out of the envelope and stares at it, frozen in shock, her heart hammering a loud bassline inside her chest. She doesn't want to open the card, but she has to. Even after yesterday's undisputable proof, she's masochistically hungry for more.

So she does. She reads the brief verse and then the handwriting inside:

Happy belated six-month anniversary, baby. I've been counting the days until I could give you this in person. All my love forever, Fletcher. xxx

The tears welling in her eyes make a Monet painting of the words. She swallows thickly and blinks, the tears spilling onto her cheeks. She sniffs and quickly wipes them away before sliding the card back into the envelope, putting everything back in the shoebox, and then returning it to the wardrobe.

She closes the doors, crosses over to the bed to collect the clean linen, then leaves, escaping to her own bedroom where she drops the linen on her own bed before locking herself in her en suite and turning on the shower. Once under the soothing water, she allows the sobs to break free, imagining her love for her lying, cheating husband seeping slowly out of her body and then circling down the drain, where it belongs.

'Mrs Lawrenson?' The receptionist holds the door open then leaves once Carly has walked past her into the solicitor's office. After being awake most of last night in turmoil, this morning's additional discovery in Polly's bedroom has prompted her to make the first appointment she could get. Luckily, a cancellation was available this lunchtime; the universe assuring her she was doing the right thing.

Cameron Baldwin, one of the family solicitors at the reputable firm in Hull's city centre, briefly introduces himself and double-checks the scant information Carly shared with the receptionist when she called this morning. He has salt-and-pepper hair, a five o'clock shadow and his shirtsleeves are rolled up to his elbows revealing toned forearms. In Carly's mind, these things signal a willingness to show his real self rather than hide behind a suited stereotype, and that helps her relax a little.

'How can I help?' he asks.

She swallows, trying to work out how to begin. She decides to just cut to the chase. 'I need advice about divorcing my husband and taking my son back to the States. He was born in America and I'm American but I'm currently here on a spousal visa.'

'Okay,' begins Cameron, inching his chair further forward and clasping his hands together on his desk. 'You would need to prove your son is better off with you and that taking him away from his established life here is in his best interests.'

'He's only eight months old and we've only been back in the UK for two months. He doesn't have an established life here yet.'

'How long have you been married to your husband?'

'Fourteen months,' states Carly.

'And until two months ago you, your husband and your son all resided in America?'

'Yes. With my husband's daughter too. She's six.'

Cameron picks up a pen and makes a few notes on his desk pad. 'Can I ask the reason behind you seeking advice today?'

'You can,' says Carly and she takes a deep breath before launching into her raw and honest explanation. 'My husband is having an affair with our nanny. Such a cliché...' She huffs out a brief laugh and rolls her now watery eyes. 'It's been going on for months. My son – Sonny – recently had a breathing pause and was treated in A & E, but they made me think I caused it. I'm not sure I did now. I also have a history of post-natal depression and other problems after the complicated birth of my son, and I may not be the best mother in the world, but I do love him, very much, and now the thought of losing him on top of my marriage imploding...' She turns her head and blinks furiously, trying to keep the tears at bay.

Cameron subtly pushes the box of tissues on his desk towards her.

Carly waves them away and breathes deeply again, pulling herself together. She needs to be stronger than this. She looks back at Cameron, as steely as she can.

'If I pursue this divorce, my husband will use my mental health struggles against me, so what can I do to make sure I don't lose everything, and he pays for what he's done?'

CHAPTER TWENTY-FIVE

WEDNESDAY

For the first time in weeks Fletcher wakes up and Carly is still beside him. For a split second, as he floats towards consciousness, he almost reaches out, slides his hand over her hip and onto her stomach, then down between her legs. His erection wants attention and it's been a long time since he felt a warm body in his own bed. His eyes flutter open and he realises where he is and what's happening, or rather what's not happening. His erection begins to deflate.

'Morning. You not swimming today?' he asks, rubbing his eyes with his thumb and forefinger.

Carly turns her head to face him, wearing a pained, pinched expression. 'No, I think I've got a stomach bug, I've been up half the night.'

'Really? I didn't hear you.'

'I used the downstairs toilet. I didn't want to disturb you.' She turns back over, away from him. 'I think I'm going to have to ring Gavin and call in sick.'

'But it's only your second week... are you sure that's a good idea?' he asks, placing a hand on her arm.

She sits up slowly and looks down at him. 'I think it'd be a bad idea to go into work and pass it on to Gavin and the clients. I can't help being sick.'

'No, no, of course not. Sorry. Do you think it might be a side effect of your medication?'

Carly shrugs. 'More likely something Eaden has passed on from school – you know what germ factories they can be. It'll probably just be one of those twenty-four-hour things. I'll stay up here out of everyone's way though, make sure I don't pass anything on to Sonny. I don't want him getting poorly again.'

'Good thinking. I'll go down and help Polly with the kids.' Fletcher gets out of bed and pulls his old faithful Lyricsmiths T-shirt and a pair of jogging bottoms on. 'Do you want me to bring you anything up – herbal tea?'

She nods and offers him a small smile. 'That'd be nice. Thanks.'

'Okay, coming right up.'

Carly listens as Fletcher goes downstairs and greets the children loudly in the kitchen. She marvels at his ability to rile them up instantaneously, make his very presence feel like an occasion, something to whoop and cheer about.

She exhales, blowing her cheeks out as she flops back down onto her pillow and stares up at the yet-to-be-painted ceiling, her stomach cramping at the thought of them all downstairs with Polly, not even noticing her absence. She might not really have a stomach bug, but she does feel sick with worry about what her future may or may not hold.

She thinks back to the advice Cameron Baldwin gave her yesterday, about establishing 'the best interests of the child' and proving that Sonny is better off with her. Her mind turns over ideas about how she might be able to prove that so Fletcher can't counter her actions with a prohibited steps order or a child abduction claim, because she hasn't gone through the traumatic ordeal of carrying and birthing a baby and creating a family with Fletcher only for him to snatch it all away from her in favour of *some girl* – their new nanny, for Christ's sake.

The thought of returning to her parents' squalid little trailer in rural America with her tail between her legs, a washed-up model, a failed mother and a humiliated divorcée is too much to bear. Although with Sonny in tow, as well as a post-baby butchered body and post-husband broken heart, she'd fit the local demographic to a tee.

Interrupting her thoughts but true to his word for a change, Fletcher brings Carly a cup of herbal tea in bed and magnanimously instructs her to relax, declaring that he will take care of everything today.

She stews in their marital bed while he showers, already feeling guilty about letting Gavin down and about not swimming this morning. She imagines her muscles slackening and fat cells expanding inside her body and feels disgusted at the thought. She'll have to skip in the garden later to counterbalance her inertia even though she already feels weak at the thought of it. What if her not being in good enough shape is a contributing factor to Fletcher's infidelity, leading to his preference for young, nubile, perfect Polly?

She shakes the thought from her head and chides herself. Fletcher has been unfaithful because of urges he's had and choices he's made, not because of things she has or hasn't done. She knows this yet the knowledge brings no comfort. Instead, it brings mess and complications and decisions that need to be made, actions that need to be taken. She's not sure she has the strength to keep up the façade, to do what needs to be done, to play those cheating secret-keepers at their own game. Is she smart enough to steal control?

Fletcher exits the en suite after his shower, dresses quickly and leans over to kiss her on the forehead. 'Right, I'm off. Feel better soon, okay?'

Carly nods, staying prone. A stranger in her own home, she listens to him shout goodbye to the children and close the front door behind him, then she hears Polly bringing Eaden and Sonny upstairs to get them dressed and ready for the day, without even popping her head round the bedroom door to confirm proof of life. She texts Gavin a brief but sincerely apologetic message then puts her phone on silent, face down on the bedside table, and closes her eyes against it all.

Carly wakes with a jolt and realises she must have fallen asleep. She checks her phone and sees that it's gone 9am. She can't remember the last time she was still in bed at this time. It was definitely before Sonny was born, perhaps even before she and Fletcher got married, in those halcyon days of their early relationship when she believed his false promises and declarations whispered during their nightly pillow talks.

With trepidation, she opens a new message from Gavin, but it's kind, wishing her a speedy recovery, and her guilt momentarily makes her feel worse than she did before. Then she remembers the reason she needed to be at home today and she's immediately galvanised. Pushing back the duvet, she gets up, slips her robe on over her nightdress and pads downstairs to the kitchen, taking her undrunk, cold cup of tea with her.

She pours the liquid down the sink, drops the bag in the island's integrated bin and leaves the cup on the counter.

A piece of paper catches her eye on the table, and she wanders over to look at it. It's one of Eaden's drawings, a family portrait. Underneath the figures there are faintly written names in pencil that Eaden has gone over in crayon. Carly finds herself in stick-figure form on the end, next to Sonny, but right in the middle, pride of place, is Polly. Her eyes narrow; is it that obvious even to a little girl that the nanny has usurped Carly's role in their lives? Or has Polly prompted Eaden to create this drawing, just like the one Carly found in her shoebox yesterday? Is this Polly's pattern – a cuckoo in many nests?

Carly hears the front door open then close. A few seconds later, Polly steers Sonny's pushchair into the hallway and starts a little as she sees the other woman standing by the table. She recovers quickly and smiles.

'Morning. Fletcher says you're not well?' She phrases this as a question, as though speaking to an invalid.

'No. Stomach bug.' Carly grimaces. 'I was just getting some more herbal tea. The one Fletcher made me went cold.'

'I can do that for you?' Polly offers. 'Sonny will be fine in his pushchair for a few more minutes.'

'Don't be silly,' Carly replies and crosses back over to the island. She reaches across for her cup and her robe's sleeve rides up, exposing her arm which is black and blue from banging it against the steering wheel after she discovered Fletcher and Polly together on Monday. She feels Polly's stare and pretends to be embarrassed, pulling her sleeve down again. She begins to make herself a fresh cup of herbal tea. 'It really was my own fault this time,' she says quietly, over her shoulder.

'What do you mean?' Polly asks, brow furrowed.

'I make him angry.' Carly pauses, enjoying Polly's confusion and discomfort. She rubs her arm gently, as though soothing the affected area.

Polly gapes at her for a few moments. 'Fletcher doesn't seem the abusive type,' she says eventually, a tremor of emotion in her voice.

Carly nods, biting her lip. 'Yes, that's what I used to think too. And he never used to be, not towards me, anyway. I obviously can't speak for Pippa, his first wife.'

'What do you mean?' Polly asks again as her head snaps back, her eyes wide.

'Well, Pippa died. In a horrible, tragic collision,' she says softly. 'Little Eaden was in the car too but thankfully her car seat was robust enough to protect her. But my point is that Pippa can't tell her side of the story, can she? Who knows how he treated her in the years they were together, and Stella would never think or speak badly of – or hear anyone else speak badly of – her darling son even if she witnessed any questionable behaviour herself.'

Carly takes a sip of her tea and continues, 'He can be so loving and protective and generous; he used to surprise me with presents – jewellery, shoes, my Chanel bag – and we couldn't get enough of each other in the beginning. It was a whirlwind. I was obsessed with him, I felt like a teenager again. Yes, he liked it rough in the bedroom, but he never hurt me deliberately, never crossed any boundaries I wasn't comfortable with.' She smiles coyly. 'I always remember he used to call me his "north star", his "pure delight". Bit of an obscure reference from an old Lyricsmiths' song. Do you know it?'

Polly shakes her head.

'Of course, he had to explain it to me because they're an English indie band – his favourite band – who I wasn't really aware of, being American, plus Fletcher's era is a bit before mine, but I loved the sentiment behind it. And I truly believed him, more fool me.' She sniffs and crosses her arms. 'Now I have to be so careful around him and I'm telling you, woman to woman, that while you're living under his roof, you might want to be careful too.'

CHAPTER TWENTY-SIX

L ater, after showering and dressing in comfortable but flattering loungewear, Carly finally emerges again from her bedroom and pauses, trying to gauge where Polly is in the house. From the landing, she sees that Sonny is down for a nap and Polly's door is open, her room empty.

Carly wonders if she's missing today's illicit rendezvous with Fletcher or whether she might just be grateful for the break from all that sex. Surely thrush must be a concern. Then, through the arched landing window, Carly spots Polly and the neighbour Meryl chatting over the adjoining garden wall. She frowns at the sight; yet another person that Polly seems instantly friendly with – she really is a fast worker, that one.

Taking advantage of the opportunity to investigate without interruption, Carly goes down the uncarpeted stairs to the office. It's one of the smaller, windowless rooms in the large house, in between the double garage and the utility room. Although carpeted, its freshly plastered and whitewashed walls are bare, and it only contains a desk and chair, an iMac computer, a floor lamp and a large faux plant. Boxes filled with files and books and stationery are stacked neatly along the back wall, waiting for the custom shelving unit that Fletcher intends to build. She never usually comes in here – it's solely his domain – so she feels a slight thrill as she closes the door and sits down at the sleek walnut desk.

Moving the mouse to wake the computer up, Carly is greeted with a password prompt, as she knew she would be. She types in what she knew his password used to be when they lived in Brooklyn but it's incorrect, as she anticipated it would be. An unfaithful liar doesn't keep the same password for long. She sits and thinks for a moment, running through variations of the old password in her head. She tries one. Incorrect. She begins to type another then stops and deletes it quickly before trying something else. Just like that, she's in and looking at the wallpaper photo of Eaden with a newborn Sonny. Fletcher may be wily but he's not that imaginative.

Next, she navigates to his search history. It only goes back a week, so it seems he does clear it regularly, but a few days' worth might be enough. She starts with the earliest and works her way through to yesterday, checking all the sites he's visited. Despite her suspicions, she's still shaking when she closes the tab and takes her hand off the mouse. She places both palms on the desk to ground herself and breathes slowly and deeply, trying to calm her hammering heart.

It all flashes through her brain again like a startling slideshow: custody advice sites and forums, deportation advice sites… and schoolgirl porn. Young schoolgirls. Her stomach twists, and she reflexively clamps a hand over her mouth, feeling like she might vomit. She refused to entertain that particularly sick fantasy the one time he suggested it, but it's clearly still something he's very much into. Her watery eyes roam the desktop as she tries to refocus on her search. The screen is a mess of documents and folders, most labelled with capitalised surnames, which she assumes are his clients' names, but some are saved under street names or dates.

As she's trying to make sense of it all, she spies a folder labelled with their surname and frowns. She clicks on it and as she quickly scans the contents, she feels like she's been sucker-punched in the stomach. This time the documents are labelled clearly, and they all begin with the same word: her name. *Carly meds. Carly behaviour. Carly outburst.* She opens the *outburst* one and is horrified to find it's Perry's typed account of her confronting their Chestnut Avenue client last week.

She stares rigidly at the document, dumbfounded that Fletcher has roped Perry into this. *Family really does stick together,* she thinks bitterly, although she's burning with rage and regret for giving them something so sensational to document in the first place. Panicked thoughts pepper her mind: *has the red-haired woman written one too? And her wife, whatever her name was? What about Stella?*

Carly's head swims at the thought of all the people Fletcher could corral into backing up his claims that she's an unstable liability, a terrible wife, an unfit mother. And she's been playing right into his hands.

She allows herself a few minutes to weep, to wallow in the whole sorry situation, then she sits up straight, wipes her tears and swallows thickly. She takes a deep, restorative breath, expels it slowly, and asks herself one question: *what next?*

Opening the internet browser, she steels herself and types in *T³ Design Studio* followed by *New York.* It's on the first page of Google. A fancy website featuring curated images instantly loads. She clicks on the 'meet the team' tab and sees a gallery of stylish black-and-white portraits. Husband-and-wife team Edward and Theodora Miller are listed as CEOs. Searching further, she finds a mobile number in the 'contact us' tab. Adrenaline still spiking, she instantly rings it, knowing that they're five hours behind and it'll be morning there.

A male voice answers and Carly feels homesick upon hearing the familiar accent.

'Hello, could I please speak with Mr or Mrs Miller?'

'Edward Miller speaking,' he replies.

She's surprised to have got him direct without going through a receptionist or PA but she noticed he introduced himself as Edward and not Teddy. Obviously Teddy was a nickname reserved for or used by Polly. She launches straight into her reason for calling. 'I'm contacting you in relation to Polly Blake. She interviewed for a nanny position with my husband recently and gave your name as a reference. I'm just following up.'

There's a pause. 'I find that highly unlikely,' Edward replies curtly.

'Oh, may I ask why you say that? Is there anything I need to know about her?' asks Carly, secretly thrilled with his immediate honesty.

He gives a mirthless laugh. 'If you want to employ a homewrecking little bitch, go right ahead. However, if you value your marriage, I'd advise against it.' His tone is stone cold.

Despite her current situation, Carly is surprised to feel slightly affronted on Polly's behalf. He must have played his part too.

'That's a bit rich,' she feels compelled to say. 'It takes two to have an affair.'

'It does indeed,' he replies, a hard edge to his voice. 'And the two in this equation were Polly and my wife Teddy.'

In the garden, after exchanging pleasantries for a few minutes, Polly plucks up the courage to ask what she really wants to ask Meryl.

'Do you remember last week when you said that something's not quite right with this family and that Fletcher and Carly are a fiery couple, or "smouldering couple" was the phrase I think you used?'

'Yes, dear, of course I remember,' replies Meryl, an inquisitive expression on her face.

'What did you mean by that exactly?' asks Polly.

Meryl looks over at the house and tilts her head slightly, as if Fletcher and Carly are there, am-dram performers behind the windows.

Polly glances down at Sonny's baby monitor to check that he's still sound asleep. Carly may be home but he's still her responsibility and she never wants a repeat of that dreadful day she found him unconscious.

'Well, from what I've personally observed, disregarding anything Stella has said,' Meryl begins, 'Fletcher seems a very laid-back chap except when he's around Carly. The few times I've seen them together, whether to say hello in person or just spotting them coming and going, there's an obvious tension there. It seems to radiate from him especially, like heat.'

Polly's brow creases as she ventures her next question. 'Have you ever seen Fletcher lose his temper?'

Meryl looks at her curiously. 'I haven't, no. Why do you ask?'

Polly folds her arms across her body and shrugs, affecting nonchalance. 'I just want to be able to understand the family dynamic better. To support them. They've all been through a lot.'

The older woman clucks her tongue and shakes her head. 'It's your job to support the children, dear, not the parents. You shouldn't feel obliged to stay if either one of them, or both of them, are making you feel uncomfortable in any way.'

'Oh, no, it's nothing like that, I was just being nosy really. Everything's fine,' Polly states. 'I'm sure it'll be fine,' she modifies after a moment's pause. 'The kids are gorgeous.' She conjures up what she hopes is a convincing smile.

They say goodbye and Meryl returns to her gardening while Polly goes back inside, makes herself a hot chocolate using one of the sachets she bought herself and steals upstairs to her bedroom to wait until Sonny wakes up. She closes the door behind her, feeling awkward in the house while Carly's here too, especially after their conversation this morning.

Her head feels fuzzy and she's desperate to talk to Fletcher, but she knows he won't appreciate her ringing him at work to discuss it and it's not the sort of thing she wants to message him about. She resigns herself to waiting until they can be alone, to talk privately, hopefully tomorrow when Carly's back at work. She sighs and curls up on her bed with her drink and her turbulent thoughts. All she seems to do lately is wait.

CHAPTER TWENTY-SEVEN

THURSDAY

Polly is sitting at the table opposite Eaden when Fletcher and Perry enter the kitchen.

'Look who's here, munchkin,' says Fletcher to his daughter.

Eaden pauses before taking her next mouthful of cereal and shouts, 'Uncle Perry!'

'Now then, sunshine, how's it going?' Perry leans down as though he's going to kiss Eaden's cheek but blows a raspberry on it instead. She dissolves into giggles as he bops Sonny on the nose and strokes his head.

'They've missed you,' Fletcher tells him, eyes crinkling with affection as he watches them all.

'I've missed them too. All work and no play makes Perry a busy boy though.' Perry winks at Fletcher then gestures for Eaden to move along the bench seating. 'Scoot.'

Eaden happily wiggles over as Polly reaches across and moves her bowl for her.

Fletcher laughs at his cousin's remark. 'All work and no play – yeah, right.' He gestures towards Polly. 'Perry, this is Polly. Polly, this is my cousin and business partner, Perry.'

Polly says hello at the same time as Perry says it's good to meet her. 'Finally,' he adds. 'I've heard lots about you – all good, don't worry.' He smiles.

Polly flicks a glance at Fletcher, but he doesn't meet her eye as he hands Sonny a slice of banana.

'Daddy, can Uncle Perry stay for breakfast?' Eaden asks.

'Not today, Eadie-pie,' Perry answers. 'I've already had my breakfast, I'm just here to pick up your daddy so he can help me collect some heavy building supplies.'

'Because Daddy's much stronger than Uncle Perry,' Fletcher jokes, winking at Perry.

Perry laughs. 'I will have a cuppa though.'

'You sit with the children, I'll make it. Coffee?' Polly offers, standing up.

'Great, thanks, Polly.'

'Coffee, Fletcher?' she asks.

'Sure, thanks. The good stuff from the machine though, not that instant crap in the jar.'

She nods and crosses over to the island, taking out her phone and firing off a quick message to Fletcher, asking if she'll see him later. If Perry's taking him to work, he won't be able to drive home when he pleases, and she won't get the opportunity to talk to him about what Carly said yesterday.

As she crosses back over to the table with the coffees, she sees Fletcher get his phone out and read the message. He taps out a reply and puts it back in his pocket. She feels her own vibrate.

'Right, I'll take these two monkeys upstairs to get dressed and ready for school,' she says, lifting Sonny out of his highchair and patiently waiting for Eaden to clamber ungainly over Perry. He tickles her as she does, which provokes raucous giggles, delaying them further. Finally, Polly and the children exit the kitchen, leaving the cousins at the table.

As soon as she gets upstairs, she puts Sonny back in his cot for a few minutes and directs Eaden to the bathroom to brush her teeth. Then she looks at her phone, at the message saying *not today* with three sad-face emojis, and her heart sinks.

Downstairs, Fletcher takes the children's breakfast detritus over to the sink in the kitchen island then rejoins Perry.

'Look at you, all domesticated.' Perry chuckles and takes a mouthful of his coffee.

'Fuck off!' Fletcher laughs in response. 'I am domesticated! And besides, Polly's the nanny, not the maid. She shouldn't have to do it all herself.'

'True. Little fox though, isn't she? You didn't mention that, mate. How old is she anyway?'

Fletcher shrugs. 'It's irrelevant.'

'Bit of a risk to bring in a hot young nanny when Carly is all jealous and territorial though, isn't it?'

Fletcher pinches his bottom lip and turns his head, checking there's nobody within earshot before he speaks again. 'She claims she was ill yesterday, stayed off work, but I don't know... I think there might be more to it. This is her second week in the job and she's slacking off already. I hoped that her going back to work might occupy her mind in more positive ways, leave less room for her fanciful imaginings about what I'm getting up to, or rather, not getting up to.' He sighs. 'But things are getting worse, cuz.'

'So what are you going to do about it?' asks Perry.

Fletcher glances at Perry then looks back down at his coffee. 'I've had a look online for divorce advice...'

Perry gives a low whistle, eyebrows raised.

Fletcher continues, 'Divorce advice because my wife and son are both American citizens. From what I've read, it's best to get Sonny settled, into a routine – baby classes, a network of friends and family, and so on. Prove he's better off here than there, just in case.'

'You really think she'd try to take him back to the States?' asks Perry, appalled.

'Maybe. To spite me, if it comes to that. You saw her when she came to Chestnut Avenue, all guns blazing. She's unhinged. She knows she made a massive mistake confronting Rachael but she's so paranoid she might think there's another woman, or even other women, on the scene instead.'

'Is there?' Perry asks baldly. 'Come on, Fletcher, you can tell me. I know you of old, remember. That cougar that time when we were teenagers… You've never been able to resist a hot body and a pretty face. No judgement.' He holds his hands up.

Fletcher looks him square in the eye. 'Says you! But no, there's nobody else. I've got enough on my plate with Carly and the kids. When have I got time for a bit on the side? I'm just trying to do what's best for Eaden and Sonny, and if that means being a single dad, so be it.'

'Well, I'm here for you, mate.' He looks up and taps the table, alerting Fletcher to his wife's presence.

'Perry. Good to see you again.' Carly appears in the kitchen wearing a beige trench coat with her black Chanel bag hooked over her shoulder.

Perry doesn't smile. 'Just picking your husband up. Oh yeah,' he addresses Fletcher, 'dropping these off too.' He pushes a keyring with two keys and a plastic fob bearing the number 171 in black ink across the table.

'Great. I'll get to it as soon as I've figured out how to clone myself.' Fletcher jests as he folds the keys in his hand.

'A new property you're working on?' asks Carly.

'No. Well, yes – eventually. Uncle Frank's old terrace down Boulevard near town,' replies Fletcher. 'Yet another house for us to flip when we can fit it in.'

'You'll manage, I'm sure. You secretly love having multiple

projects to juggle,' says Carly. She bends down and barely brushes Fletcher's cheek with her matte lips. 'I'm going in early, to make up for being ill yesterday. I don't want Gavin thinking I'm a slacker.' She regards them both with a cool gaze before turning. 'See you tonight,' she calls as she leaves, the click-clack of her heels echoing on the floor tiles.

'Why didn't you warn me she was behind me?' Fletcher hisses as soon as they're alone again.

Perry pulls an apologetic face. 'I honestly didn't see her until she came through the door.'

'Do you think she heard anything we said?' asks Fletcher.

'I hope not, for your sake,' Perry says.

CHAPTER TWENTY-EIGHT

FRIDAY

Fletcher slides into Polly's bed and gently presses himself against her warm back. 'God, I've missed this,' he whispers against her neck. 'It feels longer than just two days.'

Polly jerks awake and Fletcher's arm tightens around her. She unhooks it and pushes it back.

'What's wrong, baby? Are you mad at me for not being able to get home for our usual playtime yesterday?' He affects a child-like voice, and it instantly irritates her.

She shakes her head against the pillow as her worries over the past couple of days flood back in. 'No, I just didn't sleep well.'

'Go back to sleep then. I'll lie here with you for a few more minutes.' He nuzzles closer to her and emits a contented sigh.

'I heard you,' she says after a minute.

'Heard what?' he mumbles, kissing her bare shoulder.

Polly turns her head towards him. 'You and Carly arguing. Last night. I heard her accusing you of talking to Perry about your marriage troubles. I heard you shouting back at her.'

He tuts and releases his grip on her, rolling over onto his back. 'I'm sorry you had to hear that. I didn't realise we were that loud.'

'Well, you were. I'm surprised it didn't wake the children. I heard a bang too, like something falling.' She pauses. 'Or someone.'

He jerks his head in her direction. 'What are you saying exactly?'

Polly sits up and looks down at him. She presses her lips together, her accusation obvious.

'Do you think I did something to her, physically?' He sits up too, instantly puffed full of incredulity, sleep creases still lining his face. 'Fucking hell, Polly, I would never hit a woman! I thought you knew me better than that. Carly is the crazy one, making shit up, baiting me, making me look like the bad guy.'

Polly feels as though butterflies are flapping wildly inside her chest, but she powers on, albeit with a less accusatory tone. 'It's just... I've seen bruises, more than once.'

'I told you – she probably got those exercising. I don't actually know; I barely look at her body anymore, especially not unclothed, but I certainly haven't caused them.' He throws his hands up. 'If she's accusing me of abuse and she's got you believing it, who else might she convince? Imagine if I lost the kids! She's more unstable and dangerous than I thought... she's fucking poisonous! This is why we need to get Sonny and Eaden away from her.' He seizes her by the shoulders and shakes her. 'But if you're having doubts about me – about us – you need to tell me now.'

She's taken aback by the force of his grip but it's upsetting to see his abject panic, especially since her suspicion has caused it.

'I'm sorry.' Her bottom lip trembles. 'I'm just so worried. How you and Carly are now... constantly fighting... is that how we're going to end up?'

His body sags, and he strokes her shoulders with his thumbs, his voice full of concern. 'Is that what this is really about? No, baby, no.' She looks at him, tears beginning to fall. 'That's not how we're going to end up. You and me... we're different to

Carly and me. Better. You understand me. She doesn't. Not anymore.'

'Did your first wife understand you?'

His face hardens slightly, and he stills. 'I loved Pippa, and we had a happy marriage. I was devastated when she...' He turns his face into his shoulder and closes his eyes. Polly gathers him to her as he carries on talking, his lips lightly brushing her skin. '... when she died. And heartbroken for Eaden losing her mum at such a young age, not to mention her surviving the crash itself. God, the trauma that kid's experienced already...'

His voice cracks with emotion and he breathes slowly against her for a while. After a few minutes he continues, 'In hindsight, I perhaps rushed into marrying Carly, more for my sake than hers. I had high hopes for us as a family, but it's not worked out that way. If only I'd met you before her, Pol.'

'I'm sorry,' she whispers. 'For thinking the worst. I'm so sorry.'

He grips her tightly and kisses her neck, then her ear, trailing his mouth towards hers. He groans as he hears Sonny shout out his morning greeting.

'To be continued,' he says, getting out of bed, his erection straining against his boxers. 'We've got some catching up to do.'

'Can't wait,' she replies, wiping her eyes and tucking her long hair behind her ears.

'Are we good?' He waits in the doorway for her answer.

She nods and gives him her best smile. 'We're good.'

Later, once Polly has collected Eaden from school and settled her and Sonny with drinks and snacks, her phone rings. Expecting it to be Fletcher, she pulls it out of her back pocket and answers without checking the caller display.

'Missing me already, mister?' she answers, laughing.

'Polly?' Carly says.

It takes Polly a second to realise who it is. 'Oh, hi.' She grimaces against the phone. 'Sorry, I thought you were someone else.'

'Who's this *mister*?' Carly asks playfully.

'Sorry, what?' Polly says, stalling.

'No, no, I'm sorry,' replies Carly quickly, 'that's none of my business. Anyway, I'm just ringing to apologise. It's been on my mind, and I wanted to say it now rather than risk not getting the chance to later, once everyone's at home.'

'Apologise for what?' asks Polly, bending down to pick up a chunk of mango from the floor beside Sonny's highchair. She takes it across to the island's integrated bin, listening to Carly.

'For what I said yesterday about Fletcher. About being an abused woman.' She whispers the word 'abused'. 'I was feeling poorly and sorry for myself and being ridiculous. Blowing things up out of all proportion. You haven't said anything to Fletcher about it, have you?'

'No, of course not,' Polly lies.

'Good. Thank you. Fletcher wouldn't appreciate me speaking to anyone, especially someone outside of the family, about our marital woes.'

Polly registers the obvious dig but doesn't react to it.

Carly sighs on the other end of the phone. 'Not that he minds sharing our private business with Perry. I assume you heard our argument last night?'

'Argument?' Polly asks faux-innocently. 'No,' she lies again.

'Well, I'm glad about that. I would hate to think we disturbed your beauty sleep.'

'Don't worry, you didn't. Well, I'd better–' Polly is about to end the call but Carly rushes on.

'It's just that he tells that cousin of his everything, and never very favourably. Lads together. Women are so much better at keeping secrets, aren't they?' She pauses. 'Anyway, I just wanted to check that I haven't worried you at all. That there's no need to feel nervous if you're ever in the house alone with Fletcher.'

Polly's stomach flips at the implication. 'I don't feel nervous,' she says, trying to inject a lightness into her tone. She frowns into the phone, disliking the turn the conversation has taken. Does Carly really believe Fletcher would ever hurt *her*? She thinks back to his vehement denials this morning and her thoughts flounder, caught in the choppy current between her lover and his wife.

'Good. That's good. I would hate for you to worry about that. God, with all this drama already, I wouldn't blame you if you wanted to quit.' She laughs gaily. 'Anyway, I have to get back to work now but once again, I'm sorry.'

She ends the call without saying goodbye.

CHAPTER TWENTY-NINE

SATURDAY

'I'm leaving but I'll be home at lunchtime. Let's hope today's not as eventful as last Saturday, hey?' Carly raises her brows as she places her cup in the dishwasher.

'Have a good day,' Polly replies, glossing over her employer's comment. She moves Sonny's arm up and down. 'Say bye-bye, Mummy.' Sonny emits his screeched version of goodbye and Polly laughs.

Carly walks towards them, ignoring Sonny and looking at Polly. 'Did you–'

'Morning, ladies,' says Fletcher, entering the kitchen.

Carly looks at him and closes her mouth. She collects her handbag from the island.

'Is Eaden still asleep?' he asks her, reaching to get a mug from the cupboard.

Carly nods. 'Yes, little lazy bones. What time are you working until today? Remember it's Polly's afternoon off.'

'I know,' he replies. 'I said I'd pop and see Mum later, so I'll knock off, collect the kids and head there. Give you a bit of time to yourself.'

'Oh, shall I come with you to Stella's?' asks Carly.

'No need. Perry's going too – bit of an informal family business meeting.' He places a mug under the coffee machine's spout, presses one of its many buttons and leans against the counter while it pours.

'Right.' Carly sniffs. 'I'll see you later then. Enjoy your free afternoon, Polly.' She pauses to stroke the top of Sonny's head then strides out through to the hallway.

As soon as they hear the front door close Fletcher and Polly look at each other. He shakes his head and sits down at the table opposite Polly and next to Sonny's highchair, placing his coffee mug down.

'Now I'm the one who doesn't know how much longer I can do this,' he says. 'I thought I could hack it, but we're only a couple of weeks in and I already wish we could fast-forward to being together properly, especially after what we talked about yesterday.'

'Why can't we? Why don't you just file for a divorce now, or separate?' she asks.

He rubs his hands down his face and sighs. 'You've seen – and heard – the lengths she's willing to go to. We've been through this, Pol. I need to consider Eaden and make sure I can secure custody of Sonny before I even think about anything formal like that.'

She looks down and clenches her fists in her lap. 'This is messed up, Fletcher. It's not how I thought it would be – I'm here all day, mostly alone, just worrying and waiting for whatever time you can eke out for me without arousing suspicion.' She reaches across the table for his hand. 'I think you're right that Carly won't simply leave, or give you up, without a fight. She's angry and highly strung and perhaps even delusional. I don't know... I feel like she's messing with me sometimes, playing some sort of twisted game. But you need to fast-track this. I've told you before: I can't wait forever, especially not in this–' she casts around for an appropriate description '–toxic environment.'

Fletcher squeezes her hand. 'Please, just give me a bit more time, baby. Carly will mess up again – she can't help herself – and it'll strengthen my case against her. I'm keeping a record of every dodgy thing she does. Perry's written a witness statement about her Chestnut Avenue ambush too. I'm doing as much as I can to make sure I'll get custody when it comes to it. I need you here to keep taking care of the kids, to protect them from her.'

'Does Perry suspect anything, about us I mean? I kind of got the impression he did the other day. Carly says you tell him everything.'

'Well, she clearly doesn't know me as well as she thinks she does because although I've sung your praises in terms of what a great job you're doing with the kids, I haven't said a word about the amazing jobs you give me.' He sticks his tongue in his cheek playfully, but the joke falls flat.

Polly looks at him, a pained expression on her face. 'Fletcher, I'm trying to be serious here.'

'I know. I love it when you get serious.' He kisses her hand delicately, each finger in turn and she closes her eyes and sighs. He's impossible at times.

'What are you going to do this afternoon? I wish you could come to Mum's, but you'll be there with us soon enough, in your rightful place.'

Polly shrugs and pulls her hand from his grasp to take Sonny's sticky spoon off him, which makes him scream. She stands and picks him up, jiggling him on her hip to settle him. 'I'll have to occupy myself, won't I? As usual.'

Fletcher appraises her appreciatively and grins, pointing to her and Sonny, waggling his finger up and down. 'This suits you so much. You look even more beautiful when you're holding a baby.'

She raises her brows and shakes her head slowly and deliberately as Sonny grabs a handful of her hair. 'Oh no, do not get ahead of yourself, mister. We do not need any more complications right now.'

'Hey, I've got an idea,' he says excitedly, reaching out for her. 'How about I take the whole day off to spend together on Monday rather than just our usual hour? I'll ask Perry to cover for me. It'll give us something to look forward to. Give us a chance to properly reconnect after the past few crazy days. What do you think?'

'You'll ask Perry to cover for you for a whole day?' she asks. 'But what will you tell him?'

'I'll think of something. Anything. But I'll make sure our secret is safe. Okay?' He flashes one of his megawatt grins at her.

She sighs again, suddenly weary of all the subterfuge. 'Okay,' she says, relenting anyway.

ONE WEEK BEFORE

CHAPTER THIRTY

MONDAY

Fletcher returns to the house shortly after Polly gets back from the school run. He guides her straight through to her bedroom as soon as Sonny goes down for his nap.

'Hey, what's the rush?' she asks, as he practically pushes her along the landing.

'I've been thinking about this non-stop since Saturday, baby. I don't want to waste a second.' He pulls his polo shirt over his head before they're even through the doorway and throws it on the floor, then turns his phone on silent and slides it face down onto the bedside table.

'Was Perry definitely all right with you taking the day off? He doesn't suspect anything?'

'Yep, no, all good.' He pulls her towards him, kissing her neck exactly where she likes him to kiss it, but she doesn't respond as she usually does. He moves her hand down to the bulge in his combats. 'Feel how hard you make me,' he says a few seconds later when it becomes apparent that Polly is not as enthused as he is. 'Get it out and play with it.' He grabs her bum and pulls her against him.

'What did you tell him exactly?' she asks, resisting his embrace.

He pulls his head back to look at her. 'What's with all the questions, Pol?'

'I… I don't know,' she says limply. 'It just feels… weird today. Knowing you don't mind lying to your cousin.'

'I've lied for *you*. So we could spend some quality time together.'

'So we could spend most of the day fucking, you mean,' she says.

'No,' he protests then cocks his head to the side and smirks. 'Well, yes, I did hope… but not just that. I want to feel close to you again, baby. I thought you wanted that too.'

She takes a step back from him and crosses her arms. 'Secretly screwing in your spare bedroom while your wife's at work is not quality time.'

He looks perplexed. 'You've never complained before.'

She twists her head and looks at the floor, a crease forming between her eyes.

'Hey, come on.' He moves towards her, crooking his finger under her chin and turning her face back to him. 'I picked up some nice lunch for us on my way back this morning. We could have a little bed picnic later, with Sonny. And I've got something else for you too. I've been saving it for a special occasion, but this is the perfect time. Wait there.'

He darts out of the room and returns quickly, brandishing a parcel.

Despite her conflicted feelings, she beams as he proffers it on bended knee like he's serving her with a precious offering. She takes it from him and places it on the bed then opens it carefully, savouring the anticipation. Inside the wrapping she finds a short, pleated grey skirt, a white shirt that looks a couple of sizes too small for her, a tie, and knee-high white socks. A schoolgirl's outfit.

'What's this?' she asks, feeling herself flush.

'You're going to look so sexy in this,' he says, laying the garments out on top of the sheets. 'Let me dress you up.' He can barely contain his glee.

'Another fantasy?' she asks. 'What about the cheerleader and French maid outfits we've already got?'

'I thought we'd expand the collection.' He slides his palm around the back of her neck and kisses her, urgently and forcefully, pushing her down onto the bed next to the clothes. She lets him, trying to get into it, trying to clear her mind of all her niggles and concerns, trying to relax and enjoy what he's doing to her. But she feels detached.

It's as though she has left her body and is watching Fletcher getting excited about undressing her then redressing her like a mannequin, a blow-up doll, from afar. He's so desperate to pleasure her, for her to pleasure him, that he seems slightly rabid, animalistic. He makes it clear he wants to rut her like an animal first, practically tearing off their clothes before folding her down onto the bed, and she pictures him grunting and sweating behind her and she can't stand the thought of it all of a sudden. She wants an emotional connection, not just a physical one.

'Wait,' she says firmly, just as he's about to plunge himself into her. She feels him tense and his breath is heavy.

'What? Baby, I don't think I can wait.' He's gripping her hips tightly, the tip of him against her and she can hear a tinge of impatience, or maybe annoyance, in his voice.

'No, stop.' She softens her voice. 'I'm... I'm finding it hard to relax. I can't seem to switch off. Maybe we should just take a break. Try again later – we've got all day, haven't we?'

'I've got just the thing,' he says and reaches down to his combats on the floor by the bed.

She twists round and sits down on the bed and widens her eyes in surprise as he pulls out a blister pack of pills.

'Tablets?' She is appalled he has even thought of this, let alone got them to hand. 'I'm not taking drugs right now!'

'It's just diazepam. They're Carly's. It'll help you relax.' He pops a pill out of the pack and holds it in his palm.

'No, Fletcher. I need to pick up Eaden – *your* daughter – later, with Sonny in tow. I've never taken diazepam before. What about the side effects? I can't be off my face in charge of them.'

'That's not for hours and any side effects will have worn off by then. And if you're worried, I'll collect Eaden from school,' he offers.

'And how will you explain that to Carly? Eaden might say something. No, this is meant to be a day for us to reconnect, not take drugs.'

He looks at her ruefully, admonished. 'You're right,' he says. He kneels in front of her, stroking the sides of her thighs, the tablet folded in his hand. 'I just feel like I've put you through so much these past couple of weeks and all I wanted for today was for us to feel carefree, like we did when we first met in the States. Do you remember? I'd sneak away and we'd share a few lines and spend all afternoon in a hotel bed on your day off, wrapped up in each other in every way it's possible to be, planning for this, for our future. I miss all that so much.'

She looks at him, letting his words transport her back to those delicious, dreamy days. 'So do I,' she says, with a sigh. He always knows exactly what to say to win her round.

'And now those plans are coming to fruition,' he continues. 'Maybe a bit messier than we expected but we're still on track. You and me, baby. Long game.'

'Long game,' she repeats dutifully as Fletcher gestures for her to stick out her tongue. He places the pill on it and after a moment, she swallows. He smiles widely, his dimples making an appearance, and cups her face in his palm, stroking her cheek tenderly with his thumb. 'I love you so much... let me show you how much, Miss Blake.'

She nods, lies back down on the bed and closes her eyes as he crawls on top of her.

Carly's mind is torturing her, throwing up scenario after scenario featuring Fletcher and Polly. Something was off on Saturday morning – she could sense it – and he was in a foul mood all yesterday, staying in his office for hours, rather than helping her with the children, which then caused another argument last night.

She messages him but the WhatsApp ticks stay grey. On her break, she rings him, but her call goes straight to voicemail. It infuriates her; what if she needed to speak to him about Sonny? He's not even showing her the basic respect the mother of his child deserves.

At lunchtime she drives to the Chestnut Avenue house that Fletcher and Perry are still working at. She doesn't have to wait long for Perry to make an appearance. Exiting the car, she slams the door behind her and brazenly marches straight up to him. His shock at seeing her is almost comical.

She holds a hand up to silence him before he has the chance to say anything. 'I'm not here to cause trouble, Perry, I'm just looking for Fletcher. He's not answering my calls or messages.'

Perry rubs a hand across the back of his neck and glances at the ground. 'He's... he's at the wood merchants. Probably left his phone in the car.'

'Where's the wood merchants?'

'Across town.'

'When will he be back?'

Perry laughs nervously. 'Soon, I hope. There's still loads to do here.'

'Okay. Thanks for your help, Perry.' She starts to walk away then turns again, smiling. 'You'll have to come to ours for a meal soon. I'm sure the children would love it.'

He raises his brows in surprise. 'Yeah? Sure. Thanks.'

In the car, Carly fires off a quick, apologetic text to Gavin about having another stomach upset and tells him she needs to take the afternoon off. She drives away, heading for home.

Fletcher feels himself rising up through the depths of sleep into consciousness as Polly jerks against him. She jolts out of bed and rushes through to the en suite.

'Pol?' he calls, following her.

She's crouching over the toilet bowl on her knees, her forehead resting on her arm. He places his hand on her back as she rears up and retches, expelling the remains of her stomach. She waves him away, clearly wanting space and privacy.

'I'll get you some water,' he says and squeezes her shoulder gently.

He goes to her bedside table and picks up the empty glass next to his phone. Instinctively, he turns his phone over and sees missed calls and messages from Carly and Perry, and a voicemail from Perry. He reads Perry's text first:

> Mate, Carly turned up here looking for you again. Got the feeling she wants to find you ASAP. I'm guessing you're not really ill. Told her you were getting supplies at the wood merchants. What's going on?

He sees it was sent more than fifteen minutes ago. Forgetting about Polly's water, he listens to the voicemail as he walks across to the main bedroom at the front of the house and looks out onto the driveway. Perry's voicemail more or less repeats what was in the text, but it escalates Fletcher's panic. As he listens, he sees the gates swing open and Carly's car waiting to pull in. His heart thuds hard in his chest as he runs back through to Polly, who is shuffling out of the en suite on her way back to bed.

'Carly's home! You get back in bed and I'll deal with her.' He yanks on his clothes and shoes and leaves the room.

The front door opens just as he reaches the bottom step and he and Carly lock eyes.

'Oh, hey,' he says, running his hand through his hair then resting it casually on the banister. 'What are you doing home?'

Carly calmly closes the door and drops her keys into the bowl on the console table. 'I wasn't feeling well. What are you doing home?'

'I popped in to get some paperwork on my way back from the wood merchants. When I got here, I heard Polly being sick, so I've sent her to bed. I've just seen your calls and messages; sorry I missed them.'

The silence stretches between them for a few seconds. 'Right. Poor Polly. Must be something nasty going around,' says Carly.

He nods. 'Yeah, seems so. Anyway, I need to get back to work, so are you okay with Sonny? I'll ask Mum to collect Eaden.'

She nods and he moves to kiss her on the cheek, but she turns her face away. 'I wouldn't want you to catch anything.'

'No. Okay. I'll see you later.' He grabs his keys and opens the door.

'Don't work too hard,' she warns, heading upstairs. 'Oh, and say hi to Perry for me.'

CHAPTER THIRTY-ONE

Polly wakes again in a panic, and according to Carly's designer clock on the bedside table, it's just before she's due to leave to collect Eaden from school. Still slightly fuzzy and fragile, she dresses as quickly as she can, splashes some water on her face, brushes her teeth and pulls her long hair back into a low ponytail. She shrugs on an oversized hoodie as she goes downstairs then stops, shocked, in the hallway as she spots Carly in the kitchen with Sonny. She's horrified that she'd completely forgotten about the baby.

Guilt explodes within her at the vague memory of Fletcher announcing Carly's surprise appearance earlier and she's further panicked to realise she doesn't know what happened or what Fletcher said to his wife because her phone is still upstairs in her jacket pocket, and she hasn't checked it since just before he returned home this morning. There's nothing she can do now though; she's just going to have to face the other woman head-on.

'Polly, how are you feeling? Fletcher said you were sick,' Carly calls from the table where she's sitting, drinking herbal tea. Sonny is in his bouncer at her feet, contentedly flapping one of his crinkly fabric books about. It feels jarring to be on the stage instead of in the audience for a change.

'Yes, I was. I'm really sorry. I feel better now, thank you.' She points to the door. 'I'm just going to collect Eaden from school.'

'No need, I've arranged for Stella to pick her up today so you can get some more rest.'

'Oh, right, okay.' Polly pauses. 'Why are you home already?'

'I wasn't feeling well either, so I came home at lunchtime. I feel better now too.' Carly smiles.

Polly nods and waits awkwardly for a moment. 'Good. Well, I think I'll pop out for a walk anyway. Get some fresh air.'

She leaves the house, pulling her hood up and shoving her hands in her pockets, then slowly circles the tree-lined block a few times, trying to make sense of the day's events. Shame colours her face, heating her cheeks. She wonders what messages she's missed from Fletcher but feels no desire to rush back to the house to check her phone.

She can't remember all the details clearly, but she does recall allowing Fletcher to persuade her to take diazepam and understands that they've had a very close call. The whole house of cards could have completely collapsed today. There's a part of her that wishes it had, that Fletcher's hand had been forced so that all this craziness would end. She's not sure it's worth it anymore.

A while later, as she completes another circuit and approaches the house once again, she looks up and comes face to face with Meryl deadheading flowers in her front garden.

'Hello, Polly dear,' Meryl says, standing and brushing down her corduroy trousers before moving closer to her front wall. 'Goodness me, you look a bit peaky. I've just seen Stella bring Eaden home – have you got the afternoon off?'

'Well, yes, I suppose I have.' Polly's eyes immediately fill with tears.

Meryl's expression conveys concern and sympathy. 'Come

on,' she says, rounding the wall and putting an arm around Polly on the path. 'Come inside and we'll have a nice cup of tea.'

Polly sniffs and nods and allows the kind neighbour to guide her indoors.

A few minutes later, Meryl places a full teapot on her kitchen table next to the cups, milk jug and sugar bowl she's already set out. Polly smiles gratefully as she pulls her hood down, sadly acknowledging that she already feels more at home here than she does next door.

'So, did you and Fletcher begin your affair before you moved in or has your relationship developed since you've been living under his roof?' Meryl asks plainly. Her words are stark, but her expression is soft.

Polly gapes at Meryl who merely smiles knowingly and pours the tea as she waits for an answer. 'Sorry, what?' Polly forces a laugh, trying to feign ignorance.

Meryl stirs their cups of tea then pats Polly's hand, clicking her tongue. 'Your secret's safe with me, dear.'

Polly's cheeks burn and she takes a moment to measure her response. She realises lying is futile. 'How did you know?' she asks, nibbling a neon-green-painted fingernail.

Meryl meets her gaze. 'The clues were there, and I just pieced them together. Remember, I'm a retiree with plenty of time on my hands to observe and overthink. And I do chat to Stella occasionally too, so I've probably got more of an overview of the Lawrensons' marriage than you. It wasn't difficult to work out, I'm afraid.'

Polly covers her face with her hands. 'I'm so embarrassed. I can't believe I'm that transparent. You haven't said anything to Stella, have you? Oh God, does she suspect too?'

'No and no,' states Meryl confidently. 'You don't need to worry about either of those things. Now, you don't have to answer this if you don't wish to, but do you really know what you're doing? There are many ways the situation could unfold and no matter what, there will be consequences. Not necessarily bad ones but consequences nonetheless.'

Polly curves her hands around her cup and stares at her tea. 'I thought I knew what I was doing but now I'm not sure.'

'Has he pressured you in any way?' asks Meryl.

Polly looks across at the older woman, shaking her head vigorously. 'No, no, it's not like that; we love each other, we really do.'

'All right,' says Meryl, bringing a biscuit barrel over to the table. 'I just wanted to make sure. And if you ever want to talk about it, I'm here. No judgement whatsoever. Biscuit?' She takes the lid off the tin and pushes it towards Polly.

Polly wipes her eyes and manages a watery smile before she takes a shortbread finger. She eats it in silence before taking a swig of her weak, sweet tea. It's just what she needs, and she begins to feel a bit better, her head much clearer.

She leans back in her chair and begins to tell an attentive and – true to her word – non-judgemental Meryl the story of how she and Fletcher first met eight months earlier, in Brooklyn. About how Meryl was right when she told Polly on her first day that Fletcher had let Eaden simply point at a map after Pippa's death and that's where they ventured off to.

And about how, just over a year later, on a nondescript January afternoon, she and Fletcher got chatting in a coffee shop queue after he heard her English accent and told her he was mainlining caffeine after the birth of his son who "never sleeps". How he never lied to her about having a family but shared how unhappy he was over their subsequent friendly get-togethers on her days off from nannying for an American family in New York.

Polly tells Meryl how he made his and Eaden's move there sound like an adventure when really it was a ridiculous, spontaneous decision he made in the throes of grief. And eventually, when they were wrapped in each other's arms in hotel beds as the weeks went by, he whispered his concerns about how absent a mother – and stepmother – Carly was.

Then, when his Uncle Frank died, he told her he had to leave, that he was going back to the UK to run the family business with his cousin, as well as surround himself with a proper support system because Carly wasn't interested in being a stay-at-home mum.

Meryl pours them both another cup of tea as Polly helps herself to another biscuit.

'And what happened next, dear?' asks Meryl.

'By that time, my nannying job there had ended, so Fletcher asked me to come back to the UK too. He was so excited. We both were. We began planning how we could make things work and after I left, I stayed with a friend down south for a few weeks while he and Carly prepared for coming back here. We kept in touch the whole time we were apart, FaceTiming most days. We even managed to meet up a couple of times when he flew back for family visits. We pretended one of the meetings was my nanny interview. I met Eaden that time too.' She hangs her head and bites into the shortbread.

'You didn't go home to your family?'

Polly shakes her head. 'I don't have any family. It was just me and my dad after my mum left us when I was a baby. And he died before I went to America. He left me a bit of money so in a way, I did the same as Fletcher – upped and left. I thought, what job will give me somewhere to live too? Nannying seemed the obvious choice. So, I made it happen. I wanted to get as far away from my old life as I could. And now I can't think of anything better than being part of a proper family. It's all I've ever wanted.'

'I'm sorry to hear about your father, dear. And your mother. Terrible thing losing a parent when you're young.' Meryl then asks, 'Is this your first serious relationship – with Fletcher?'

Polly hesitates then nods as she finishes the biscuit.

'I think I'm beginning to understand how this has all come

about,' says Meryl, patting Polly's arm. She takes a sip of her tea and then furrows her brow, a thought occurring to her. 'But why did Fletcher let Carly renovate his house to her taste if he wants you to live there with him eventually? Or are you planning on moving somewhere else together?'

Polly shrugs. 'He said he had to choose his battles, to do whatever it took to make sure he got Sonny over here. That meant her coming too. She might not be a great mum, but she is his biological mother, and Sonny is an American citizen. Fletcher claims Carly's completely unhinged; jealous, possessive, paranoid... the list goes on. He's worried about how she might react or what she might do if he tells her he wants to separate or divorce. And about the effect it might all have on Eaden. It's a delicate situation and how the house is decorated is the least of his worries right now. I'm just trying to build a strong relationship with the children ready for the future.'

Meryl sips her tea, digesting all the information. 'I mean this with the greatest respect, Polly, and tell me to mind my own business if I'm crossing a line,' she says, 'but you're very young. Are you sure you want a ready-made family with a middle-aged man who will have already had two marriages behind him by the time you're free to be together properly?'

'I might be young, but I know my own mind and I know how I feel,' Polly snaps.

'Of course you do, dear. I apologise.' Meryl holds her palms up in supplication then folds her arms back down on the table. She glances at Polly again. 'I'm just saying be careful, for your own sake.'

After leaving Meryl's, Polly gets home to find Stella, Eaden and Sonny sitting together on the sofa in the kitchen. Stella greets

Polly warmly and Eaden jumps up to hug Polly's legs then sits back down next to a collection of her toys.

'Carly said you're not well today?' enquires Stella.

'I wasn't but I'm feeling much better now,' she replies. 'I'm so sorry if collecting Eaden disrupted your day. It won't happen again.'

'Nonsense,' Stella scoffs. 'Spending time with my granddaughter is never a disruption, and if you're ill, you're ill. We're a family, we pull together.'

'Polly, you're back.' Carly enters the kitchen. 'Did the walk do the trick?'

'It did, thank you.'

'The benefits of exercise!' Carly beams at her.

'Are you feeling better too?' Polly asks.

'Oh yes, I'm absolutely fine now. Bit of family time worked wonders.' She gestures to Stella and the children and Polly struggles to hide the surprise she feels at Carly's alien statement.

'I won't interrupt then but I can do the children's bath and bed routine later if you need me to?' she offers.

'No, no, Fletcher and I will do that tonight. You go upstairs and chill out.'

'Okay. Thanks.' She smiles and says goodbye to Stella.

Polly walks out to the hallway but before she even sets foot on the bottom step of the staircase, she hears Carly say her name. She turns around and the other woman is right behind her, as stealthy as a fox.

'I just wanted to ask,' Carly whispers furtively, 'when I came home at lunchtime, Fletcher was just coming downstairs. He looked a bit flustered and said he sent you to bed after he heard you vomiting. Was that the truth?'

Polly raises her eyebrows. 'What do you mean?' Her pitch is higher than usual and she's sure she's giving herself away. She couldn't feel more guilty; it's as if someone has branded the word on her forehead.

Carly glances back towards the kitchen then turns to face Polly again. 'Okay, I'm just going to ask it straight out: did he behave inappropriately towards you in any way?'

Polly hears the question, but she can't believe her ears. Alongside the disbelief, a tiny part of her is glad that it's this question Carly's asking and not a different one.

Polly's laugh is short and sharp. 'What? No.'

'Did you feel unsafe when he came home unexpectedly... I mean, were you worried about being alone in the house with him?'

Polly shakes her head as well as verbalising her answer. 'No.'

Carly persists. 'Did you pretend to be ill to get him to leave you alone?'

'No, Carly,' says Polly in a firm tone. 'I was genuinely ill. He suggested I go back to bed and offered to bring me some water. He was kind. He looked after me.'

Carly smiles tightly. 'Okay. I just wanted to make sure... after what we talked about the other day. You haven't spoken to anyone else about it, have you?'

'No, of course not. I told you that.' Polly places one foot onto the next uncarpeted step, desperate to get away from this dangerous conversation. Fletcher's right – Carly's unhinged, changing the narrative to suit herself. Now she's alluding to being a battered woman again. Polly can't handle this right now, not after the day she's had.

'Good. Thank you. I know I can trust you. Right now, you're the only true friend I've got.' Carly turns on her heel and returns to the kitchen as Polly races upstairs to the privacy of her room, her stomping feet mirroring the vigorous thumping of her heart.

CHAPTER THIRTY-TWO

Fletcher arrives home late to find his children already in bed, his mistress upstairs in her bedroom and his wife sitting in the front lounge speaking to someone on the phone. From the doorway he hears the tail end of the conversation and ascertains she's talking to Gavin, apologising profusely for going home sick today when she was off ill last week too. She ends the call and looks up at Fletcher as he enters the room.

'Everything okay?' he asks and sits on the arm of the sofa.

'Gavin's being so nice about me being off sick, it's making me feel even more guilty.'

'Yeah, that sounds like Gavin; he's a nice guy. Perhaps a bit of a soft touch though. He's taken you on in good faith – partly based on my say-so – but you being off sick twice so soon into the job isn't reflecting well on you, or me,' chides Fletcher.

Carly scowls. 'I might have known you'd be more worried about yourself than you are about me. I can't help it if I'm ill. Just like I couldn't help that my infant son was rushed to hospital, and I had to leave early that day too.'

Fletcher sighs. 'You seemed really positive about starting this job, about having a new career opportunity and time to focus on yourself again. What's changed?'

She crosses one long, lean leg over the other. 'Nothing's changed. I'm still excited about where it could take me. Possibly even starting my own injectables business down the line, after some proper training. But, if I'm being honest, I feel a bit haggard and old there amongst all the beautiful – and mainly younger than me – clients. Gavin even suggested some treatments that I would benefit from, which means that he thinks I need cosmetic work!'

'That is his job, Carly. I'm sure he wasn't trying to be insensitive. Perhaps you're being a bit *over*sensitive about it?' Fletcher looks at her pointedly. 'And you know that beauty is subjective. I bet plenty of the clients wish they looked like you.'

'Yeah, right.' She laughs mirthlessly and rolls her eyes. 'I was a model. Emphasis on *was*. My heyday was over a decade ago. Nobody wants to pay to look at me or wear their clothes anymore. I'm past-it and invisible.' She pouts.

'Come on, don't start torturing yourself over this again. I thought that was the appeal of this new job – to be able to help other women who might feel like this too, to encourage them to become better versions of themselves. That's what you said, wasn't it?'

She nods, surprised he'd remembered her exact words. 'Yes, but–'

He interrupts. 'Do you want me to have a word with Gavin, ask about organising some training courses for you sooner rather than later? I'm happy to if you think it would help. But you'd need to prove you were serious about it – no more sick days unless absolutely necessary.'

Carly shakes her head, indignant. 'No, Fletcher, I do not need you speaking to my boss on my behalf. I am more than capable of advocating for myself.'

He holds both hands up, a gesture of surrender. 'Okay, okay, I know you're more than capable. I'll stay out of it, Little Miss Independent. Just don't say I didn't try.' He stands and heads for the door but stops when Carly says his name.

'Thank you.'

Softly spoken, the words surprise him, and he turns back to her.

Carly glances up at him then looks away. She takes a deep breath. 'Thank you for the offer… to speak to Gavin. I'm grateful for your support. I do appreciate it, even if it doesn't always seem that way. I appreciate all that you do for this family, especially employing Polly so I am able to go back to work.' She looks back up at him. 'She's a good kid, isn't she?'

He rubs the back of his neck and nods.

'Do you think she's okay?' she asks.

'What do you mean?' he asks, frowning.

'This sudden illness today. She doesn't seem herself at all. I hope all the tension in the house isn't affecting her. We need to do better. We don't want to lose her, do we?'

He gazes at her. 'No, we don't.'

'Well, it's been a long day. I think I'm going to treat myself to a bubble bath before bed.' She stands and pats his chest before walking past him out of the room.

Now that the effects of the diazepam have fully worn off, Polly is restless. She hears Fletcher come home and then she hears Carly's heels on the bare wooden stairs and then, a minute later, water running into the bath.

Reunited with her phone, Polly has been scrolling through all the messages Fletcher has sent throughout the day, calm and almost gleeful at first, pleased they got away with it, then more urgent the longer she took to reply.

She finally messaged him back when she returned from

Meryl's, but they haven't actually spoken. Although she talked a good game at Meryl's, eloquently explaining her and Fletcher's whirlwind love story, she's struggling to shake off the anxiety that's been building all day. Since last week, if she's being honest with herself, and it's now threatening to explode out of her. She gets up off the bed and goes over to the wardrobe, kneeling to retrieve her memory box from the bottom. She rereads Fletcher's card and holds it against her chest, her heart. She closes her eyes, trying to see their future in her mind's eye, reminding herself what it's all about.

She snaps her eyes open as she hears a knock at the door. Carly says her name. Panicked, Polly drops the card back into the open shoebox and shoves it back in the wardrobe. Closing the doors, she crosses over to the bedroom door and as she does, she spots her *Prick Tease* lip gloss on the floor, peeking out from behind her bedside table. It must have fallen down there. She quickly grabs it and puts it in her hoodie pocket.

Carly knocks again and Polly opens the door a crack. The running bathwater has stopped, and the other woman is standing on the landing holding a cup of hot chocolate.

'How are you feeling now?' She tilts her head to one side.

'I'm okay.' Polly points behind her to the bed. 'I was going to get an early night.'

'I brought you one of your hot chocolates. I noticed the sachets in the cupboard. Have you had anything to eat? Do you want me to get you something?'

'No, honestly, I'm fine. I'll take the drink though.' She smiles and opens the door wider, holding out her hand for the cup.

'I'll bring it in for you.' Carly sweeps into the room and places the hot chocolate down on the bedside table. Polly clutches the lip gloss in her pocket, relieved she retrieved it moments ago. Carly steps back towards the door but instead of leaving through it, she closes it and turns back around.

In that instant, several thoughts and emotions rush through

Polly's brain and body and she stares at the other woman expectantly, not daring to speak.

Carly presses her lips together and briefly scans the room before dropping a whispered bombshell. 'I've decided... I'm leaving Fletcher.'

Polly blinks, astonished.

'You mustn't tell him, you mustn't tell anyone, I'm telling you this in confidence, okay, because I need your help to get my ducks in a row.' Carly's words jumble out like consecutive dominos falling.

Polly nods her head without conscious thought, her still-addled brain struggling to process the words she's hearing but not truly comprehending.

'I'm going to move out as soon as I can, somewhere temporary for now. A bolthole. I'll just take the essentials and a few toys so Sonny has some familiarity, and then arrange to collect the rest of my things later. You'll come too, of course. You're primarily Sonny's nanny rather than Eaden's so you go where he goes. Same rate; don't worry. I'll need to carry on working to pay the rent too – and I do want to work however generous the divorce settlement ends up being – so I'll need you.'

Polly's mind is a bubbling whirlpool. She blinks again, which seems to reboot her system. 'You're leaving him? But why?'

Carly smiles sadly. 'Polly, you know why. You've seen what he does to me, emotionally and physically. I'm a black-and-blue nervous wreck! I know I said I was being ridiculous and blowing things up out of all proportion, but I need to face reality now, for my own sake.' Tears well in her eyes and even through her own brain fog, Polly's first thought is to wonder whether the emotion is genuine or if Carly is simply an excellent actress.

She thinks for a moment, wondering what on earth to say, how to play it. Everything's escalating by the hour, and she feels utterly blindsided. She tucks her hair behind her ears, watching Carly recover her composure. 'Is moving somewhere new actually necessary?' she asks eventually, as her brain function returns. 'Why not just stay at the Fraisthorpe house for a while? Give yourself some time and space to think?'

'Yes, that was my first thought too but it's not safe there for Sonny, not when it needs so much work doing to it. And it'll be so cold over winter. And besides that, I don't want Fletcher to come after us; it's the first place he'd look.'

Polly's attention is caught by a new message flashing up on her phone, which is on the bed. The display name shows as three heart emojis and the message simply contains a question mark. Fletcher must know that Carly is in here with her.

Carly looks over at it too but doesn't comment. Polly's grateful that she's too wrapped up in her own drama to ask any questions and brings her focus back to the matter at hand.

'I know I'm asking a lot,' continues Carly, 'but please say you'll help me. I want to start putting things in motion in the next day or so.'

Polly's lips part in further surprise. 'That soon?'

'No time like the present. Right, I'm going to get in the bath; I've got a lot to think about. Goodnight, Polly. Enjoy your hot chocolate. We'll talk again soon.'

Polly sits cross-legged on the bed and waits a few minutes to give Carly time to ensconce herself in the bathroom before she rings Fletcher. Although communicating with each other while Carly is in the house is usually restricted to messages only, she feels this is too important to discuss in a message thread. Despite Carly's request to keep things just between them and all the worries she herself has about Fletcher's behaviour lately, Polly's pull towards the man she loves is still too great.

'What's going on? Why was she in your room?' he asks in a hushed tone.

'She practically barged in, under the pretence of bringing me hot chocolate,' she whispers in reply.

'Pretence? Why, what was the real reason?'

Polly takes a deep breath and glances at her closed door. 'Fletcher, she just told me she's going to leave you.'

'What the fuck!' His exclamation is so forceful she moves the phone away from her ear for a second. 'Where the hell has this come from? We had a fairly pleasant conversation about her career earlier. She *thanked* me for my support. Told me she appreciated me. This is crazy! What else did she say?'

'She said she's going to take Sonny with her.' Polly finds it difficult to contain her smile. Things are finally coming to a head – Fletcher will have to take action now and then this stressful, suffocating situation will be over.

'Bitch!' He expels the word with such venom she almost feels its blast. She can hear his heavy breath and movement and visualises him pacing downstairs. She gets up and goes over to the window, needing to eject some energy too. As she looks down, she sees him exit the house through the bi-fold doors, head thrown back, and phone held by his side. He strides to the end of the garden and as he comes back, he puts the phone to his ear and looks up at the house. From the patio, he zones in on her in the window.

'You know what? If she takes him, it's abduction,' he says. 'I'll call the police straight away and they'll get him back and then she'll never get custody. And then if you say you've seen her self-harm, she'll have no abuse case against me. Pol, this could actually work in our favour. Fast-track things, just like you want.' His voice lifts with his mood.

Polly's smile disappears. 'But I haven't witnessed her self-harming, Fletcher. You want me to lie about that?'

'She's lied about me, hasn't she? Or do you secretly believe her vile version of events?' He moves and she can see his face clearly in the patio lights. He looks outraged again.

'No, no,' she rushes to reply. 'I just don't think two wrongs make a right. What if it all blows up in our faces?'

He runs his hand through his hair and stares up at her. 'We need to play her at her own game.'

'This isn't a game though, Fletcher. These are our lives... and the children's lives,' implores Polly.

'I know, I know. I'm sorry. Poor choice of phrase but you know what I mean. You can't let her get in your head, baby. It'll all work out. Trust me. I love you.' He ends the call and walks back inside.

Polly draws the curtains, places her phone face down on her bedside table next to the untouched hot chocolate and gets into bed, pulling the duvet up over her head.

Out in the hallway, Carly steps back away from Polly's bedroom door and returns to the bathroom, smiling to herself.

CHAPTER THIRTY-THREE

THURSDAY

Polly looks over as Carly walks confidently into the kitchen before she leaves for work. She gestures for Polly to move away from the children on the sofa and join her at the island.

'It's on. I've found somewhere,' she whispers, the corners of her mouth curving into a smile.

'Already?' asks Polly, unable to disguise her surprise. 'But it's only been a couple of days.'

Ever since Carly announced her intention to leave Fletcher on Monday, Polly has been trying and failing to allay her growing anxiety, despite furtive and often frantic conversations with Fletcher, who remains convinced they should give Carly enough rope to hang herself, metaphorically speaking. Polly still isn't sure, and she feels tightly wound, shackled to a cause she's rapidly losing faith in.

'I told you I wanted to move quickly, in all senses of the phrase,' says Carly breezily, the epitome of a woman who has everything under control. 'Once I've made up my mind about something, there's no stopping me. And luckily, I have friends in the right places – Mallory's husband has a place near the city centre and he's currently between tenants. Mallory's persuaded him to let me have it at a discount too for a "friend". It's serendipity.' She smiles serenely.

'Carly, I—' Polly begins but the other woman cuts her off with a wave of her hand.

'It's all arranged. I want to move a few things there tomorrow and Saturday, and then leave for good on Sunday.'

'This weekend!' Polly's eyebrows shoot up. 'Are you taking the day off tomorrow then?'

'No, I can't take any more time off work — I still feel awful for having to abandon Gavin on Monday and we've got back-to-back appointments all week, thanks to the success of the last open day. Everyone's already thinking about freshening themselves up for Christmas and the new year, it seems. No, I need you to take a few things to the new house for me tomorrow. I'll call you with the address in the morning. It'll give you a chance to have a nosy around as it'll be your new home too. I'll tell Fletcher I need you to run errands for me and to leave his car here. Perry can collect him. They'll both love the extra boys' time together anyway,' she states triumphantly.

Polly shakes her head and looks over at the children who are both mesmerised by the early morning cartoons on the TV screen. It's a change to their routine but Polly's glad she suggested it. They deserve a bit of calm before the impending storm. 'I need time to think about this, Carly, it's all happening so fast.'

'What's there to think about? You're employed as Sonny's nanny. Yes, you help out with Eaden before and after school too, but you're mainly here for the baby. That was the deal Fletcher and I struck. So, wherever Sonny is, that's where you need to be too. Unless you want to resign, in which case I'll find a replacement. I would be extremely sorry to lose you and it would cause me quite the headache this week, but I would respect your decision.'

Polly gapes at her employer, lost for words. She hadn't even considered that being an option.

Carly huffs out a sigh, clearly growing impatient. 'Look, I'm asking for your help for my son's benefit, not forcing you to do something against your will at knifepoint. There is a difference.' She pauses. 'I need an answer, Polly. Now.' She crosses her arms and waits.

Polly presses her teeth down on her tongue, subconsciously mirroring the pressure she's feeling from Carly. She can't leave Sonny; she's going to be his stepmother very soon, they're going to be a proper family. 'Okay, yes, okay. I'll help you,' confirms Polly, regaining the power of speech. What other choice does she have? Fletcher needs her to just go along with it for now.

'Good.' Carly nods once. 'Now one last thing: does Fletcher suspect anything about this?'

Polly shakes her head, not trusting herself to utter a word in response to that particular question.

'Good,' Carly repeats. 'So, here's what's going to happen. Remember it's Celeste's party this Sunday – Eaden's friend from school?'

Polly nods, bristling at the memory of Mallory, Celeste's mother, practically shoving the invitation in her hand at the school gates a couple of days ago and crisply instructing her to pass it on to Carly, like she was nothing but a postal worker.

'I'll tell Fletcher I'll take both children to it. It'll buy me a few hours. I made sure I told him how much I appreciated all he does as a father the other night, so he'll think I'm doing it to give him a parenting break, but I'll actually drop Eaden at Stella's first.'

'What will you say to Stella about why you're not taking Eaden to the party?' asks Polly.

'That she's upset about her mum or something – the anniversary of her death's coming up. I might even mention Pippa to Eaden, make it realistic. And then I'll take Sonny to the party, show my face and explain Eaden's absence, then we'll go on to Mallory's husband's house. Simple as that. We'll lay low and settle in for a short while, then I'll begin divorce proceedings.'

'But won't Stella tell Fletcher that you've dropped Eaden off at her house?' asks Polly, her brain quickly processing what Carly is telling her. 'Why wouldn't you just bring her home if Fletcher's here?'

'Clever girl!' says Carly in a condescending tone. 'This is where I'll need your help again. I'm going to suggest to Fletcher that he spends the day at the Fraisthorpe house making a start on the renovation, which he hasn't had any spare time to do up to now. I'll remind him that the winter months are fast approaching and the sooner he starts, the sooner he'll be able to finish it in time to let it out next summer. Which means another income into the business. He finds money a great motivator. As a co-owner, that's what Stella wants too. Of course, it will also benefit me in the divorce.' She smiles.

'How am I supposed to help with that?' asks Polly.

'You're going to go too.'

Polly blinks. The surprises keep coming. 'Why?'

'To keep him there as long as possible, obviously, so I can do what I need to do. You can take the mood boards and floor-plans I've already mocked up, pretend I'd forgotten to give them to him before he left. Then, instead of coming back here, you'll meet Sonny and I at the new place. When Fletcher gets home, he'll realise we've gone. And if he calls the police claiming I've kidnapped Sonny or some such lie, I've got physical and photographic evidence of his abuse.'

'You've been taking photos?'

'Of course I have,' says Carly. 'Otherwise, it would just be a case of *he said, she said*, wouldn't it?'

'Wow, you really have thought of everything.' Polly bites her lip and looks across at the children again, tight knots of turmoil twisting in her stomach.

Carly's mouth settles into a smug smile. 'I hope so. It's my armour against my despicable husband – no chinks whatsoever. So, any more questions or are you all set with the plan?'

'No more questions,' states Polly.

'Thank you, Polly. I appreciate what you're going to do for me, and I won't ever forget it.'

Just after midnight, as arranged, Fletcher and Polly secretly rendezvous downstairs in the utility room. Polly relays her conversation with Carly to him.

He nods repeatedly while she talks, listening carefully, arms folded across his old, faded Lyricsmiths T-shirt.

When she has finished, he takes a few steps to the back door and looks out through the glass onto the garden, deep in thought. She feels disconnected from him. Not that long ago they wouldn't be discussing anything during a snatched, illicit moment like this, preferring to kiss and touch and fondle instead. So much has changed in such a short time and she doesn't like it one bit. She feels she's not only losing the idea of what their future could – and should – look like, but she's also losing herself in the process.

'Okay.' Fletcher's voice jolts her back to the present moment. 'I'll go to the Fraisthorpe house, as she suggests, then when I come back here and find Carly and Sonny gone, I'll wait a few hours then ring you to ask if you know where they are. Don't pick up – I'll leave a voicemail sounding worried. You'll then call me back and tell me she's taken Sonny, that she threatened to sack you if you didn't help her, that she's unhinged and been self-harming. We'll make it realistic so there's a record of it on our phones. I'll then ring the police and they'll take it from there. That should be enough to prove her lies and make sure she won't get custody.'

'Fletcher, this is getting really complicated. I feel caught in the crossfire between you. I don't know what to do for the best. I don't want to lie to the police.' Polly wraps her arms tightly around her torso, trying to comfort herself.

He grabs her roughly by the shoulders, digging his thumbs into her collarbone and hisses his words at her. 'Polly, none of what we'll say are lies. Not technically.'

'Ow, you're hurting me.' She pushes him back, rubbing the soreness away. 'Claiming I've seen Carly self-harm first-hand *is* a lie. It's wrong.'

'Why do you keep saying that? We've already agreed what to do for the best. And not just for us but for Sonny, and Eaden too. Or do you want to allow her to splinter this family for good?'

She leans back against the worktop, dejected. 'I'm worried, Fletcher. I'm… I feel like I'm caught in her web, just stuck right in the middle, the shadow of a black widow looming over me. I can't cope with this. It wasn't supposed to be this way.' A lone tear escapes and she lets it run down her cheek.

He sighs and pinches the bridge of his nose between his thumb and forefinger. 'I know, I know, and I'm sorry. I wish it was cleaner cut, I really do, but the end will justify the means. It might not be exactly the way we planned it, but it'll still work out how we hoped.'

Hanging her head, she worries at the satin belt of her robe with her fingers.

He stands in front of her and lifts her chin upwards. Looking into her eyes, he says, 'Hey, you know what?' He smiles. 'You're my north star, my pure delight. I need you, Miss Blake.'

She gasps as she realises it's the same line Carly told her he used to say to her, sung by his favourite band whose T-shirt he's wearing right now. As her eyes fill with more tears and her stomach sinks with the weight of more sorrow, a part of her heart shatters too.

CHAPTER THIRTY-FOUR

FRIDAY

On Friday morning, Polly is still giving Fletcher the cold shoulder. He's so confused and for the life of him can't work out what he's said or done that has upset her so much. Having replayed last night's conversation a few times to himself and found nothing he regrets saying, he has concluded that it must just be the culmination of stress that's making her so moody.

As Polly hasn't thawed, he's worried too, about whether she's going to stick to the plan. He *needs* her to say she's witnessed Carly causing herself harm; surely she will if she loves him and wants them to be a proper family after all this is over. He knows that's what she wants more than anything; she's told him enough times. It's what she's always wanted. Or at least she did.

Perry arrives to collect him for work, and he tries to say goodbye to Polly on the landing, outside the children's bedroom, but she looks through him with watery eyes and doesn't respond.

He thunders loudly down the uncarpeted stairs, makes sure his car keys are in the bowl on the console table, and stomps out to Perry's van. One of the worst aspects of all this for him has been keeping such a massive secret from his cousin. Despite

Carly's claims that he tells Perry everything, he doesn't. He hasn't wanted to because he intends to present his relationship with Polly as fresh and new when he's been separated from Carly for a while. He wants Perry, and his mother, to accept her into the family, no awkward questions asked, assumptions made, or accusations voiced.

His dad was unfaithful – there were several indiscretions over the years that he knew of – and he knows Stella won't stand for her son being a cheater too, no matter how miserable his marriage is. She never found out about his infidelities when he was married to Pippa, and he's not going to voluntarily tarnish his good reputation now.

Stella has often cited the damage an affair causes to a wife's psyche, how unfaithfulness insidiously erodes trust and respect, and gnaws away at the simple day-to-day joys of a marriage. She also expressed her surprise, and concern, at how quickly he moved on from Pippa with Carly. If she had confirmation that this time his serious relationships actually overlapped, she'd be disappointed.

The whole situation infuriates him though. His anger is a viscous liquid, slowly rolling and boiling inside him, and he wonders whether to abort the whole thing altogether, call Carly out, tell her he knows what she's planning. But then she might not be gone on Sunday, like he wants her to be, leaving him with all the sympathy a wronged husband and father deserves. God forbid she stays and suggests marriage counselling or some such shit. He does understand how Polly feels to an extent because he wants an end to it all too, but what he can't get his head around is Polly's repeated reluctance to tell a little white lie to make sure the final nail is hammered securely into Carly's coffin.

'Everything okay?' asks Perry, glancing at the house before moving the van's gearstick into reverse.

'Fine and fucking dandy,' replies Fletcher with a scowl.

After a fitful night, Polly watches from the children's bedroom window as Fletcher climbs into Perry's van. He attempted yet again to engage with her before he left for work, but she had no words left for him. His anxiety was palpable, which she privately enjoyed because it finally seemed as though it matched the intensity of hers.

Rather than driving straight off, Fletcher and Perry exchange a few words and both look up at the house. She steps back from the window, out of sight, paranoid that Perry is in on everything too. What did Carly say – 'lads together'? She wonders if they're secretly having a laugh at her expense; the gullible nanny who's only good for a recycled song lyric Fletcher probably uses on all women. Maybe Perry has one of his own too, although she didn't get the sense he was that type when they met. But what does she know? She's not the best judge of character. First Teddy, now Fletcher. Out of the sizzling frying pan and into the scorching fire.

Polly gets the children dressed and ready for the day, grateful for the distraction, then they all set off on the school run. After seeing Eaden safely into the playground, her stomach flips as Carly phones. *There's no way out now*, thinks Polly. Carly shares the address for Mallory's husband's house and informs her that the things she wants her to take to the house are ready in the garage, with a spare key – Polly's new door key.

Once home, leaving Sonny safely fastened in his pushchair, Polly retrieves Fletcher's set of keys and opens one of the garage doors. Inside, stacked neatly, are two large boxes that Carly has labelled with Polly's initials as well as two plain black holdalls. Not designer, to Polly's surprise. With a deep sigh, she opens the boot of Fletcher's car and begins transferring everything.

Meryl appears next to the open gates at the end of the driveway. 'Hello, dear, going somewhere?'

Polly looks across at Meryl and the older woman's concerned expression is enough to burst her flimsy floodgates.

'Oh, Polly, what on earth's the matter?' Meryl asks, crossing the gravelled distance between them and placing her hand on Polly's heaving shoulder. Sonny looks up at both women as he contentedly sucks his dummy, oblivious to all the drama.

'It's all gone too far,' Polly says, her voice thick with emotion.

'Whatever do you mean?'

Polly raises her hands then slaps them back down against her thighs. 'I've nowhere else to go and I love him, I do, but I don't know if I can trust him. How can I be sure he won't do to me in the future what he's doing to her now?' The words pour out of her like liquid; she's unable to stop them, even if she wanted to.

'I see. So, things haven't improved then?' Meryl asks gently.

'I should have listened to you. I'm so confused.' She covers her face with her hands and shakes her head, her long hair hanging limply down over her shoulders, remnants of neon-green nail polish still visible on her bitten-down fingernails.

'Come on now, you mustn't get yourself worked up like this,' says Meryl, glancing down at Sonny. 'Would you like to come for a cuppa – calm down a bit? You could even have a lie down in the spare bedroom, if you'd like? I'll entertain the little one. Perhaps you shouldn't be on your own right now.'

Polly drags the heels of her hands across her cheeks, roughly wiping her tears away. She sniffs loudly and pulls her shoulders back, standing up straighter. 'No, no. Thank you. There are things I need to do today, and they can't wait. I'm sorry, Meryl. You must think I'm a pathetic, emotional wreck. I promise I'm not normally like this.' Her laugh is shallow.

'All the more reason to accept help then, if you're in distress,' Meryl says kindly.

'No. Thank you,' Polly states again, her voice firmer now. 'I just need to get through the next couple of days and everything will be fine.'

'Well, if you're sure, dear. You know where I am if you need me.' She smiles warmly then turns and leaves, throwing a concerned glance back over her shoulder when she reaches the gates.

Polly manages to move the boxes and bags and her own suitcase into Mallory's husband's house, return the car home and then collect Eaden from school. She gets through it all by repeatedly reminding herself that her and Fletcher's long game will be over this weekend. Every hour she spends pretending to help Carly is another hour closer to a life with Fletcher and the children. A proper family. Something she has dreamed of since she was a little girl.

She loved her dad so much, but he just seemed to wither more each year after her mum left. He worked hard, he provided, but he checked out emotionally while he was at home in between twelve-hour shifts. She was either left in the care of casual teenage babysitters or, as she became a teenager herself, left to her own devices. She has no idea if her mum is still alive or not and she can't bear the thought of poor Eaden ending up without a proper, loving mother too. She doesn't deserve that, and she doesn't deserve her current, cold stepmother either.

Polly doesn't want to lie about Carly, it doesn't sit well with her at all, and although she's not happy about Fletcher parroting some well-worn lyric to her, she honestly doesn't believe that he has ever abused Carly physically. So she has decided that she is prepared to lie, after all, to prove her commitment to him, to go against her instincts because the trade-off will be worth it.

Once she's got the children settled – Eaden at the table and Sonny in his bouncer – Fletcher arrives home. She twirls, surprised but also pleased to see him.

'Hey, munchkins!' he addresses the children and kisses them in turn. Then, to Polly, he asks, 'Can we talk? Please?'

After a moment, she nods.

'Okay, go upstairs, give me a few minutes, and then come back down again.'

'What? Why?' she asks.

He smiles widely, the dimples in his cheeks working their magic on her.

'All will be revealed. Go.' He mimes shooing her away and she complies.

Five minutes later, she returns to see that he has moved Eaden onto the sofa, turned on the TV and put her headphones on. She's already engrossed in the animation, barely blinking as she robotically transfers halved strawberries and apple slices from a bowl to her mouth. Sonny is on the rug in front of her, his dangling mobile positioned above his bouncer and a dummy in his mouth. Neither of them are uttering a sound.

Fletcher is sitting at the table and he gestures for Polly to sit opposite him. She likes that he's created space for them to talk privately and it bolsters her mood marginally.

'How did it go today?' he asks.

She frowns. 'Tough, at first. I had a bit of a meltdown when I was packing up the car.' She pauses. 'And then another when I put my suitcase in my "new room".' She makes air quotes around the words. 'I hate that I've had to move my own things under the pretence of living there. It makes it feel real.'

'I know, but it is just pretend.' He reaches across the table and takes her hand. 'What we have is real.'

'I want to believe that so much but...' She shakes her head, tapping her fingertips on the tabletop.

'But what? Please tell me, Polly. I know I probably haven't handled all of this very well, and I'm so sorry if anything I've said or done has hurt you. Believe it or not, making a plan with my girlfriend to leave my wife isn't something I've ever done before. Shouldn't it be reassuring that I'm not great at handling it?' He gives her a lopsided smile and strokes her knuckles with his thumbs.

'Can I ask you something? And I want you to be honest,' she says.

'Okay.' He sits up straighter and waits expectantly.

Polly presses her lips together and looks straight at him. 'What you said last night: "You're my north star, my pure delight". Did you mean it?'

'Of course I did. Lyricsmiths, legends that they are, may have sung the words but it's exactly how I feel about you.' He treats her to one of his megawatt grins.

'Did you mean it when you said the exact same thing to Carly too?'

The smile slips from his face. 'Ah,' he says as he understands his mistake. He grimaces. 'Is that what you were so upset about?'

'I don't want repeated patter, Fletcher, I want honest feelings. I want to know what you're really thinking. I'm not Carly and I don't want our relationship to be anything like yours and hers.'

'You're overthinking it, baby, but I am sorry. I may have said something like that to Carly once, probably in the very early days, but I genuinely can't even remember saying it. With all my heart, I truly believe that you are the most perfect woman for me. We won't ever be like Carly and I have been. I respect you. I love you.' He lets go of her hand and picks something up from the bench seat next to him, grasping it in his palm. 'Look, I wasn't planning to do this just yet, and definitely not like this, but I can't wait another day, especially with all this... craziness going on.'

Polly gasps in shock as he opens his palm to reveal a small red box. A ring-sized box.

He lifts the lid to show her the gold-and-diamond solitaire inside. 'I want you to be my wife, Polly Blake. Will you marry me?'

Tears shine in her eyes and instantly, all the doubts and worries that have been weighing her down for the past couple of weeks rise like bubbles and pop into nothingness.

CHAPTER THIRTY-FIVE

SUNDAY

Carly enters the kitchen with wet hair and wearing her robe.

'But Daddy, I want to spend the day with you,' Eaden says to Fletcher, pushing her bottom lip out, her face crinkled with disappointment.

'Daddy has got to go to the seaside house to start fixing it up and once it's all done, we'll be able to go there for weekends and holidays,' Fletcher replies.

Eaden brings her lip back in and thinks for a moment. 'And birthday parties?'

'Yes, and for birthday parties. It might even be ready in time for Sonny Jim's first birthday in January if I get a move on with it.' He reaches out and runs his palm gently over his son's head.

'Yay!' cheers Eaden.

'So today, when you're at Celeste's party with Sonny and Carly, you can think about the seaside house and feel excited about all the fun we'll have there next year.'

'Okay, Daddy,' she says, mollified.

Carly lightly touches her hand to Fletcher's back. 'You all set for today? Ready to get your hands dirty?'

He looks up at her from his seat. 'I am. Are you all set for a day out with the kids?'

She looks at Eaden and then Sonny in his highchair. 'Absolutely. It'll be good for us.' She smiles and crosses to the island. 'We'll be leaving in an hour,' she says, taking two cups out to make drinks. 'Could you please make sure Eaden's ready, and I'll sort Sonny out. I don't want Polly disturbed on her day off.'

'Sure, no problem,' he throws back over his shoulder.

'Great. Thank you.'

She takes the drinks upstairs with her, the herbal tea to sip while she gets dressed and the hot chocolate for Polly. It's a small gesture but she wants Polly to know that she's considering her needs. It sets a tone.

Carly places her drink in her bedroom then takes the other to Polly's door and knocks lightly. Considering she's got a momentous day ahead she feels remarkably calm. There's no answer so she knocks again then opens the door, whispering Polly's name. Inside, she sees the younger woman sleeping, oblivious to her presence. Carly creeps in, intending to leave the cup on the bedside table when something catches her eye. Polly's left hand rests on top of the white duvet cover. And on her third finger is a sparkling gold-and-diamond solitaire ring that Carly has never seen before.

Polly's nerves are jangling.

When she opened her eyes this morning there was a cup of hot chocolate by the bed and she feels sure that if Fletcher had left it there, he would have tried to wake her up. So, it must have been Carly. And stupidly, she slept in her brand-new engagement ring, too love-drunk and excited not to. She suspects Carly spotted it, and if she did, what is she thinking now? After Fletcher's unexpected proposal last night, she floated up to cloud nine, away from all the stress and overanalysing and overthinking, but now she's come back down to earth with a bump.

A while ago, from the landing, she listened to Fletcher saying his goodbyes to Sonny and Eaden and then Carly before heading off to the Fraisthorpe house, just like it was a normal Sunday in the life of the Lawrensons. She marvelled at the ordinariness of it, incongruous against her inner anxiety. Then Fletcher had glanced up the stairs and winked at her and her belly flipped, and she breathed deeply and renewed her determination.

After he had left, in the work van that he'd borrowed from Perry under the pretence of taking all the tools for the repairs he was going to get on with, Carly summoned her downstairs and laid out the plan for the day one final time. Then Polly left too, waving to Sonny and Eaden as Carly packed them into her car.

Now she is driving Fletcher's car to the Fraisthorpe house.

Carly believes Polly is going there under relative duress, delivering her folder of mood boards and suggested floor-plans for Fletcher to reference while he's making a start on pulling the house to pieces in order to put it back together again. Mirroring their lives. And then Carly expects Polly to meet her and Sonny at Mallory's husband's house later, while a supposedly oblivious Fletcher goes home to confusion and emptiness and abrupt, unexpected separation from his wife and baby son.

Whereas Fletcher believes she is going there so they can spend the day together. To revel in their newly engaged status. To make proper plans for the future. To beat Carly at her own game, as he called it.

Polly finds it difficult to get her head around the dual narratives, to marry her perception of herself with the part she feels she's currently playing: the fiancée of an already married man who's also a widower.

She feels a spark of shame when she recalls that as her and Fletcher's affair became more serious, she was more than happy to match his deviousness. To plot Carly's downfall. She *wanted* to wreck their marriage because out of the ruins she was going to forge a ready-made family of her own. A foundation that she and Fletcher would then build their future on. She honestly felt it was what she deserved – a chance to rebuild her life out of the rubble of her and Teddy's ravaged relationship. Teddy choosing Edward over her in the end mutilated Polly's heart. But then she met Fletcher, and got another chance at happiness.

She reflects on the fact that the past couple of weeks have been tougher than she originally imagined, but as she drives, she frequently glances at her engagement ring as it sparkles in the sunlight. She slipped it back on after she left and the solitaire diamond galvanises her, injecting her with hope and optimism and love.

Polly arrives at the house by the beach and parks by the front door, which faces the large patch of scrubland the row of houses stands on. This side of the house is scruffy and barren, a lot less aesthetic than the beach side. Still, she hopes the land won't be developed upon with anything that might spoil the privacy of the existing properties. She gets out of the car, leaving Carly's large zipped folder in the boot and suddenly awash with a wave of giddiness, she rushes inside and upstairs and into her fiancé's arms.

'Hi there, Mrs Lawrenson-to-be,' he says when they finally break their embrace.

She gazes up at him, beaming. 'Hi, yourself, Mr Lawrenson.'

'I have a surprise.' He crosses over to the kitchen area and retrieves two champagne flutes from a bag and a bottle of champagne from the ancient under-counter fridge.

Polly widens her eyes and presses her lips together. 'Fletcher, I'd love to, but we can't,' she says. 'We both need to drive later and then we'll be dealing with the police. We need clear heads.'

'We'll just have one glass,' he says, popping the cork and pouring the glittery liquid into the flutes. 'This is an occasion that requires a celebration!'

Polly frowns. 'Which part? Our engagement, or your marriage and your family as you know it ending?'

Fletcher hands her a glass and holds the other up for a toast, unaffected by her snarky comment. 'Our engagement, of course. And my children are my family, and you, so only one aspect is ending and I'm not sorry that it is.' He clinks her glass against his and takes a swig.

Against her better judgement, she does the same, enjoying the sensation of the champagne going straight to her head despite herself.

He encourages her to raise it to her lips for a second sip. 'That's my girl,' he says, smiling.

CHAPTER THIRTY-SIX

Polly wakes in the downstairs bedroom of the Fraisthorpe house a few hours later. She can feel Fletcher's warmth against her back and can hear his soft, rhythmic breathing.

The thin curtains are still open, but the small room is darker and colder. She feels strange, hungover, and thinks back to earlier. Fletcher suggested they take their champagne to bed and once she had emerged from the bijou bathroom wearing only her engagement ring, he was already naked himself, holding two more full glasses of fizz, clearly ready and eager to escalate proceedings. They celebrated vigorously then fell asleep, but Polly feels as though she slipped into unconsciousness rather than a slumber.

She extends an arm and feels around on the bedside shelf for her phone, then recalls that she left her bag upstairs with her phone inside. She groans as she eases her head off the pillow and swings her body out of bed. On the way out of the room she picks Fletcher's discarded Lyricsmiths T-shirt up off the floor and puts it on. He doesn't stir.

Polly makes her way upstairs unsteadily, clinging onto the wobbly banister as she goes, and emerges into the main living room, surprised to see a stormy sky beyond the rain-splashed picture window, varying shades of grey blanketing the North Sea. She shivers, a full body tremble, which causes her head to hurt more and she screws her eyes shut, wondering again why she feels so groggy after just two glasses of champagne. She crosses over to the sink and downs a mug of tepid tap water as she can't find a glass, then she locates her bag and takes out her phone. She is surprised to see two missed calls from Carly and a text message, given that it's a deviation from the plan that Carly believes she is sticking to:

> Polly, I'm sorry to ask but can you get home sooner than planned? I need help with Sonny.

Polly's heart starts beating wildly, which only makes her head pound more, and she sinks down onto the shabby sofa, feeling torn and drowsy. After a few minutes, through the brain fog, she realises she's felt this way before, recently, after Fletcher gave her diazepam.

Lurching back towards the kitchenette, she starts opening drawers and rifling through their contents, looking for evidence of the tablets. As she's on her knees about to upend the bin, Fletcher appears in the doorway in his boxers, still bleary-eyed from sleep.

'Are you okay, baby?' he asks, frowning down at her. 'Come back to bed.'

'I know what you did!' she roars.

'What?'

She tips the bin over, its sparse contents spilling out onto the lino. Straight away she spots it – an empty blister packet – and she snatches it up, waving it in front of him.

He falls to his knees next to her, his slumped body language screaming his guilt.

'How could you?' she cries.

His face is still scrunched up from sleep, but she can see how shocked he is by her reaction. 'I'm sorry, Pol. I knew how worried you were about today, and I just wanted you to be able to relax, to enjoy being here, just us. I didn't think you'd be able to do that without a bit of help.'

'Help? How does drugging my drink without my knowledge or permission help me keep track of all the fucking chaos I need to deal with today? And never mind that it's illegal!'

'I know, I know, but–'

She cuts him off with a sharp look. 'Yes, I was worried about today, and today isn't over yet. Carly's called twice and left a message – she needs help with Sonny, so I need to drive there now to support her. And then I need to switch sides and back you up when you report Sonny's kidnapping to the police! How am I meant to do all that when my head's a mess?'

'What's wrong with Sonny?' he asks.

'I'm not sure, she didn't say anything else in the message and now I've got no service so I can't phone her back.'

'It'll be a ploy,' says Fletcher after a pause. 'She's just asserting her power as your new employer and making you dance to her tune. Ignore the message. We need to stick to what we said we were going to do.'

'How can I ignore it? What if there's something wrong with him – what if he's had another breathing pause? Do you really want to risk it?'

He sighs and chews the inside of his lip for a few seconds. 'No,' he says eventually. Then, 'I'll drive you back, in the van.'

'To where Carly's staying? What if she sees us? It'll blow everything up.'

'Okay, I'll just drive you back home then. Don't go to her new place at all. We'll get home to find her gone and take it from there. It's just a slight tweak to the plan.'

'But all my things are there, remember? My worldly possessions are in that suitcase. And if something has happened to Sonny, I would never be able to forgive myself if I didn't check he was all right. And neither would you. No, I need to go.'

'Okay, okay. But first...' He stands up, takes her by the elbow and guides her towards the patio doors. 'Get some fresh air. You'll feel better.' He opens one of the sliding doors and steps out onto the balcony into the lashing rain, pulling her with him.

She twists out of his grip, her rising panic palpable. 'No, Fletcher, get off me! I need to go right now.'

He reaches out again and grabs her tightly. 'Polly, calm down, you're acting as crazy as Carly!'

She gapes at him. 'You did not just say that to me!'

Instantly, he's remorseful. Shaking his head, he says, 'God, I'm sorry, baby.' He pulls her to him, roughly, trying to force an embrace.

'No! Let go of me, you're hurting me!' She breaks free and lashes out, scratching his neck with her fingernails.

'Fuck!' he shouts, staggering backwards, clamping his palm over the scratch and reaching out with his other hand to steady himself. He misjudges and falls awkwardly against the balcony, splintering the already rickety handrail.

He rights himself just in time and sees that she's kneeling on the floor near the patio doors, crying, rocking, trying to rub away the red imprint of his fingertips from the tops of her arms.

He steps towards her slowly, as though approaching a wounded animal, repeatedly apologising.

'I'm so sorry, Polly. I didn't mean to hurt you.' He kneels beside her, tentatively placing a hand on her shoulder. 'Please, baby, listen to me. I'm the crazy one – crazy about you.'

She shrugs his hand off and looks up at him, tears coursing down her blotchy cheeks, tear-soaked strands of hair sticking to her anguished face. 'She was right, wasn't she?'

'Who?' he asks. 'Right about what?'

She stares at him, at her supposed husband-to-be, at the man who chose to give her a pill without her knowledge and grabbed her forcefully and called her crazy.

Shaking her head, she stands, one arm outstretched, fingers splayed, silently warning him to keep his distance. His eyes flick to something behind her and she feels a strange shift in the charged atmosphere.

'Who the fuck are you?' asks Fletcher.

Polly snaps her head around and is astonished to see a scruffy man standing there, as though he has been teleported into the room. As though data is being downloaded into her brain, she immediately takes in that he's wearing a green utility jacket and frayed jeans and a determined albeit slightly wild expression. His clothes are soaked from the storm. She registers that he has a cleft lip showing through a patchy beard. He is brandishing a kitchen knife, his stare fixed on Fletcher.

She blinks and in that mere split second of time, the man charges silently at Fletcher as Fletcher raises his arm instinctively to block the knife's blade from slashing or penetrating his skin. It's like watching players in a video game, as though they're characters on a screen rather than right in front of her. *This can't actually be happening*, she thinks helplessly.

The two men wrestle as Polly looks on, utterly dumbstruck and unable to move, to hide, to help the man she loves. Fletcher is taller and broader but he's struggling to overpower the lean, wiry intruder, perhaps due to the after-effects of the champagne or from being wrongfooted by the surprise.

A second later, the knife streaks to the floor, the tip of its blade piercing through the lino, leaving it embedded vertically. Fletcher's face contorts as he tries to manoeuvre the man over to the patio doors and Polly understands what he's trying to do. They grunt and gasp, locked in a macabre dance as they engage in their battle of wills.

Suddenly, the man lifts his knee and Fletcher releases his grip, clutching his groin, his eyes screwed up with pain. He drops down and the intruder takes full advantage of the weak moment with a left hook to Fletcher's ear. There's a sickening sound as Fletcher's head strikes the corner of the kitchen peninsula, and then he slumps onto the floor.

Polly cries his name, fresh tears now blurring her vision. Adrenaline spiking at realising she now needs to defend herself from this stranger who means them harm, she yanks the knife out of the floor and lunges forward as though she's performing a choreographed stunt move. Feeling like she's watching herself from above, she barrels into the intruder, propelling him out through the open patio door. He falls against the broken balcony fencing and automatically reaches out for her to anchor himself to, but she steps back into the doorway, lip quivering and hands shaking. Empty hands, she realises. The already damaged balcony splinters against his weight, then gives way completely. He's gone as quickly as he appeared. Now you see him, now you don't.

A gurgling sound behind her brings her back to reality and she spins around to see Fletcher lying on the dirty, dusty lino next to the kitchen peninsula. She kneels next to him. There's a trickle of blood underneath his head.

'Fletcher...' She takes his hand. 'What just... why... what...' Her teeth are chattering and she can't get the words out.

He opens his eyes; they're bloodshot. 'Go,' he commands. 'I'll say it was me.'

'I'm calling the police,' she says, looking around for her phone but not letting go of his hand.

He squeezes hers to get her attention and she looks back at him.

'Stick to the plan. I'll get the knife.'

'You're bleeding...' she says, her eyes full of fear.

'It's okay... I'll be okay in a minute.' He swallows and grimaces. 'I'll say it was me. Go to Carly. Stay with the kids. Please.'

'What are you saying?' She starts to sob. 'No... no... we need to face this together. That man attacked us in our own home. It was self-defence.' Snot streams from her nose to her top lip and she uses the sleeve of his T-shirt to wipe it away.

He shakes his head slowly, his pain obvious. 'Stick to the plan,' he repeats. 'I'll ring the police. Tell them about this... Report the kidnapping. Two birds, one stone.'

'You'd lie for me?' she asks, stroking his face tenderly.

'It's not a lie,' he says forcefully. 'You left already, before he got here. That's our truth, okay? I'll take care of it.' His eyes bore into her, pleading with her to do as he asks. She understands. He'll lie for her, so she'll lie about Carly self-harming. It's a fair trade, a pact, an act of love. She nods.

'I love you.' She squashes her lips against his, her tears dripping onto his face then trickling into the blood on the floor, their earlier argument forgotten in the wake of this new warped reality.

'I love you too, Miss Blake,' he says. 'Now go.'

Gathering her things and shoving her leggings and trainers back on, she finds both their phones then reluctantly leaves after pressing Fletcher's into his palm, ready to call 999 in a few minutes.

As she gets in the car and reverses, she vacillates, desperately wanting to go back inside yet knowing it's already too late – the police will be on their way soon enough. Instead, suppressing more rising sobs, she turns the car, puts it into gear and speeds away.

CHAPTER THIRTY-SEVEN

Carly leaves the children's bedroom and heads to the kitchen to rejoin Stella and Eaden, calling Fletcher on the way.

'Still no answer.' She frowns, placing her phone down on the table next to their half-empty cups a minute later. 'But Sonny was asleep before I finished his story. Must be all the party excitement catching up with him – he loved all the attention.'

'Shall *I* try him again?' asks Stella, fiddling with her pearl earrings.

'We've both called him several times now.' Carly looks away, tapping her top lip with her finger. 'Am I being silly for worrying?' she asks her mother-in-law, turning back to face her. 'It's just that he said he'd be home for supper. I roasted a joint of beef and it's his favourite. It's not like him to just go AWOL.'

'You're right, it's not. And it's especially strange that Perry says he's not heard from him or had any luck contacting him today either. Normally they're constantly connected,' comments Stella.

A pensive expression creeps across Carly's face. 'I know.'

'Granny, is Daddy okay?' Eaden looks up from her colouring book.

Stella pats her hand. 'I'm sure he is, poppet. He's probably just put his phone down somewhere and forgotten where it is. Silly Daddy!' She smiles but it doesn't reach her eyes. Getting up from the table, Stella jerks her head, signalling for Carly to join her by the island, leaving Eaden to her colouring.

'Should we maybe think about calling the police?' Stella whispers, her eyes full of concern for her only son. 'This really isn't like him.'

'The police?' asks Carly. 'Already? He's not classed as a missing person yet. We'll just be wasting their time calling now.'

Stella shakes her head. 'Oh, I don't know. I've just got a bad feeling, that's all.'

'Why don't I take a drive to the Fraisthorpe house? He might have fallen ill or lost his phone like you say. Or the van might have broken down somewhere with no signal or something. It was stormy there earlier according to my weather app.' She shrugs. 'Listen to me... I sound like I'm trying to convince myself, don't I?'

Stella sighs in sympathy, evidently pleased they're united in a cause for once. 'Yes, but you're only thinking what I'm thinking. It might be worth you going to check if he's there and I could always ring you if he comes home while you're out.'

'Okay. If you don't mind staying with the children?'

'Of course not.'

Carly glances at the clock propped on the worktop. It's gone 7.30pm. 'Okay, well, I'll get Eaden ready for bed and then I'll set off.'

'I can do that. You go,' says Stella.

'No, I'll stay to help. She's already aware that something's not right – clever little thing – and after her upset about Pippa this afternoon, I want to reassure her a bit.'

Stella nods. 'Good idea. Poor little mite was in bits over her mum when you dropped her off this afternoon. And then when she perked up, she was disappointed she missed out on Celeste's party. What brought it all on, do you think?'

'We were looking through her scrapbook before we left, and I gave her another picture of Pippa I found to stick in. It just set her off. As I said earlier, I gave her the option of coming with us or going to your house and she said she wanted to stay with you. We missed her though. I know I haven't spent much time with the children since we moved but I do want to remedy that, Stella.'

Stella smiles again, with warmth this time. 'I'm glad to hear that.' She touches Carly's arm. 'Come on then, let's get the little lady bathed and settled in bed and then you can go and see what on earth my son is playing at.'

'You watch, he'll probably waltz through the door any minute, cross with us for worrying about him.' Carly winks at her mother-in-law.

'Yes, maybe he will,' replies Stella, the desperate note of hope clear in her voice.

CHAPTER THIRTY-EIGHT

'Drive safely. If he's there, ring me straight away,' Stella says to her daughter-in-law as they stand in the hallway after putting Eaden to bed.

Carly picks her car keys up from the bowl on the console table, opens the door, and presses the button to open the electric gates. 'And if he comes home while I'm gone, ring me straight away.'

They exchange half-smiles and Carly steps out into the dark night, activating the sensored light.

'What on earth…' Stella's hand flutters to her chest at the sight of two men, one in a smart suit and one in a police uniform, just beyond the gates, waiting for them to part. Carly automatically steps back inside and stands beside Stella.

The visitors reach the door and the man in the suit introduces himself as Detective Inspector Greaves and asks for Mrs Lawrenson, looking between the two gaping women.

'Yes?' both Stella and Carly reply.

'Mrs Carly Lawrenson? Wife of Mr Fletcher Lawrenson?'

'That's me,' says Carly. 'And this is my mother-in-law, Stella.'

'Could we step inside a moment, please?' DI Greaves asks.

'What's this about?' asks Carly as Stella reverses further into the hallway, her jaw slack once more.

'It's better if we talk inside,' he replies.

Carly nods and arcs her arm in the direction of the kitchen. 'My children are asleep upstairs but please come through.'

Once seated around the table, Carly asks again, 'What's this about?'

Stella reaches out and clutches her hand, an alien gesture between them, eyes still fixed on the detective.

In a practised though sympathetic fashion, DI Greaves shares the reason for their visit. 'I'm very sorry to inform you that we were called to Seaview Cottage on Cliff Drive in Fraisthorpe earlier this evening and we found Mr Lawrenson injured and unconscious.' He pauses.

Stella lets out a distressed cry, her hands flying to her mouth.

'We also found the body of Benjamin Robinson just outside the property.'

Carly squints at the detective, frowning, one hand grasping her neck. 'I'm sorry... Who? What?'

DI Greaves repeats the facts, speaking gently but clearly. He directs the information towards Carly but keeps glancing over towards Stella who is now trembling uncontrollably.

'A body? What do you mean? Are you saying Fletcher had something to do with it?' asks Carly.

'We don't know yet, we're still investigating. All we know so far is that we received a 999 call from Mr Lawrenson's phone, but the first responders confirmed that he was unconscious upon arrival, and that Mr Robinson was deceased.'

'Where is Fletcher now?' asks Stella.

'He was taken by ambulance to Bridlington Hospital. He sustained a head injury. He's in a coma.'

'We must go to him, Carly.' Stella's eyes well with tears.

Carly blinks at her. 'Who'll stay with the children?'

'I could ask Meryl to sit with them?' she suggests, wringing her hands. 'I'm sure she would.'

DI Greaves catches Carly's attention. 'Mrs Lawrenson, we need you to stay here to answer a few questions. I won't keep you any longer than absolutely necessary.'

Carly nods. 'You go on ahead,' she says to Stella. 'I'll pop over and speak to Meryl as soon as we're done here and be right behind you.' She gets up and passes her sniffling mother-in-law a tissue from the box on the worktop.

Stella wipes her nose and crumples the tissue in her clenched fist. 'All right,' she says. Then, 'Excuse me, please. I just need a few moments and then I'll phone a taxi. I don't think I'm up to the drive.' She rises from the table and walks shakily out to the hallway, turning right towards the downstairs toilet.

Carly watches her mother-in-law leave, shaking her hands by her sides as though trying to expel her nervous energy through her fingers. Her mind turns over the information DI Greaves has just shared. *Benny is dead and Fletcher is unconscious? That's not what was supposed to happen.* She stops, places a hand on her chest and sits back, ready to hear more details from the detective.

He takes out a pen and a small notebook with a black cover. Flipping it open to a clean page, he asks his first question: 'Why was Mr Lawrenson at the Cliff Drive property today?'

'Erm...' She looks at the detective with watery eyes. 'The plan was to renovate it over the winter when it won't be used. He went today to make a start on that, so we can use it next year as a family, as well as rent it out.'

'Had he arranged to meet anyone at the property today? Perhaps Mr Robinson? Did he know him?'

Carly shakes her head and a tear spills onto her cheek. She brushes it away with her index finger. 'No. Well, not that I know of. Unless Fletcher used him as a casual labourer? But if anyone else was going to be there to help him it would have been his cousin, Perry, but Perry hasn't been able to get hold of him all day, has he, Stella?' she asks as Stella reappears in the kitchen with her coat on.

Stella shakes her head. 'None of us have been able to reach him, detective. This obviously explains why. My taxi will be here in a few minutes. I'm going to wait outside. I need some air.'

Carly gets up and properly embraces Stella for the first time since she became a Lawrenson. 'I'll let you know when I'm on my way. Ring me if you find out anything about how he is before I get there.'

Stella nods, clearly still shell-shocked.

DI Greaves half turns his head as Stella leaves, then he looks back at Carly. 'Mrs Lawrenson–'

'How did the man die? What happened?' she interrupts.

'It appears he was stabbed and then fell from the balcony.'

Carly gasps. 'Stabbed?' she repeats.

'Mrs Lawrenson, where were you while Mr Lawrenson was at Seaview Cottage this afternoon? Just so we can get a full picture of the day.'

Carly blinks several times, trying to process everything the detective is telling her. She didn't want Benny to *die*. She needs to think on her feet. 'Erm… I was at a children's birthday party in Levisham with Sonny, my infant son. My stepdaughter Eaden was supposed to be there too – it was for Celeste, one of her school friends – but she wasn't feeling well so I dropped her off at Stella's – her grandmother's – on the way.'

'Celeste?' He pauses for her to give a last name.

'Reynolds,' Carly supplies. 'Her mother, Mallory Reynolds, will be able to confirm Sonny and I were there.'

'Whereabouts in Levisham?'

'Riseholme Grange children's farm. Mallory booked it exclusively for the party.'

DI Greaves jots down Carly's answers in his notebook.

'Thank you, Mrs Lawrenson, that's very helpful.' He clears his throat and shifts in his seat before looking back up at her, an awkward expression on his face. 'We also found a bottle of champagne and two glasses at the Fraisthorpe property.'

'Champagne?' asks Carly, ensuring there's a confused pitch to her voice. 'Why would he be drinking champagne when he's working on the house? And who with? That doesn't make any sense.'

'Could he have been drinking champagne with Mr Robinson?'

Carly purses her lips as she stares at the detective, understanding the implication. She admires lateral thinking. 'That's an interesting theory but I do think that's highly unlikely.'

DI Greaves moves smoothly on to his next question. 'Given that you were at a children's party, do you have any idea who else might have been there with your husband? We'll obviously test the glasses for fingerprints, but it would help us narrow things down if you could tell us who else knew about the house or had access to it?'

Carly makes sure to chew her lip thoughtfully before she answers. 'Just us,' she says, shrugging. 'Just our family.'

'Okay. Did any–' He stops abruptly as Carly grasps his arm and looks directly at him with wide eyes.

'Polly,' she says. Her bottom lip wobbles and she lays her palms flat on the table as though to steady herself.

'Polly?' he repeats.

'Polly Blake, our new nanny, she knows about the Fraisthorpe house too. She's been before, with me, and she knew Fletcher was going there today.'

'Where is she now?' asks the detective.

Carly swallows and gazes steadily at him. 'It's her day off. I messaged her earlier asking if she wouldn't mind coming home sooner, as a favour, but she hasn't replied, and she hasn't answered my calls either.'

Polly has never felt more scared, worried or alone. She's been sitting in Mallory's husband's terraced house – Carly and Sonny's temporary new home – for hours, slowly going out of her mind, checking her phone every few seconds, and going over and over the moment she released her grip on the knife's handle and realised the blade was embedded in that man's stomach as he fell backwards off the balcony. *I'm a murderer*, she thinks, freshly appalled at the notion every single time it loops through her brain.

Despite messaging Carly that she's here, and trying to call her now that she's got service again, Polly's phone remains silent. She keeps alternating between packing her things and going 'home' – to Fletcher and Carly's house – to wait it out without knowing where Carly and Sonny are, or staying put until they finally arrive, or even going back to Fraisthorpe. Every time she makes a decision and gets up to leave, she imagines Fletcher talking to the police, explaining about attacking the intruder, then telling them that Carly and Sonny are missing, that his wife has taken his son without his knowledge. However, she feels sick with fear that when the police eventually question her, they'll see straight through her – that she stabbed the man not Fletcher, and that she helped his wife take his son, even though she believes Carly to be a danger to the baby. It's all terrifying.

But the longer she stays here, the more intense the feeling grows that something is very wrong. Yet surely sitting tight must be the safest option right now, she feels, away from all the intense drama currently unfolding.

She breathes deeply. She sips water. She tries to stay calm, to trust that everything is going to be okay but all she feels is a ferocious whirl of turmoil and trepidation inside her.

She's still so angry that Fletcher didn't tell her about drugging her drink with diazepam – yet how can she doubt his love for her when he's willing to lie to the police on her behalf? And if he's prepared to do that, she can definitely lie about Carly in return. Can't she? But then if Fletcher ends up going to prison – God forbid – she'll need Carly. She'll need a job and somewhere to live and a way to still be in the children's lives while she waits for Fletcher to serve time for a crime she committed, albeit accidentally. Sort of. And living with Carly without Fletcher would be a hell of its own.

But then a terrible, terrifying thought pierces her psyche, worse than anything else she can think of: what if Fletcher has chickened out and told the police the truth, condemning her to a murder trial? Would it go to trial, or would she be automatically sentenced? She doesn't even know how the justice system works. Can she really trust that Fletcher has done what he said he was going to do or was that a lie too? She honestly doesn't know anymore.

She stands. It's all too much. Suddenly full of resolve borne from pure fear, she runs upstairs to collect her meagre belongings from the spare bedroom. She hesitates for a moment then decides to leave her memory box and all its contents behind. It's time for a new start. She learned a few coping mechanisms when things blew up with Teddy in New York and she'll implement them again this time around.

On her way back out, she detours to the bathroom, yanks her engagement ring off her finger and drops it down the toilet. As she stares sadly at the gold-and-diamond solitaire beneath the water, she thinks about how her hope of a new life with Fletcher has gone the same way – down the toilet. She so desperately wants a proper family of her own and now, in order to get that, she realises she has to leave this twisted one behind.

As she reaches the bottom of the stairs, she pauses beside the unpacked boxes and holdalls she brought on Friday and pulls out her phone to send a final message to Carly. As soon as she's sent it, she turns her phone off, opens the door and comes face to face with a tall man in a suit and a woman in police uniform.

'Polly Blake?' the tall man asks. Polly knits her brows together and nods. 'I'm Detective Sergeant Hawkins and I'd like to ask you a few questions about Fletcher Lawrenson and Benjamin Robinson.'

CHAPTER THIRTY-NINE

'What's happening? What's this about?' Polly has been waiting in the small, square, strange-smelling interview room in the Pickering Road police station for a long time, working herself up into a frenzy, and now that DS Hawkins has returned, she's imagining the worst and desperate for information. She was expecting the police to catch up with her to ask about Sonny's alleged kidnapping – although perhaps not so soon – but why do they need to question her about Fletcher and the other man they named, who she can only assume must be the intruder? Has Fletcher sold her out as she thought he might?

'Miss Blake, thank you for coming in to speak with us. This is a voluntary interview, which will be recorded. Would you like legal representation at this stage?'

'Do I need legal representation?' she asks, her voice cracking.

'Just a yes or no answer, please.'

She stares at the detective, wishing she could read his mind because her gut is screaming at her that she's going to hear something bad, and she'd just rather *know* than wonder. 'No,' she states.

DS Hawkins nods and the female police officer presses a

button on the recording device. DS Hawkins states his name, the other officer's name, Polly's name, and the date out loud, and then they wait until the long intrusive buzz has ended.

Detective Sergeant Hawkins and his silent colleague exchange a glance then they both look back at Polly.

'Miss Blake, were you at Seaview Cottage on Cliff Drive in Fraisthorpe earlier today? It's a property belonging to Fletcher Lawrenson and his mother, Stella Lawrenson.'

'Yes,' confirms Polly without hesitation, wanting to get to the nitty-gritty.

'Was Mr Lawrenson there at the same time?' he asks next.

Polly clasps her hands in her lap and squeezes her fingers together. She swallows. 'Yes, he was there too.'

'And Mr Robinson?'

'Who?' She bounces a confused look from DS Hawkins to the other police officer, deciding to stick to the version of the truth she and Fletcher agreed on – that she left before the other man even arrived.

DS Hawkins clears his throat. 'In your own words, in your own time, could you please tell us what happened at that property today?' He sits back in his chair and fractionally adjusts his tie, indicating he's ready and willing to listen to her version of events.

'Why? What's this about?' she asks again, hoping to bypass more questions and get straight to the heart of the matter, even though she knows that's not going to happen.

'Miss Blake, please just take us through the events of today,' the detective requests again, a firmer edge to his voice now.

Polly picks up the plastic cup of water they gave her earlier and drains the last drops. As she places the cup back down, she feels herself shaking. She puts both hands in her lap.

Over the next few minutes, Polly explains what happened during the time she and Fletcher spent together at the beach house as honestly and concisely as she can. When she talks about their affair she feels her cheeks flame with shame, and when she tells them about their argument, her heart squeezes with pain. But she lays it all out for them, exactly as it happened, up to just before the intruder surprised them. When she has finished, she nods once and looks the detective squarely in the eyes.

'So, when you left the property, Mr Lawrenson was alive and well?'

Her brows furrow. 'Yes, of course he was. Well, I scratched him, his neck, as I explained, when we argued, but other than that he was fine. A bit hungover maybe.' She absentmindedly rubs the tops of her arms, still slightly sore from where Fletcher grabbed them.

'And neither of you saw or talked to anyone else while you were at the house? No visitors, no neighbours...?'

'No,' confirms Polly immediately.

DS Hawkins opens the folder that's been lying in front of him since the interview began. He takes out what looks like a piece of paper and slides it towards her. 'So can you explain how this might have happened?' he asks.

She looks down at the paper and sees that it is a photograph, taken in the dark but with bright lights illuminating the central object. Like a magic eye pattern, it takes her a few seconds to understand that the object is in fact the stranger's dead, crumpled body and with that clarity comes the horrific realisation that she is being questioned in relation to it, which means Fletcher hasn't told them what he promised he was going to tell them. It's her worst fear realised.

She opens her mouth and tips her head up to look at DS Hawkins, her eyes like saucers as he describes what she's looking at for the benefit of the recording. Her bones begin to shake, and the sensation increases and increases until it reaches a crescendo, resulting in an anguished, guttural sob. For the man she still loves in spite of his false promise, and for this seemingly never-ending, most awful day of her life so far that has resulted in being trapped in this squalid interview room being interrogated by a smug detective.

She slams her hands on the table, her emotions rising then bubbling over, like hot lava from an erupting volcano. DS Hawkins blinks in surprise.

'Fletcher stabbed that man!' She swipes her hot tears away and takes a breath. 'He told me to go! He was fine when I left!' She swallows. 'I need to speak to Carly. She's expecting me.'

'Carly Lawrenson, Fletcher Lawrenson's wife?' asks the detective?

Polly nods.

'Mrs Lawrenson is currently speaking with one of my colleagues. She has already alluded to the fact that you and Mr Lawrenson were having an affair.'

Polly shakes her head. 'No, she can't have done. She was paranoid that Fletcher was carrying on with one of his clients, but he wasn't. We were in love. But we were always careful, and Carly and I were friendly. She didn't know about us.'

'When did your affair begin?' he asks.

Polly takes a juddering breath and closes her eyes. They feel gritty, like salt or sand grains are stuck under her eyelids. She opens them again, moves the gruesome photo away and carefully presses her palms together on top of the table. She looks down, fixing her stare on her ragged thumbnails, flecks of neon-green nail varnish still clinging on.

'We met by chance eight months ago, in America. He lived there with his family, and I lived there with the family I was nannying for. We fell in love quickly. Then he had to move back to England, and we decided that I would come home too and become his children's nanny. We continued our relationship in secret.' She's surprised by how calm her voice sounds, at odds with the maelstrom of emotions churning inside her. 'I'm not proud of that decision,' she states, feeling like she has to make this fact clear.

'You say you were in love, yet you claim he drugged you this afternoon.'

Polly's eyes instantly mist over again, and she sniffs. 'He did. I saw a different side to him. A side that Carly claimed was there, but I didn't believe her. Until today.'

'What did Mrs Lawrenson claim?'

'That Fletcher was abusing her physically. She told me she had taken photos of her bruises. She asked me to help her leave him. She rented a new place for her and Sonny and asked me to move their things there on Friday, ready for them to move in today. That's where you found me tonight. They were supposed to be there too.' She frowns, the thought having only just occurred to her. 'How did you know I was there – at Mallory's husband's house?'

DS Hawkins scratches his cheek and regards Polly thoughtfully. He doesn't anwer her question. A moment later, there's a knock at the door and another officer pokes her head in and apologises for the intrusion, stating that she has information to pass on from DI Greaves. The detective announces to the tape that he's pausing the interview and leaving the room temporarily.

A few minutes later, during which neither Polly nor the remaining officer speak, he returns and resumes the recording.

'So, how were you helping Mrs Lawrenson leave Mr Lawrenson today if you were at the Fraisthorpe property?'

'Carly asked me to keep Fletcher there while she left the family home with Sonny,' replies Polly. 'But I'd already told Fletcher her plan. He convinced me that Carly was deranged, mad with paranoia, an unfit mother, and that he'd get full custody if she took Sonny without his permission. But then this afternoon he grabbed me after I confronted him about spiking my drink – I've got the marks to prove it. It was like he was possessed.'

'Were you scared of Mr Lawrenson?' DS Hawkins asks.

She blinks a few times then looks away. A minute later she

says, 'In that moment, yes. I was. It made me think that maybe Carly was telling the truth, that he had been abusive towards her, that maybe her taking Sonny away from him was for the best.'

'He got rough with you, after drugging you without your knowledge or consent, and you fought?' DS Hawkins summarises. 'Is that correct?'

She nods.

'So, was it possibly self-defence?'

'Was what self-defence?' asks Polly, baffled.

'Knocking Mr Lawrenson unconscious.'

CHAPTER FORTY

'Unconscious? What? No!' cries Polly. 'I've already told you – he told me to go after he stabbed the intruder! He definitely wasn't unconscious then. Is he awake again now? What did he tell you?'

'So now you're saying that you were there when Mr Robinson arrived at the property?'

'Yes. I'm sorry. I didn't want to lie about that but we agreed that I would. Whatever Fletcher's said, he told me to go...' she repeats. 'And that's the truth.' She wraps her arms around herself.

'The house next door is empty, but we've spoken to the occupants of the other two houses in the row, and although neither of them was in all day, they haven't reported seeing anyone suspicious or hearing anything concerning when they got home. One of them, however, does recall seeing a car matching the description of Mr Lawrenson's car...' DS Hawkins consults his notebook. '"...driving off extremely fast, like a getaway car" around 7pm.' He looks at Polly. 'Obviously, that could not have been Mr Lawrenson.'

Polly presses her dry lips together and moves her head slowly from side to side. Her nostrils flare as she stares at the detective, but her eyes are full of tears and fear. She's so confused. Has Fletcher dropped her in it or is this happening because he's not able to protect her? Whatever the situation, she needs to do whatever it takes to protect herself.

'We have also spoken to a Mrs Meryl Bennett, who lives next door to the Lawrenson family home, and she reports that you said...' He glances down at his notebook again. '"It's all gone too far" and "I just need to get through the next couple of days and everything will be fine" in a conversation with her on Friday morning. Can you explain what you meant by those statements?'

Polly wipes her nose with the back of her hand and sniffs loudly. 'I meant that their marriage – Fletcher and Carly's – would be over, and Fletcher and I would be together. That's all. That's all I meant by that. Meryl knew about mine and Fletcher's relationship. You've taken that completely out of context.'

'Okay.' He nods. 'So what was the context of the apology text you sent to Mrs Lawrenson just before we located you?'

Polly shrugs. 'Just sorry for not waiting longer for her and Sonny to get to Mallory's husband's house. I had already waited for ages, and I just wanted to leave. I couldn't get hold of her and I had a really bad feeling so I decided to put the whole sorry mess behind me.'

'So you weren't apologising for having an affair with Mrs Lawrenson's husband?' DS Hawkins raises an eyebrow.

'I am sorry for that but that's not what I was apologising for in the text,' says Polly, through clenched teeth. 'And correct me if I'm wrong, but having an affair isn't a crime.'

'No, but causing serious physical bodily harm to your lover during the course of that affair may be.'

'He wasn't badly hurt!' she shouts. 'I told you that!'

He sighs heavily. 'The problem, Miss Blake, is that Mrs Lawrenson is bewildered by your claim that she was going to leave her husband. She states that she hadn't secured a new home for her and her son and that despite suspecting your affair, she wanted her marriage to work. In fact, the house we located you at – 171 Boulevard – belongs to Perry Lawrenson, and was previously owned by his father Frank Lawrenson before his death. Fletcher Lawrenson also has a set of keys to the property and Mrs Lawrenson confirms that those keys are missing from a drawer in Mr Lawrenson's office.'

Polly shakes her head, struggling to believe what she's hearing. 'Perry's house? But Carly told me it was her friend's husband's house and asked me to move her and Sonny's stuff there – on Friday, like I said. She left the packed boxes and bags in the garage.'

'Mrs Lawrenson has informed my colleague DI Greaves that the boxes and bags of old clothes and accessories in her garage were the result of a clear-out. She claims she asked you to donate them to a local charity shop on Friday, which she believes you did. Furthermore, she states that any boxes and bags currently at 171 Boulevard contain Frank Lawrenson's belongings, which were packed up after his death.'

'No, that's just not true.' Polly shakes her head again and looks straight at DS Hawkins. 'She didn't. I didn't.'

Just as Polly feels her head is about to explode, there's another knock at the door and the same officer as before interrupts the interview. DS Hawkins once again excuses himself after asking Polly if she would like more water. She nods, her brain whirring rapidly, trying desperately to comprehend what he's just told her. *If it was really Perry's house, was he in on it too?* wonders Polly. *Were he and Carly having an affair of their own?*

Before she can properly unearth the potentially outrageous theory, DS Hawkins returns with a fresh plastic cup of water. It's room temperature but she gulps it down gratefully, hoping it'll ease the tight band of pressure circling her brain.

He smiles, resumes the recording, then changes tack from where they previously left off. 'Let's talk about Benjamin Robinson.'

The detective pulls two more photos from the folder. One is a close-up of a knife handle sticking out of a bloodied stomach and the other is a headshot. The skull of the head in the image is badly damaged.

Polly's vision swims and her heart pounds as she stares at the photo. *Fletcher didn't get the knife like he said he would.*

'You said earlier that Mr Lawrenson stabbed Mr Robinson?'

She looks up again and nods.

'Talk us through what happened.' He makes a circling gesture with his hand.

Polly huffs out a shaky breath. 'He just appeared... in the house, holding a knife. Threatening us. He must have broken in while Fletcher and I were arguing. We didn't see him at first. He just went for Fletcher and they fought. Fletcher got the knife off him and stabbed him.'

'There's no evidence of forced entry.'

'Maybe we left the door unlocked by mistake then! But he was still trespassing!' Polly clamps her hands to the side of her head and scrapes her bitten nails down her temples.

'Or maybe Mr Robinson appeared after you attacked Mr Lawrenson,' DS Hawkins suggests. 'And you stabbed him to prevent him from telling anyone what he had stumbled into – a lovers' tiff gone badly awry. Perhaps he heard your argument and simply wanted to help you. Yes, he may have technically been trespassing, but he became collateral damage in a different crime.'

Polly shakes her head vigorously and doubles down on her lie. It's her word against Fletcher's. 'No. Fletcher stabbed him after he broke in.'

The detective sighs, but it is not the sigh of a weary man, it's a sigh that precedes a winning card being dealt. 'Okay.' He nods. 'In that case, there's one last thing I'm curious about, Miss Blake. My colleague has just confirmed that Mr Lawrenson's fingerprints aren't on the handle of the knife that was plunged into Mr Robinson's torso... but yours are. Can you explain that?'

CHAPTER FORTY-ONE

D I Greaves returns to the table after making a lengthy phone call in the garden. While he was on the phone, Carly spoke to Stella, who had just arrived at Bridlington Hospital. The older woman was clearly trying to put a brave face on, but Carly heard her voice catch with emotion a few times during their brief conversation. She already knows that tonight has united them, created an unbreakable bond between them, and she feels sure that they'll support each other as they navigate whatever comes next.

The other police officer returned from speaking with Meryl next door a while ago and now he's standing at the kitchen island, dutifully making hot drinks for them all. Carly has no idea what Meryl might have said but she hopes her neighbour has lived up to her stickybeak reputation and given them even more fuel for the fire.

DI Greaves informs Carly that he has been liaising with his colleagues at the police station who are currently interviewing Polly. He solemnly poses his next question.

'Abuse?' Carly repeats, blinking twice. 'Absolutely not,

detective. No.' She shakes her head. 'Our marriage wasn't perfect and, yes, we disagreed sometimes but we've been through a lot together, especially this year, what with the baby and the move back here. Why on earth would our nanny, who only joined our household three weeks ago, think my husband was abusing me?'

'She claims you've been documenting the abuse with photographs.'

'What? That's ridiculous,' scoffs Carly, feigning anger sparking. 'Thank you,' she says as the PC places a cup of herbal tea and two cups of coffee on the table and sits down next to DI Greaves. 'She must have seen the bruises I've collected during my workouts and jumped to the wrong conclusion. I take regular progress photos but that's all.'

The detective turns the corners of his mouth down and holds the handle of his cup without picking it up. 'Mrs Lawrenson, Miss Blake has now confirmed that she and Mr Lawrenson have been in a serious relationship since meeting in America in January of this year.'

This new and unexpected extra piece of information pierces Carly's heart like a blade. She knew it; she knew something was off in America all those months ago. It seems Fletcher had the audacity to bring his mistress here like she was a treasured transatlantic souvenir, unpack their sordid relationship with the rest of their luggage and then resume it, hidden in plain sight. She should have trusted her gut at the time.

Appalled, she looks away, down the length of the kitchen towards the darkness of the bi-fold doors. She remembers peering through them, feeling like a private eye, hoping to spy on her husband and her nanny, before actually catching them in the act – red-faced rather than red-handed – in Polly's room upstairs.

She swallows down her disgust, shakes her head softly and turns back to DI Greaves. 'No, that can't be true.' She forces a smile. 'Our son was born in January. Fletcher dotes on him, on both of his children. Men don't cheat as soon as their babies arrive.' After a pause she looks at the detective with much less certainty. With a slight tremor in her voice she asks, 'Do they?'

The detective gives her a small, sympathetic smile and leans forwards slightly. 'Miss Blake has told my colleagues that she and Mr Lawrenson orchestrated her job here and that Mr Lawrenson told her he was going to end your marriage so they could be together. That's why they were drinking champagne – she claims they were celebrating that fact.'

Carly shakes her head. She doesn't need to pull on her acting skills to pretend to be upset by this concrete confirmation. She looks at the DI and PC's pitiful expressions and sees herself through their eyes: the ageing, hoodwinked, less attractive, easily replaced wife. Despite needing them to see her that way, the shame and discomfort of it overwhelms her and she breaks down, crying not only over her husband's betrayal but also for what he forced her to do to take back control. Her original plan went awry but this outcome still works to her advantage. Three words turn over in her head: *Thank you, Benny.*

She composes herself, needing to ask her next question. 'If Polly and Fletcher were celebrating, as you say, how did Fletcher end up injured and unconscious and how did that poor man end up dead?'

'Miss Blake is still helping us with our enquiries. As soon–' His phone rings and cuts him off. 'If you'll excuse me,' he says, answering the call as he steps away from Carly towards the hallway.

She takes a small sip of her now tepid, stewed herbal tea then pushes the cup away. The PC offers her a small smile before collecting all their barely touched drinks and taking them over to the sink.

DI Greaves returns to the table. He nods once at the PC

before addressing Carly. 'Mrs Lawrenson, that was my colleague DS Hawkins. Miss Blake has just been charged with the manslaughter of Benjamin Robinson and the grievous bodily harm of your husband.'

CHAPTER FORTY-TWO

TWO MONTHS LATER

Carly enters the visitors' room at HMP New Hall and gingerly takes a seat at one of the metal picnic-style tables, nearest the far wall. It is one of about fifteen and bolted securely to the floor; they all are.

She glances around the space and it's as miserable as she imagined. There are three small windows, all covered with black bars. They are too high up to see out of, but they let the meagre winter light in. *Not a pleasant place if you're claustrophobic,* Carly muses.

The stench is appalling: a cocktail of damp, bleach and body odour and she scrunches her nose up as she waits.

A loud buzzer sounds followed by a heavy door unlocking then the hustle of a collection of bodies moving. She twists her head towards the women spilling out into the depressing space. Some smile or laugh with joy at the sight of whoever is here to see them, catapulting themselves forwards with eagerness, some shuffle in, struggling to hold back tears, but most maintain a neutral expression and steady gait, their emotions locked down but their hunched bodies hinting at their melancholy.

Polly's emotions, however, are conveyed transparently on her face: anger and hatred. And something else too perhaps – wariness?

Carly suppresses a smirk. 'Hello, Polly. You look well,' she lies when her former nanny reaches the table. 'Thank you for accepting my request to visit.'

The young woman's greasy hair is tied back in a low ponytail, a few loose, lank strands hanging down to her chin. Her once pearlescent skin now lacks lustre, her lips are chapped, and the coy yet cocky expression has completely disappeared. She's wearing concrete-grey sweats and sliders with socks.

After just a few weeks of imprisonment, Polly seems to have aged years. Carly wonders if it would be too cruel to slide an *Image Aesthetic Clinic* business card across the filthy surface between them, recommend a few treatments for when she gets out, at a discounted rate of course. She'll need them if she's ever going to recover her youthful, girlish glow. Then again, if the upcoming trial goes the way she hopes it will, Polly's twenties may be long gone by the time she gets out of prison.

Polly slumps down opposite Carly, chin down, eyes up. 'What do you want?' she asks.

Carly smiles and twists on her seat, crossing one leg over the other. She's glad they can slice straight through the small talk. 'I came to say thank you.'

'Thank you?' Polly screws her face up. 'What for?'

'Well, outwardly, obviously, I am the wronged wife, but you saved me from him, Polly. I thought that deserved a thank you. Face to face.'

'I didn't hurt him! He was conscious when I left!' cries Polly, sitting up straighter. A prison officer throws her a sharp glance and she shrinks back down in her seat. 'He told me to go. He wanted me to be with the kids because he thought you were a terrible mother and he didn't trust you with them. He was willing to sacrifice himself for me because he loved me more than you!'

The words sting but Carly sticks her bottom lip out in an

exaggerated show of sympathy. She keeps her voice soft and low as she replies, 'Poor Polly. Fletcher really did mess with your head, didn't he? I saw how he changed you from a bright, beautiful homewrecking bitch into a shrivelled, snivelling shell of your former self. What did he promise you, hey? That he was going to leave me and set up home with you?'

Polly presses her lips together and looks away, nostrils flaring.

'Is that why he wanted to hole up in his Uncle Frank's house so you could pretend to be a proper couple for a few days? Was his plan to leave me while I was taking our children to a birthday party? But what I don't understand is why didn't you both go straight there – why go to the Fraisthorpe house first? What happened there that made you want to cause him grievous bodily harm? Did he change his mind about wanting you?' Carly taunts her. 'Did that poor stranger get caught in your crossfire? Or was your cheeky threesome a bit rougher than planned? Did they forget the safe word?' Carly giggles.

'What?' Polly gapes at the other woman. 'You're fucking crazy!' She speaks through gritted teeth as she stabs a finger against her temple. 'It was you. I know it was. A random man with a knife magically appeared at that house – the house that just happened to be the place you instructed us to go to. In fact, your mood boards were in Fletcher's car. Maybe they still are – they're going to check! You were behind it all. I've told my solicitor so.'

'Crazy?' Carly smiles serenely. 'I'm not the one about to go on trial for manslaughter and GBH. And I'd be careful about insulting the only friend you have left, Polly.'

It's Polly's turn to scoff. 'You've lied about everything – leaving Fletcher, the abuse, Frank's house belonging to Mallory's husband. I've had a lot of time to think these past few weeks, and I see it all clearly now. What was that intruder meant to do... kill Fletcher? Kill me? Or both of us? You're not my friend. You never were.'

Carly picks an imaginary piece of fluff off her cashmere coat sleeve while she pretends to consider Polly's accusation. 'It's a shame you see it that way because I think I *was* a good friend to you,' she says after a few moments. 'I trusted you. I confided in you about the problems I was experiencing in my marriage. I was honest all along – you were the one keeping sordid secrets, sleeping with my husband right under my nose. When I found out about the affair, it hurt more than the abuse, Polly. Wronged women should stick together, but I suppose, in a way, we have, because what you did proved you believed me in the end. You would have been a battered wife eventually too because his pattern is to move on to the next shiny, new, young thing as soon as the one he's got has borne his children and morphed into an older, less taut, less stunning, two-dimensional version of herself. I'm just grateful you stopped him before he got to me the way he got to Pippa.'

Polly is horrified. 'What are you trying to imply? You said Pippa died in a car accident.'

'Did I? Or did I just say it was a horrible, tragic collision?' Carly twists her face into a mock-sad expression.

'You're lying again! You've lied about everything,' Polly repeats. Tears drip down her flushed face and she scrubs them away roughly.

Carly clucks her tongue. 'There you go again. First, I'm crazy, then I'm a liar. Whereas the simpler explanation might be that you're the delusional one.'

'Fuck you.' Polly spits the words at her. 'I'm not delusional. Fletcher knows the truth and when he wakes up, he'll–'

'He'll what?' Carly cuts her off and leans forward, her eyes narrowed. 'Back you up? Say you didn't hurt him? Say he killed that man not you? Are you sure about that, Polly? Or might he wash his hands of you the same way Edward and Theodora Miller did – choose to keep his family together rather than throw it all away on a cheap little cuckoo whore?'

248

Polly clenches her hands into fists and scrubs her knuckles against her cheekbones, her elbows banging against the edge of the table. Her tears splash heavily onto the brushed metal surface, weighted with sadness.

Carly observes the other woman's decline victoriously after playing her Teddy trump card.

'Now you listen to me, Polly. You can tell your solicitor whatever bizarre theories you like but facts are facts: there weren't any of mine or Sonny's possessions in the Boulevard house that the police finally found you at. And there were no mood boards in Fletcher's car. Just a few of Eaden's drawings and collages zipped into the folder. The police already checked and that's all they found. I was at Celeste's party with Mallory and all the other school mums when, by chance, a burglar broke into the Fraisthorpe house. It was random, yes, and terribly unfortunate, and it ended in the worst way possible for you, but I understand why you did what you did. You were only defending yourself, against Fletcher and the intruder. Hopefully the jury will see that too and be lenient with your sentence.' She sits back and smooths her perfect chignon.

Polly looks up, her face a mask of anguish. 'No... you were behind it all. I know you were,' she snivels.

Carly stands, puts her hands in her pockets and looks down at Polly. She smirks.

'Prove it.'

EPILOGUE

September 2020

Carefully, Carly lays out the vials and places the brand-new wrapped needle next to them, all ready for her first client of the day.

She turns and surveys her newly renovated clinic space – Fletcher's old office. A few months ago, she started her own fledgling injectables business from home after completing the intensive training that Gavin recommended and mentored her through. The room now has its own outer door so her clients – mostly the other school mums, who have rallied round her offering plenty of support and sympathy – have a dedicated entrance. It's become important to Carly to set and maintain clear boundaries.

As she prepares the room – sanitising the surfaces, unboxing an expensive designer candle, choosing a tranquil playlist – her mind wanders casually over the myriad events of the past year.

Unsurprisingly, she and Stella have grown a lot closer since last September. United in grief and disappointment in Fletcher Lawrenson and his inability to be a decent and honourable man, yet still playing the roles of doting wife and mother while he remains oblivious to it all in The Spire's intensive care unit. He's currently the sole coma patient being treated there.

Carly and Stella take it in turns to visit every week. They used to go daily but that's just not sustainable long term. Life has moved on – for them at least. Carly is grateful to have someone to share the burden of the visiting commitment with and Stella's very handy to have around to look after the children whenever Carly wants to pursue her own interests.

One of those interests is Gavin. He wasn't too disappointed to lose her as an employee, not now they often share a bed rather than a workplace, all hush-hush of course while she's still in marriage limbo. Now there's a man who appreciates what he's got and is willing to invest (and inject) his time, affection and aesthetics expertise into her. He's nowhere near as handsome as Fletcher but she thinks she's learnt her lesson there – it's better to be the trophy than to try to win the trophy.

And, of course, Stella being here so often means there's no need for a nanny anymore. Carly often wonders what would have happened if she hadn't put up so much resistance to Stella in the first place – would Fletcher have been able to convince her to employ Polly regardless? She guesses she'll never know.

But she is now extremely thankful for her mother-in-law and the freedom she gives her from active motherhood. Carly is involved in her children's lives, obviously, but it's important to keep a sense of self too.

Surprisingly, Perry has been a huge help through it all too. She feels bad now for assuming he belonged in the same category as his despicable cousin. He was so shocked by Fletcher's clandestine affair with Polly that he flatly refused to entertain the idea of renovating the Fraisthorpe house either while Fletcher's enjoying his deep sleep or when – if – he wakes up. Respecting his feelings, Carly and Stella made the executive decision to sell Seaview Cottage as a doer-upper project at a knockdown price. It sold much quicker than expected given its macabre recent history.

Eaden began grief counselling earlier this year given that she's now effectively lost both her parents, but she's beginning to warm to Carly more and more each day, especially since they decorated her bedroom in a woodland theme together. The seaside concept didn't seem appropriate anymore after what happened at the beach house. She particularly loves foxes; Carly hopes she doesn't grow up to be as sly as one, just like her father.

As for Sonny, he's happy and settled and doesn't seem to miss Fletcher's presence at all. He's going to be a mummy's boy; she will make sure of it. Social services deemed there to be no cause for concern in their follow-up appointment after his A & E visit, so that's another bad memory erased too.

Carly chuckles to herself as she remembers her recent wicked suggestion to Stella that perhaps they should make a memory book for the children, featuring Fletcher, just like she did with Eaden for Pippa, but Stella rather tartly informed her that her son wasn't dead yet. It's been their only tense moment since Fletcher fell into his coma.

Carly doesn't think Stella quite gets her sense of humour yet, but she's confident she will, in time. In her opinion, Fletcher isn't the kind of father she wants to encourage the children to remember anyway, even if he is still hanging on in there collecting bedsores. He's not the kind of husband she wants back either. Hopefully his brain activity will eventually atrophy along with his body.

With the clarity of hindsight, she sees that when she first met him, he was looking for a replacement for Pippa. She understands now that replacing women with newer, younger versions was his pattern and he was the type of man who liked the chase. She acknowledges she allowed that to happen initially, and she may have fallen pregnant 'accidentally on purpose', knowing that she was a practically destitute former model and that a baby would be her meal ticket to a better life.

She saw how much Fletcher adored Eaden, and despite his many character flaws, he was actually a good father back then. A good provider. However, she didn't realise how much of herself she would lose, both physically and emotionally, in the process of becoming a mother. But sustaining a few emotional and physical scars and battling severe post-natal depression was bearable in the grand scheme of things because it eventually led to this life she now loves.

Benny's life, however... That's the one regret she does have. It was a lot easier than Carly had expected to persuade the homeless man, who had lost his own family due to a sordid affair, to help her keep hers. Wronged partners united for a one-off, well-paid job – a supposed break-in gone wrong. Money that Benny was determined to use to steer his life back on track and fight for access to his son – the only thing he truly cared about in the world.

While Benny was at Fraisthorpe, creeping along the beach in order to access the house from the rear steps without being seen, Carly was at Celeste's party with Sonny, enthusiastically parading him around Mallory and the other mums, taking selfies and cute pictures of the children, to secure her alibi. Thanks to Mallory's predictable need to document everything she ever does and then post it all on Facebook, Carly and Sonny feature in a lot of her photos too, all uploaded the same day.

It's a shame that Benny blundered killing Fletcher and became collateral damage, but it worked out even better than she hoped in the end. If everything had gone to plan, if Polly had left the Fraisthorpe house earlier, like she was supposed to following Carly's calls and text, Fletcher would have been dead, and Carly would have executed her original plan to frame Polly for his murder, painting her as the groomed mistress gone mad. But the punishments they've received now seem even more fitting: coma patient and convict.

As she lights the Jo Malone candle – a luxurious atmosphere is paramount – Carly wonders what 'poor' Polly is doing right now. The scarlet woman did not come across well at all in the jury's eyes, nor in the court of public opinion, at her trial several weeks after Carly visited her in prison. And it turns out she was only nineteen, not twenty-four as she originally claimed. Carly always suspected as much; Fletcher really did like them young.

Polly was found guilty of manslaughter and GBH and sentenced to seven years' imprisonment – thanks to fingerprint evidence at the scene and on the knife embedded in Benny's stomach, a lack of any other conscious witnesses and her own flimsy testimony in court, which still consisted of pinning all the blame on her lover despite the concrete evidence to the contrary. Carly suspects she took her solicitor's advice to stick to her original defence and not use any of her other random theories as alternatives. And if Fletcher dies, she may be charged with his manslaughter too.

Carly and Stella both attended her sentencing and after an ashen-faced Polly was taken down to the holding cells, Carly made a beeline for the newly promoted DCI Greaves and thanked him for his sensitive handling of the case. He agreed that justice had certainly prevailed.

Carly double-checks that everything is perfect and then puts her phone on silent. Her clients always get her full attention as she works her magic on their faces. She enjoys nothing more than subtly altering appearances and skewing reality.

THE END

ACKNOWLEDGEMENTS

Wow – book two already! This really is a long-held dream come true. Therefore, there are a few people I would like to thank for helping this author dream of mine finally become a reality, whether they helped physically, virtually or emotionally.

Thank you to the amazing team at Bloodhound Books, especially Betsy, Clare, Abbie, Vicky and Katia. After initially entering their #PitchHound blurb contest in August 2022, I was thrilled to be offered publishing contracts for three psychological suspense novels, and I have felt extremely valued and supported ever since.

Thank you to my husband, Richard, for often answering random questions about things I know nothing about when I need to include a niche detail in a story (cars, gaming and football, mostly!) and for occasionally brainstorming weird and wonderful plot ideas with me. Most importantly, thank you for always giving me the time and space I need to write. Thank you also to Caroline, Phil and Sharon who are amazing supporters of and cheerleaders for my books. And to anyone – whether friend, family member, acquaintance or complete stranger – who has ever messaged me personally to say lovely things about my books, please know that those surprise messages are always an absolute joy to receive. Thank you.

What's Mine Is Yours is the fastest novel I have ever written, thanks to Self Publishing Formula's *How to Write a Bestseller* online course created by Suzy K Quinn, and her subsequent Facebook bootcamp challenge during March 2021, in which all participants wrote 2,000 words per day. Writing is a discipline and this brilliant course taught me invaluable practices I'll carry through to my future books – of which I hope there will be many!

Finally, thank you to readers for choosing to spend your precious time with Carly, Fletcher and Polly. I hope you enjoyed reading their twisted story as much as I enjoyed writing it!

ALSO BY C.L. JENNISON

The Desperate Wife

A NOTE FROM THE PUBLISHER

Thank you for reading this book. If you enjoyed it please do consider leaving a review on Amazon to help others find it too.

We hate typos. All of our books have been rigorously edited and proofread, but sometimes mistakes do slip through. If you have spotted a typo, please do let us know and we can get it amended within hours.

info@bloodhoundbooks.com

Printed in Great Britain
by Amazon